Michael Kerawalla

Turoon

The Ocean Planet

Fantasy Novel

Michael Kerawalla

Turoon
The Ocean Planet

Fantasy Novel

Bibliografic Information of the German National Library:
The German National Library lists this Publication
in the German National Bibliography; detailed bibliographical
Data are retrievable in the Internet via http://dnb.dnb.de.

Translated by Michael Kerawalla
Editor: Birgitta Wolf

Production and Publisher: BoD – Books on Demand, Norderstedt
Cover-Design and Illustrations: Michael Kerawalla

ISBN: 978-3-7386-4277-3

For Sabine

Content

The Book...8

Preface... 9

What happened before.................................. 11

The abduction.. 13

In a strange world...................................... 17

Slave...42

A brief friendship...................................... 69

Escape... 93

Dangerous encounters...................................119

Betrayal...137

In the polar sea..144

In the dome of the sea-elves........................... 155

Natural forces..168

In the empire of the Qails............................. 178

Return...186

Crystal thieves..207

Good friends... 216

The Fire-Crystal..227

Liberation...231

Home again..234

A visitor from Turoon.................................. 244

Life..247

Acknowledgement..250

Turoon and its inhabitants.............................251

Explanation of the term „cavitation".............. 274

The Book

The Velbe-girl Saira lives a happy and carefree life on planet Wuun. She is about to graduate as a magician and is already her master's best apprentice. But one day she gets abducted from her home planet to the waterworld Turoon. After being transformed to a deep-sea creature, she is supposed to work as a slave in a mine for the rest of her life. For the first time, she experiences the horrors of slavery: the dull, harsh physical work, the daily oppression and humiliation by her overseers and the cruelty and coldness of her masters. But Saira is not willing to simply accept her fate. She finally manages to escape with her instructor Cherou, and a long, adventurous and mostly dangerous chase across the ocean takes place. During their escape, the two refugees are drawn deeper and deeper into a network of plots, betrayal, war and destruction, and finally, the destruction of the entire planet seems imminent! Will they be able to change the seemingly inevitable fate of their world, free the slaves and bring peace back to their home? And which part does the mighty Fire-Crystal with its awesome magic power play?

The first great deep-sea fantasy epic, full of suspense and action, plots and ambushes, emotion and passion, magic and mysticism!

Preface

Michael Kerawalla has written an exciting fantasy novel entitled "Turoon", a mystery thriller that has it all: suspense and action, plots and ambushes, emotion and passion, magic and mysticism. Out of these ingredients he weaves a colourful epic, which can easily compete with the great bestsellers of this popular genre. But with "Turoon" he enters completely new territory. At the beginning of the third millennium after Christ, the moon seems more familiar to us than a huge part of our terrestrial world: the largely unexplored depths of our planet's oceans. We are ready to step into space, and yet we do not really know our own oceans.

The Velbe girl Saira is dragged out of her carefree life on planet Wuun, and abducted to the waterworld Turoon. After transformation into a deep-sea creature, she is supposed to work for the rest of her life as a slave in a mine. She is terrified by the mind-numbing daily work of the slaves and their frequent oppression by their cruel, horribly sadistic guardians, for whom having power means that they can revel in the humiliation of the weaker ones at their mercy. Saira rebels against her seemingly unavoidable fate. She succeeds in escaping with her instructor Cherou. Will she ultimately be rescued, or does she flee towards an even worse, even harder future, which may culminate in an apocalypse, the end of the world?

Michael Kerawalla has the perfect skill of a mystery writer. He takes us to Saira's home. We follow the apprentice girl magician into the strange world to which she is abducted, into a hell seemingly without escape. We sympathize with Saira, we share her worries and her hopes. Is it Michael Kerawalla's art of storytelling that fascinates us, that makes us rush from page to page? The author has, without doubt, a great talent to enable us to experience Saira's adventures so very intensely.

But that is not the only reason why we cannot stop reading "Turoon". As exotic and strange as Turoon's world may be, it is somehow familiar to us. In the broadest sense, our blue planet is a waterworld too. Life developed in water before it stepped onto the land. Our earliest ancestors lived in the "primeval ocean". In the thrilling description of this far world, we recognize over and over our own planet of origin. Like never before, the real-life problems of our oceans (and with that, life on planet Earth), are described so thrillingly and, in the best sense of the word, so enjoyably: over-fishing, the dying of the corals, the destruction of the seabed by trawl-nets, water-pollution, the warming and changing of the ocean-streams.

Michael Kerawalla's opus does not point a cautionary finger or deliver a moralizing lecture. It offers thrilling entertainment in a unique underwater mystery novel, a perfect mental movie, which should absolutely make its way onto the big screen. It takes us to distant worlds and confronts us again and again with the destruction of the former terrestrial paradise known as "planet Earth". And there is more. His book describes – as a modern mystery tale set in a time of utopian science fiction – the seemingly hopeless fight of men against an overwhelming fate. But is the battle against adversity and appalling destiny truly hopeless? Or does a spark of hope still glow, for freedom and for peace?

Michael Kerawalla has not written a long theoretical discourse about burning needs and crushing problems, but a thrilling novel that takes our breath away. The crescendo at the end makes "Turoon" a supremely memorable reading experience.

Walter-Jörg Langbein

10

What happened before

Peace reigns once again on Wuun. According to legend, the Gods of the Light once hurled a piece of Wuuns sun onto the planet. Since then, the Sunstone guards this world and controls its development. It preserves life against all influences of the dark side, and so a paradisiacal world came into existence, whose inhabitants live in total harmony with nature. For millions of years the sun dedicated its power to the stone, but gradually its light grew dimmer. One night the dark side invaded unnoticed this world of beauty and peace. It put the Craggots, one of the peoples of Wuun, under its spell, and with their help established an unrivalled reign of terror. A prophecy foretold that one far-away day a Velbe would terminate this reign. So the Velbs, one meter tall, human-like inhabitants of the forests, were mercilessly hunted, caught, or killed. But two Velbe mothers in two different villages succeeded in hiding their children during an attack. The first child, a boy named Keh, was later found by the Guardians of the Light, the servants of the Sunstone, and was raised under their care. The second child, a girl named Hri, was discovered and raised by the Toddles, another race of small, human-like forest dwellers. Both lived a secret life and did not know about each other for a long time, while no other free living Velbs existed for many a year. One day the Guardians of the Light sent Keh on a long journey. He was the chosen one, the one who would end the terror reign of the darkness and bring back peace to Wuun. During that journey he met Hri, whose village was raided and destroyed some time later. She followed Keh and became his constant companion through many dangers and adventures. Both of them finally fulfilled the prophecy and put an end to the reign of darkness. Because all the peoples of Wuun were helpful to each other, the original sense of harmony soon prevailed again and the wounds of the past were quick to heal. Today the inhabitants of Wuun again live together in peace, and nothing reminds them of the awful times they lived through before. These times only live on in the memories and stories of the people, stories that are told over and over again as a constant reminder to all. Keh and Hri live in a village with other Velbs. Their daughter Saira is almost grown up now, and has decided to be a great magician one day. This is why she works as an apprentice to Torem nearly every day. Torem is the master magician of the Velbs, and Saira has become his best student.

The abduction

Keh loved this long walks in the endless forests of Wuun. It had taken a long time for him and Hri to become used to the fact that no danger threatened them here any longer, now that the terror reign of the darkness had ended. Before, they could only move through the forests with utmost caution, for they were in constant fear of being discovered and killed by Craggot patrols. But this awful era had been over for a long time, thanks to their own involvement, and they finally lived a happy life after that long time of deprivation and danger. Now, as their daughter was almost grown up and mostly went her own way, they had more time for themselves again and they enjoyed, among other things, these long walks in their world's beautiful forests. Hri once got stabbed down by a Craggot during the fulfilment of the prophecy. But the Gods of the Light had compassion and gave her back her life. The pain that Keh had felt during this short time had been so unbearable that he had taken even greater care of Hri ever since. Both of them thoroughly enjoyed the time they spent together. Their daughter had grown into a splendid and beautiful young girl who enjoyed the same love and affection, that Keh and Hri had for each other. Saira was supposed to have lessons with Torem today, but when Keh and Hri returned to their cottage, Saira was still there.

"Oh, we thought you had already gone to Torem!" Hri said surprised.

"Yes, I know I'm late!" Saira admitted and packed her utensils. "What will we eat today?" she asked inquisitively.

"Your favourite meal," Hri answered and smiled.

"Oh, great!" Saira said with enthusiasm.

"But only if you are back in time, otherwise I'll have eaten it all," Keh teased his daughter, grinning.

"Mama, you can't allow that!" Saira became indignant and turned to Keh. "Paps won't fit into his clothes any more!" she giggled.

"Don't you get insolent, young lady!" Keh scolded in feigned annoyance and threatened her jokingly with his fist, after which Saira hurried to reach the door.

"You'll leave me some of it, in any case," she grumbled.

"Only if you are back in time," Hri grinned and winked at Keh conspiratorially.

"Oooh, you are mean!" Saira scolded, pretending to be annoyed.

"You just go, we'll certainly leave enough for you!" Hri called laughingly, and Saira ran out waving briefly. Hri looked after her with an amused shake of her head.

"Do you really want to leave her some of that good meal?" Keh asked with a grin, which earned him a disapproving look from Hri.

*

Saira hurried to reach the prophet hall. Slightly out of breath she finally opened the door and nearly ran into Torem.

"Please excuse me, Master, for being late!" she stammered breathing hard.

"That's all right," Torem answered with a smile. "The day is still long, just recover your breath first."

Saira put down her utensils and gave her master a thankful glance, while she took a moment's rest. After her breathing had calmed down, she stepped closer to the big round platform in the centre of the hall. Above it rose a tall crystal dome, through which one could observe the stars by night. Complex magic symbols were engraved in the walls of the spacious hall. Numerous shelves were arranged beneath them, carrying many different herbs and tinctures as well as many types of tools and containers for all kinds of purposes. Every time she looked around the big hall, Saira was impressed anew. Torem was busy with the adjustment of an astronomy tool and did not pay any attention to Saira. At that very moment a bluish fluorescent pane suddenly appeared directly beside her, which quickly grew large, while crackling flashes shot through it.

Torem's head jerked around and he wanted to shout a warning to Saira, but it was too late! The flashes enfolded Saira who was much too surprised to react. She only gawped at the shining disc while she was being drawn right into it and disappeared. Then the strange phenomenon simply dissolved. Horrified, Torem stared at the point where Saira had just stood. Then he raised his magic powers, but he could not bring back the shining disc. The magic phenomenon had not left any traces behind so that he could not pursue it. After some time, he gave up trying and called the Guardians of the Light in the Temple of Lights for help. The tall, solid figures were shaped like Velbs, but they were more than twice their size. Deep wrinkles on their faces bore witness to the fact that they were very old. They immediately contacted the Sunstone. It had observed the phenomenon too, but had not been able to detain it either. The Guardians of the Light promised to do everything within their power to bring Saira back. But even the Sunstone did not succeed in pursuing the spell. They only discovered that it was some type of portal through which Saira had probably been hurled into another world. But they could not determine for the moment where this world was located and what type of world it was. So the guardians of the light and Torem were left extremely concerned, damned to inactivity. How could Torem explain this to Keh and Hri? What would await Saira in that foreign world? She had gained some experience as a magician already, and so was not completely helpless. Torem had taught her how to behave in an emergency. But would these skills help her in the other world? Would she be able to survive there? In despair, Torem conjured up a demon who appeared a short time later above the big, round platform of the prophet hall. It was Tarul, whose solid figure hovered above the platform. His long drawn-out body with the mighty head nearly reached the top of the crystal dome. The metallic blue shimmering skin was covered with protuberances, which were moving constantly. His three big, yellow eyes offered a strong contrast to his dark body. After a short welcome, Torem described to him what had happened. The demon could not help him either, but promised to assist with the search. Demons had much better chances of finding the origin of the portal, because they moved between the dimensions. The shape of the demon dissolved a short time later, as he started the search. So Torem finally remained alone in the big hall. Full of anger about his helplessness he walked up and down restlessly. He was highly concerned about Saira. He could not imagine what might happen to her now. He was ultimately responsible for her. At first, panic rose in him, but finally rationality prevailed. He had to stay calm and continue to try to do everything within his power to find Saira. Again, he raised all his magic powers. But whatever he did was in vain, the Velbe girl remained lost for the time being.

In a strange world

It was always the same! They just abducted some being from its world of origin, transformed its body, and afterwards he had to take care of the rest of it. This time they had brought him a land-dweller. That would make things even more complicated. Now he would first have to teach it how to swim with its new body and practise the echo location with the aid of the body's own sonar system. In addition, the shock would turn out to be significantly worse, when his new protégé realized that it now lived in the sea and its body was similar to that of a deep-sea creature. Many had not survived this shock or had gone mad after a short time. Well, he just had to wait, until his new protégé woke up. It was a female being, that much he could make out at least, because the head and the upper body had barely undergone a transformation. She seemed to be quite young, which obviously increased her ability to adequately overcome the shock. Furthermore, she had a really pretty face, and her slender body would make it easier for her to swim. She was lying on her back in front of him with her eyes still closed, breathing a little clumsily, but regularly. It could not take much longer for her to awaken. But that was all right. It meant that for the moment, he did not have to work in the fire-stone mines with all the other abducted creatures. If everything went well, she would soon be able to start her compulsory labour with the other slaves. The Masters disliked it very much if new slaves took too much time before they could start working. He just hoped that she was not too squeamish, otherwise, right from the start, her chances of survival would be few. She finally stirred. The typical twitches flashed through her body, which she had not properly under control yet. Her luminous organs began to flicker, and then she opened her eyes and looked at him in puzzlement. She wanted to rise up, but did not succeed. He placed a hand on her upper body and pushed her gently back onto the bed. "Lie still," he said to her in a friendly tone of voice. "Have no fear, I won't harm you." With his other hand he patted her head tenderly, which pacified her a little bit. "Can you understand me?" he asked gently. She nodded and uttered a throaty sound. "Well, listen to me carefully! You have been abducted from your world to this place, called Turoon. This planet is a waterworld. There is no dry land, so they have transformed your body to enable you to live here. You look almost like me, only your head and parts of your upper body have retained their original shape." He got up and began to hover beside her with light movements of his fins, so she could see him clearly. His strong upper body carried a hairless head with big, dark eyes and a narrow mouth. Two strong arms arose from the upper edge of his body. His long-drawn abdomen tapered markedly and carried at its end a short tail fin, while the legs were missing all together. But the most impressive parts of his body were the broad, triangular wing fins, which reached from his shoulders to almost the end of the abdomen. They were mostly transparent and carried many luminous oval organs, which emitted a steady, blue-purple light. She looked at him with the utmost surprise, while he continued his explanation. "You will at first have some problems in controlling your new body, and it will be difficult for you to speak, but that will cease after a while. You are breathing water now, which will cause you some difficulty at first, but you will soon become familiar with that too. I will teach you everything you need to know, and will train you to control your body quickly. By the way, my name is Cherou. After a few days, you will have become familiar with everything. Then you will work in the fire-stone mines, just like all the others. The work is very heavy, we are constantly watched, and we are not treated well, but at least we get enough to eat. We are nothing more than working slaves for the Duumars, but you will learn about this some time later. Now it is most important that you learn to control your body as quickly as possible. Do you understand?" he asked emphatically. The girl nodded hesitantly while she looked at him horrified. "Yes," she managed to verbalize huskily. It looked as if she had overcome the initial shock quite well.

"Don't be afraid, you are still under my protection during the first few days, so nothing can harm you. You will quickly become familiar with life here, for it always passes the same way: working, eating, sleeping – day after day." He looked at her sadly. It just was not right to destroy such a young life, to simply misuse it for the arrogant wishes of others. But what could he do? He was a slave too, the only difference being that he had been born on this world and had gathered much experience, which was why he had been assigned to train the new slaves. He wished that he could describe for her a more pleasant future, instead of explaining to her that she would never return home and would work as a slave for the rest of her days. But that was the cruel reality! He could clearly see in her eyes that she had understood his words, and like so many times before, this nearly broke his heart. But he had to fulfil his duty, so once again he suppressed his pity and began to teach her to speak. Luckily she learned very quickly and coped quite well with the new situation. After a short time she could say her name. She was called Saira.

*

For the first time in her life, Saira was utterly terrified. She had lived a carefree and happy life on Wuun up until now. Could all that really be gone? Would she really never see her homeland again and would she really have to work here as a slave for the rest of her life? Stuck in another body, trapped forever on this world? Surely this could not yet be true, but Cherou's words permitted no doubt. "Is there really no chance of returning?" she asked desperately.

"I'm sorry," Cherou answered. "So far, none of the abducted ones has ever returned to his planet of origin. This good fortune is not permitted to any of us. The Duumars are merciless. They force us to work until we finally die in the mines. Some have indeed tried to escape from the imprisonment, but they have all paid with their lives. So banish that from your mind immediately and try to put up with the new situation. The quicker you do that, the better for you."

His hard words hurt her even more. So it was true. She would never see Wuun again, or her parents or any of the other lovely people. The idea was too hard to bear. Memories of her happy childhood appeared in her mind again. She saw her parents' faces of, worried and frightened and unable to comprehend that their daughter would never return. She saw the children of the village, with whom she had always played and cooked up tricks, now completely distraught and unable to understand that she was not there any more. It was just too much! She started to sob quietly on her bed and put her face in her hands. Desperation finally overcame her, and she cried inconsolably.

*

Cherou sank down beside her and caressed her head tenderly. He knew what was happening. He had witnessed it much too often, but it nearly broke his heart while he helplessly had to watch as the sorrow and horror broke out of the defenceless victims, when they finally realized the whole truth and with it the hopelessness of their situation. Now it would become apparent whether the new slave would overcome this shock or perish. Cherou just let her have her way. He had previously tried to comfort the desperate victims with some friendly words, but that induced aversion rather than thanks in the end. The reality was just too cruel, and pleasant words could not help. Saira's body was shaking while her tears flowed and streaked upwards between her fingers. It took a long time for her to calm down again, but finally she moved her hands away from her face and looked desperately at Cherou. This time he could not suppress a compassionate look. "Chin up, girl, you will surely make it," he tried to encourage her. "Don't worry, I will take care of you until you have settled in here." She gave him a thankful look, but kept an embittered silence. "You should first try to get used to your new body," he distracted her finally. "Just try to rise up." She turned her head to him, and her gaze seemed to return from far away, but the twitching of her body and the flickers of her luminous organs showed that she tried to comply with his request. She only managed to move her rear fin, but did not succeed in raising up. "You'd better try with your wing fins," Cherou advised and showed her what she should do. But this attempt failed too at first until Cherou pinched the rim of her wing fin. She instinctively pulled back her fins with a slight outcry and looked at him reproachfully. "I'm sorry, but this way you'll learn more quickly," he apologized. "Now you know what you have to do to use your fins." Indeed she managed to move her wing fins in a coordinated manner after a short time, and finally she could rise up. "Well done, you really learn pretty fast," he praised her. They continued the training for a while, and soon she was able to swim moderately well. Cherou also taught her to control her luminous organs, which she learned quickly too. She seemed to have overcome the shock quite well so far. The coming days would show how well she would manage to get by, but everything looked quite hopeful. Saira was soon exhausted, so Cherou ended the practice for today. Then he disappeared for a short while, and returned with a bundle of long, yellow leaves, the surface of which was covered with many growths. "This is our food down here," he explained. "We call it plopkelp."

"Looks unappetizing," Saira replied. "What's the name of this stuff again?"

"Plopkelp," Cherou repeated with a grin and mashed one of the growths on a leaf. It burst with a gentle plop, and a bubble of air ascended out of it. "That's how the plant got its name," he explained still grinning. Then he took some of the leaves and gave the rest to Saira, who carefully began to nibble. The leaves barely tasted of anything, but at least they were filling. "Tastes rather dull," she grumbled. "Is there nothing else to eat?"

"Unfortunately not in the empire of the Duumars," Cherou answered. "There are some quite delicious things out there in the ocean, but here they feed us only with this stuff. It may not be very tasty, but plopkelp contains all that we need to survive. You better get used to it right now, there's nothing else."

"Really great!" Saira scolded. "Not even anything good to eat around here!"

"Still so demanding," Cherou growled with amusement, which earned him an angry look from Saira. "Now take a rest. I have to report to the Duumars and must deal with some other things, meanwhile you won't be bothered by me," he said, winking. As he caught her worried look, he said soothingly: "Don't worry, I will look after you later. You don't get rid of me so quickly!" He saw a brief smile flitting across her face. She seemed to put up quite well with the situation. It gave him hope that she would be able to endure the mines too. Then he swam towards a big, round mark on the opposite wall. When he had nearly reached it, an opening appeared with a quiet hum, showing an illuminated corridor behind. Cherou quickly passed through the opening and waved to Saira. A moment later the wall closed as silently as it had opened.

*

The Duumar stared at Cherou with his big, yellow eyes, while the Lingit told him of his first experiences with Saira. At the end of his report Cherou briefly looked up at the octopus-like creature, who was at least five times taller than himself. He still could not stand that cold, emotionless stare. As usual, the Duumar let some time pass while he enjoyed Cherou's discomfort, until he finally gave a satisfied growl. "How long until she can work in the mines?" Thurgun asked impatiently, while he nervously drummed one of his eight arms on the floor. He was the first leader of the mine and always anxious that enough fire-stone should be dug. Some days ago, he had lost a slave in a deadly accident and he wanted to replace him as quickly as possible, so that his deliveries would reach the previous level again. His superiors would not like it at all if he produced less than the owners of other mines. He might even lose his job, but he would never let it come to that!

"She will be ready within the next three light phases," Cherou hurried to answer. "As I already told to you, she learns very quickly and she is young and strong."

"I hope so for your sake," the Duumar growled menacingly and finally turned around, so that Cherou was no longer exposed to his harsh stare. "You may leave!"

Cherou bowed down in relief and hastily left the mine's control centre. The most unpleasant part of his work was done for today. Now he could finally look after himself, relax a little bit, before he had to return to Saira and accompany her through the dark phase.

*

Saira had watched the opening and closing of the wall with amazement and now carefully swam closer. But as she stopped directly in front of it, nothing happened. The wall stayed closed. Astonished, she swam up and down in front of the mark, but the wall did not move. She stretched out an arm and quickly touched the wall. It felt completely flat and hard, but did not move. Saira also felt no magic signature, which showed that the wall was not controlled by any type of magic. It had however simply let Cherou pass through, but remained closed for her. The only thing she noticed was a weak flow of energy passing through the mark. At first this confused her. From her lessons she knew that some forms of magic existed, that she could not yet observe because of her lack of experience. But every form of magic left a clear signature behind, which even an inexperienced magician would notice immediately. So this was something completely different. She made no use of her magic skills for now, as she did not know whether she was secretly being watched. Torem had urged her to hide her capabilities in such a situation, for one could never know what might happen. So she finally moved away from the wall and began to examine her surroundings more carefully. She now noticed that the side-walls showed a slight bend, as they were forming a kind of tube. They consisted of a hard, completely flat material, the likes of which Saira had never seen before. But the most peculiar thing about the walls was that they themselves seemed to emit the diffuse bluish light that filled the room without emitting heat. Only the elves of Wuun, her world of origin, were capable of producing something similar with their magic crystals. But these walls were neither made of crystal, nor did they contain a magic spell that caused them to shine. Saira again noticed this weak stream of energy that she had noticed before at the strange opening in the wall. The room itself was divided in two by a wall. A broad, oval opening gaped in its centre. The rear part of the room, in which she had woken up earlier, contained two soft beds affixed to the sidewall, and a reflective surface, in which Saira could see herself. She was fascinated. She wore no clothing whatsoever. Her head and upper body had barely changed except for her skin and hair, which were extremely pale. And she no longer had any legs. The long stretched-out lower part of the body tapered markedly and ended in a short tail fin. Like Cherou, she now carried two big, triangular wing fins, which reached from the base of the tail fin to her shoulders. Their rims were covered with numerous luminous oval organs. She slowly sank to the ground while looking at herself, so that she had to propel herself upwards with light strokes of her tail fin again and again. She could not yet manage to simply hover in the water with slight movements of her wing fins. But in due course she would learn this too. Saira was just glad that she was able to move in a chosen direction, and already could control her new body quite well. She watched the flickering play of colours of her luminous organs with amusement, letting them light up and fade out at will. It was not clear to her for the moment why she had these luminous organs. But nature created nothing in vain. So they surely had a function, which she would likely get to know later. She finally lay down exhaustedly on the bed, and began to analyze her memories. How had she come here? She remembered the bluish disc that had suddenly appeared beside her. She had been pulled in there and finally woken up here in this new body, as a prisoner in a foreign world where she was destined to work as a slave in the future. In a world where nothing was familiar to her. She did not even breathe air any more, but water, did not walk around any longer, but moved by swimming. Water as a medium was of course not entirely unknown to her. Her world of origin had some lakes in which she had swum and dived many a time. There were big oceans on Wuun, which she had never seen, for they were much too far from the big forests where she had lived. But she had heard many stories and legends about them, which were told among the people. Fascinating stories of strange creatures and even stranger habitats. If just some of these stories were true, a completely new world waited for her out there. On the one hand, this knowledge fascinated her. On the other, it started to frighten her. Cherou had told her that he would take care of her until she had settled in, but Master Torem had shared with her a lot about other worlds, about wars, lies and plots. So Saira rather mistrusted her new instructor in this new world. She had no other choice for the moment but to be as wakeful as possible and to watch everything around her very closely. She had to learn very quickly to get around in this world. Saira was certainly not defenceless. Though she was not a fully trained magician yet, she already knew many ways of protecting herself and could well defend herself in case of emergency. It was very clear to her that those who had abducted her to this place were mighty and had great magic powers. Enormous forces were needed for the creation of such a big magic portal! Since she was still on her own for the moment, she had to be very careful, and not reveal herself too soon. She was no match for magicians with such powers. Nothing remained for her than to wait and see how the situation would develop. While she still pondered, she suddenly heard the wall opening again. It startled her out of her thoughts, while Cherou slowly swam in.

"Ah, you have already made yourself comfortable," he said smilingly. Then he sank to the floor next to her. "How are you?" he asked a little bit worried.

"I'm still quite confused," Saira confessed. "In a new body and in completely strange surroundings, I still don't know and can't understand so much here ..."

"You will find your way in due course," Cherou replied understandingly. "I will try to explain most of it to you, as far as I can. The Duumars unfortunately don't leave us much time, for you are supposed to start working in the mine in just a few light phases. But don't worry, you'll have understood most of the things by then, I promise you." He winked at her mischievously. "Now just rest, the dark phase starts soon."

"What dark phase?" Saira asked confused.

"Naturally, you can't know that, for you have never lived in the deep sea," Cherou said. "We are so deep down in the ocean here that the light from the surface can't be seen. So we use self-made sources of light, which light up or darken to the rhythm of the surface light. You must have noticed that the walls here in this room are shining. Their brightness corresponds to the light at the surface. They will slowly darken until they emit no more light. That is the dark phase. When it's getting bright again at the surface, the light phase begins."

Saira nodded knowingly. "That's why you have these luminous organs on your body, because it is constantly dark out there."

"That's right," Cherou answered impressed. "You learn really quickly," he praised her. "Here in the city of the Duumars it is, for safety reasons, never completely dark outside. Only the open ocean is dark," Cherou explained. "Tomorrow I will show you part of this site. You will be impressed," he promised smilingly. "But now it's time to retire. Would you prefer to sleep alone tonight, or should I stay with you?" he asked in a friendly manner.

Saira briefly thought about it. She still did not trust Cherou, but the thought of spending the night here all alone made her shudder.

His presence somehow seemed soothing, and if he wanted to harm her she would teach him a suitable lesson. So she finally answered: "If you don't mind, I should be glad if you stayed with me."

"All right," Cherou said, moved to the bed on the opposite wall and lay down on it. "Try to sleep now, tomorrow we'll have to face a tiring day."

"It's easy for you to talk!" Saira answered, a little reproachfully. "You haven't been put into an unknown body, infinitely far from home in a completely alien environment!"

Cherou turned to her. "Believe me, I know how you feel. You are certainly not the first slave whom I take care of and help to get settled in," he replied understandingly. "I don't know how many slaves I have prepared for their life here. I myself was born here, but I have experienced enough to know how you feel." He briefly stopped talking, then he continued: "You will need all your strength if you want to survive here. So it's really important that you make good use of the rest breaks in future. The earlier you familiarize yourself with that, the better for you."

His harsh words hit her again, but finally she realized that he was right. Only if she was well rested and fully awake would she be able to avoid mistakes, comprehend everything around her in good time and react quickly. "Please forgive me, I didn't mean to be impolite," she said quietly.

"That's all right," he replied. "I would feel the same way in your place." He hoped that this dark phase would at least pass calmly. Many slaves had not survived the first dark phase or had gone mad from sheer fear. Several times Cherou had to get out of harm's way fast, when the slaves had attacked him in rage, desperation or panic. Often, he had barely escaped alive! He would not be able to fulfil this duty much longer, because his increasing age gradually demanded its tribute. The bad experiences he had endured during this time, also had not gone by without a trace, had depleted him and dissipated much of his strength. But if he could not fulfil his duty any longer, he would be of no further use to the Duumars, which meant his certain end. He could only hope that this moment would not come too soon.

"Is there really no way I can return home?" Saira asked into his thoughts.

"I've already explained to you that it's pointless to give yourself such hopes," he grumbled annoyed. "Put that right out of your mind, this place is now your home!" Saira looked at him with a mixture of anger and despair, and he felt sorry that he had griped at her. "At least nobody has ever managed to return to his original home so far," he said conciliatory.

Saira let herself sink back and fought against the rising tears. She swallowed hard several times and managed for the moment to get her despair under control. But while she lay there, many beautiful memories came back into her mind. Her life had been so happy and so completely carefree. Now all this was supposed to be just gone, and she was supposed to spend the rest of her life here, as a slave! She knew from many of her parents' stories what that meant. Despair came upon her again, but she was not prepared to simply accept this fate. Somehow there had to be a possibility of returning home again. She lay awake for a long time, with her thoughts racing around inside of her head. But finally she came to the conclusion that her only chance was to wait until she knew her way around sufficiently. Her magic skills would surely be of great advantage here. But for the moment she only dared to use them with the utmost caution, so that no one would be able to detect her special skills too early. Then maybe she would have a chance to escape from here. These thoughts gave her a kind of pleasure, and she finally fell into a restless sleep.

*

Sometime in the night, Saira woke up out of her tangled dreams. The walls had darkened completely, although there was a bit of light that originated from her and Cherou's luminous organs. Saira was

28

surprised that despite of the dim light she could see everything around her almost as clearly as during the light phase. Apparently, the eyes of deep-sea inhabitants were extremely sensitive and still worked well at very low light levels. Cherou was fast asleep, as far as she could make out from his steady, deep breathing. His luminous organs glowed only dimly, sometimes flickering briefly. Saira avoided intensifying the light of her own luminous organs for fear of waking Cherou. She let herself sink back on her bed and tried to relax. Now she was glad that she had asked Cherou to stay the night. His closeness gave her a certain safety, and the fact that he just calmly slept beside her proved that for the moment she had nothing to fear from him. If he had not been by her side when she woke up in the darkness in this completely alien place, she would have probably been extremely frightened by now. She often had spent the night outside at her parental home, but had always woken up in familiar surroundings, quite different to this night. Cherou's steady breathing, and the certainty that nobody would harm her, let her finally slide down again into a calmer sleep.

*

Saira opened her eyes as she was slightly shaken by something. She gave a start and looked into Cherou's grinning face.

"Wake up, young fin!" he said smilingly and held a bunch of plopkelp in front of her face.

Saira looked at him in confusion until she finally woke up completely and noticed that the light phase had already begun. She briefly rubbed her eyes and then rose up.

"Did you at least get some sleep?" Cherou asked in a friendly manner and handed her some plopkelp.

"I slept little uneasily, but fairly well," Saira answered a bit sleepily and stretched her stiff body. Then she grasped the seaweed, bit into it and crossly pulled a face. Cherou looked at her and smiled, while she unenthusiastically chewed about on the leaves, and gulped the first morsels. Saira noticed his amused look. "Don't you look at me this way, this stuff really tastes completely dull!" she scolded in feigned annoyance, which caused Cherou to break into an even wider grin. "Is there really nothing better to eat here?" she grumbled seemingly desperate.

"I'm sorry, I can't offer you anything better," Cherou answered shrugging his shoulders. "Better finish it, even if it doesn't taste good, you have to remain strong," he told to her.

"Will you show me around afterwards?" Saira asked hopefully. "This room is slowly becoming too small," she confessed.

"With pleasure, but first I have to teach you some things, so that you can get along better outside," Cherou answered.

"What a pity," Saira said disappointedly. "I had hoped we could go out right after the meal."

"It won't take long," Cherou promised. "But now just finish your seaweed!"

"All right," Saira stuffed the last bunch of plopkelp into her mouth.

After she had finally finished eating, Cherou began with his instructions. "I have told you that outside in the ocean it's often completely dark. With our luminous organs we can light up our immediate surroundings, but that's not enough to get an overview. For that we use our sonar." When he noticed Saira's expression of incomprehension, he explained it to her. "We use sound to scan our wider surroundings." Then he uttered a short, steady whistle. Saira still looked at him uncomprehendingly. "Close your eyes and try to produce such a sound, too," he invited her.

Saira at first did not know what he meant, but then she did as she was told, and after some effort she indeed succeeded in producing a similar sound. The next moment she "saw" a somewhat indistinct, colourless image of her surroundings, although her eyes were closed. Her eyes popped open, and she stared perplexedly at Cherou.

"And it seems that you have just seen your surroundings," Cherou said, amused.

"Yes, indeed I have!" Saira acknowledged in surprise.

"A picture is made in your head from the sound that your surroundings reflect," he explained. "Just try it once more, while you slowly turn around, so that you also scan the other parts of the room."

Saira closed her eyes again and, after every whistle, turned a bit further, until she had turned around completely. "This is great, I could see the entire room," she said enthusiastically. "Although the images were in part quite vague."

"That will get better in time when you have gained more experience," Cherou said. "But the picture will never be completely distinct, therefore we need to use an additional method, the clicks," he explained, and Saira again looked at him with bewilderment. He uttered a sequence of loud clicking sounds at closer and closer intervals, until the sounds merged and caused a strange squeaky noise. "We have a special organ, which produces these clicks," Cherou explained and swam closer to Saira. "It is located about here." With an outstretched finger, he touched a point at the base of her throat. "Just try to concentrate on that point and will it to click."

Saira felt with her fingers for the point and noticed a bulge beneath the skin. Then, she closed her eyes to concentrate harder. After a short while she felt contact with the organ and tried to produce some sounds. It took quite a long time but finally Saira managed to produce a whole volley of loud clicking sounds. The next moment she again saw a colourless image of her surroundings. This time the section was smaller, but much more detailed and defined.

"Well done!" Cherou praised her. "I guess this time the image was clearer."

"Oh yes, much more precise and sharp." Saira confirmed enthusiastically.

"With a little bit of practice, you will soon be able to produce single clicks and exactly control their loudness and speed. It's very important that you can control this, because only then you can orientate yourself in complete darkness. Your eyes can deal quite well with very little light, but when it's completely dark they are useless for you. Your luminous organs can only lighten up your immediate surroundings. That won't help you in the open ocean where there's only water in the vast space around you. If you swim fast, you will never recognize any obstacles in time. You'll only manage that by using your sonar!"

Saira nodded. "Then it's probably better if I practice for a while, so that I quickly learn to use the sonar."

"That I would advice," Cherou confirmed. They remained in the room for a while longer, until Saira could at least control the loudness of her whistles and clicks. There would be enough opportunity later, when they were out there, to learn about orientation using the sonar. Then finally Saira was allowed to leave her quarters for the first time. She was able to pass through the opening in the wall with Cherou without problems, and found herself in a tube-like corridor. Luminaries were installed in its walls in regular intervals. Saira observed several further openings in the wall while she swam beside Cherou. Numerous junctions made orientation more difficult for Saira until they suddenly reached the end of the tube. The view that presented itself to her took her breath away. As far as Saira could see, they were above a wide plateau, which was covered with a variety of buildings, some of which were enormous and bizarrely shaped. Each building was covered with numerous bluish luminaries, which gave the area a ghostly appearance. A strange background noise of rising and falling whirring, roaring, stomping and thundering could be heard, which originated from the edge of the plateau. Very big buildings stood there with tall, tower-like outcrops, from which long, dark clouds ascended. The water flickered because of its high temperature, and the surroundings appeared indistinct. The dreadful beauty of what she saw caused Saira to feel a mixture of emotions. The strange surroundings fascinated her, but they frightened her, too.

On her world of origin, people lived as simple forest dwellers in total harmony with nature. Aside from some simple tools for metal and woodworking, they did not have technology or industry, or factories. This was the first time Saira was confronted with these things.

Cherou noticed the inner conflict of her feelings. This had happened to many of the new slaves, when they were confronted with this view for the first time. He hovered silently beside her to give her some time to get used to the situation, and to communicate a little bit of safety to her. Then he slowly turned to her and said smilingly: "I see you are impressed!"

"This is fantastic!" Saira breathed overwhelmed. "This place must house thousands of people!"

"I have never counted them, but you might be right," Cherou said amused. "Do you not have any big cities on your world of origin?" he asked carefully.

"Oh no, none of our villages are as big as this. Not by far!" Saira confirmed. Then she became aware of the background noise, and she asked Cherou where that din was coming from.

He pointed to the big buildings with the towers at the edge of the city. "Over there, in the big buildings, they produce the energy for the city by burning fire-stone. This drives big machines, which make this noise," he explained.

Saira looked at him in amazement. "What are machines?" she asked.

"I'm not really sure. I have never seen them. The slaves are not allowed to go there, and the Duumars don't like it at all if one asks too many questions about it," Cherou answered warningly. "I just know that the fire-stone we dig out in the mines is burnt there. That's why the water is so warm there that it flickers."

"Why is it not permitted to ask questions about it?" Saira asked.

"Because we are just slaves and that's none of our business, in the opinion of the Duumars." Cherou answered slightly annoyed. "You better get used to the fact that we have practically no rights and are just here for working!"

At first Saira looked at him and was dismayed as his harsh words hit her again. But then she remembered the stories that were told in her village. Stories about a bad time in the past, when their world had been ruled by dark powers. Many inhabitants of Wuun had to work as slaves in those days too, and had suffered dreadfully. Saira was born after this terrible time and had seen only happy days, which is why it was difficult for her to imagine the events they talked about. And now she was supposed to experience all of this herself!

"Come with me, I will now show you the place where you will work in future," Cherou interrupted her thoughts. "Please stay close to me, otherwise you might get into a lot of trouble," he told her warningly.

"What do you mean?" Saira asked, amazed.

"You will see soon enough," Cherou answered evasively. "Come on!" Then he pushed himself off and started to swim across the city.

Saira followed him. She was quite confused but remained close to his side. It seemed to her as if she were flying above the city, while different buildings slid by beneath her. This feeling took away some of the fear that was gradually spreading within her. While Cherou swam slowly in front of her, she took the opportunity to study some of the buildings close to her to distract herself a little from her disquieting thoughts. She could see that the buildings were made of dark, smooth rock, and not one of the buildings was like another. They seemed to be built to suit the particular fancy of their inhabitants, or they had been adapted corresponding to their purpose. No particular geometry could be detected, instead it seemed that the buildings were just arbitrarily set onto the plateau, at adequate distance to each other. This could be clearly observed from Saira's elevated position. Her fascination with being able to move in a third dimension intoxicated her and let her forget the sorrows that beset her. But then she suddenly felt the signatures of strong protection and defence spells enclosing the whole city. Some of them were so strong that even a slight touch would cause certain death! Saira shivered as she continued swimming. Although the area above the city seemed to consist only of water, escape was impossible. The layers of water at some distance above the city were sheer death traps. That was why Cherou led her at low altitude above the buildings. No wonder that many slaves lost their lives trying to escape! Lots of them must have perished at this invisible barrier, which doomed to failure any attempt to escape. After some time they reached the edge of the big colony, and Cherou headed towards a brightly illuminated rock face. He stopped at its upper rim and let himself sink down. Saira came up to him and saw a bright, nearly rectangular surface at some distance below them.

Cherou pointed at a group of creatures that looked exactly like him and were working in a line along the rectangular surface. "These are the other Lingits, with whom you will dig fire-stone," he explained.

"So your tribe is called Lingits?" Saira asked.

"That's right," Cherou confirmed.

In the back, a creature was on patrol, whose triangular body was nearly three times the size of a Lingit. Because of the four extremely long striding legs and the foremost pair of limbs, which carried strong shears, it seemed significantly taller than it was in reality.

"There in the back you can see Torg, our overseer," explained Cherou. "He belongs to the Draughs who work for the Duumars. As long as he is in a good mood he doesn't bother us, but he can get really mean. Then you better behave as quietly as possible and work as well as you can, otherwise he'll torment you with his sonar."

Saira looked at him without comprehension. "What do you mean?"

"The beings that are taller than us have a much louder sonar sound. This sound can be very painful for us, which is why it is used as a weapon by these beings. Some even taller inhabitants of the deep sea have such a loud sonar that they can stun or even kill us with it! But you will experience this often enough while you are here."

Saira looked at him in terror. This strange world seemed to her more sinister and bad with every new moment.

"You just behave as inconspicuously as possible and do what they ask you, then you won't get into trouble," Cherou told her. "And better keep out of the Draughs way. They are very unpredictable and aggressive. The overseers in the other mines often treat the Lingits worse than Torg does. Some of them are extremely cruel and malicious, and torment their Lingits wherever they can. You're lucky that you work under Torg. At least he treats us kind of well."

Saira was shocked to hear what Cherou said, and fear gradually rose in her again. At that moment Saira became aware of a giant shadow at some distance above her. A long-drawn being with a big head and a long fin edge above and beneath the tapering body moved along above her. It was at least twenty times her size.

"That's a Galanx," Cherou explained. "They patrol the empire of the Duumars. They belong to the guardians who watch everything here and are ready to fight in an emergency. In here, you are safe from them, and that is good, for their sonar is so strong that they can stun you with it for a long time! They have already foiled some attempted escapes, because they have very precise senses and can track down every being in the surrounding area. The whole region is surrounded by invisible spells too, which are hard to pervade. Some of them are very dangerous, not to say lethal for anyone who gets too close. An escape is practically impossible."

Saira almost replied that she had already noticed these spells, but she just nodded in resignation. "That's why I should stay close to you," she said.

"You learn quickly, young fin," Cherou answered grinning. "Now I shall show you your future work." He pushed himself off again and told Saira to follow him.

Slightly above and at some distance, Saira noticed another brightly illuminated area. "Is that also a mine?" she asked.

"Yes, that's the Gilgoia mine. They dig fire-stone there too. You will soon become acquainted with the Lingits who work there, for they use the same sleeping place as the Lingits from the Sergon mine where we work. Remember that name! You always have to know which mine you work in, when you are asked!"

Saira nodded and tried to memorize the name "Sergon" as well as she could. After a short time they reached another illuminated area, which was markedly smaller than the two previous mines. Cherou dived down and let himself sink to the bottom of the mine with Saira.

"This mine is too small to extract enough fire-stone. So we use it only for training new slaves," Cherou explained. Then he grasped a type of pickaxe and gave it to Saira.

Although the material shimmered like metal, it was much lighter than the metal tools Saira had previously used on Wuun. Cherou showed her a comfortable working posture, where she simply folded the lower part of her body near the tail fin and kind of knelt down. At first it was difficult for her to keep her balance this way, but in time she learned to stay upright with light movements of her wing fins.

"Now try to hack hand-sized blocks out of the fire-stone on the ground," Cherou advised her. "But be careful! You mustn't strike too hard, or the fire-stone will start to burn."

"How can something burn in water?" Saira asked surprised.

"These stones can!" Cherou said, raised his hand and repeatedly struck the floor vigorously with his pickaxe. Suddenly there was a crackle, and at one of the places where he had struck the ground little blue flames flickered up. Slowly but steadily the flames spread out in all directions until Cherou threw sand on them with a quick movement, which smothered the flames. "As you have seen, you can very easily extinguish the fire with sand. You just have to be quick enough. This is why every Lingit gets a box of sand with his tool at the start of his work. It happens over and over again that the fire-stone starts to burn while you're digging."

Saira had watched the scene with incredulous amazement, and now looked at Cherou, surprised. "That's really strange. Stones that burn in water. I've never seen anything like it," she admitted.

37

"Come on, try it yourself!" Cherou invited Saira. She first pounded timidly on the surprisingly smooth rock and produced only some very small pieces. But after some practice she finally managed to hack out adequately sized pieces without straining herself. Then Cherou invited her to strike the rock as hard as possible to produce fire. She needed significantly more attempts than Cherou, because he was clearly much stronger than Saira. But then some tiny flames flickered up off the ground and spread out slowly. Saira quickly grasped a handful of sand from the box and threw it over the fire, which expired immediately. She sighed with relief.

"Well done!" Cherou praised his protégé. "As you are so skilful and learn everything so quickly, you can start your work in the mines tomorrow."

"What, tomorrow already?" Saira called, aghast. "I had hoped I'd be spared for a few more days."

"I would gladly do you this favour, but the Duumars want me to bring each slave into the mines as quickly as possible," Cherou stated. "I can expect very unpleasant punishments if I don't comply. You can surely understand that I want to avoid that. We will work there together, so you don't need to be afraid. Only when I have to train a new slave will I leave you for a short time. You will have long settled in by then and won't need my help anymore."

"This is all going too fast. I know much too little about this new world," Saira argued desperately.

"I have already taught you what you have to know. More isn't necessary because you'll spend the rest of your time in the mine. Try to put up with it, since you have no other choice!" Cherou stated with a harsh voice.

Saira looked at him. She was horrified as it became clear to her how right he was. Then she abruptly turned away from him and sank down. "That's really not fair ..." she whispered on the verge of tears.

"I know," Cherou replied understandingly. "But I can do nothing about it. I'm a slave, just like you. Believe me, I lived here for quite a long time. If there had been a chance to change anything, I would have taken it. But the Duumars and their helpers are just too mighty and cruel. They have never given us a chance, and they won't do it in the future. We are doomed to live and die here as slaves!"

Saira briefly lifted her head and gave Cherou a short and desperate look. Then she broke down completely and started to cry inconsolably. When Cherou tried to embrace her, she pushed him away. So he sank down at some distance and waited with a sad expression on his face. This time it took quite a long time before Saira regained control over herself. The memory of her home, her parents and friends, whom she would never see again, struck her once again, and the pain was barely endurable. But nothing else remained for her than to put up with her fate. As Cherou had said, she had no other choice than to accept the unavoidable. Turoon was her new home and here she would live now, a slave for a cruel, brutal and reckless race of magicians. At least for the moment! Saira never once considered simply surrendering to her fate. One day she would succeed in escaping, and somehow she had to manage to return to Wuun. This was not her world, and she would not at all put up with a life as slave. Never! So she shook off her tears with a defiant expression and turned back to Cherou.

He was glad that she had recovered again. He knew this expression very well from the faces of the other slaves he had trained before. At least she had finally resigned to the situation. That would make it much easier for him to lead her to the mine tomorrow. He cautiously came closer to her. "Are you feeling better?" he asked carefully, at which Saira just nodded quietly. "Then we should use the remaining time to practise your sonar skills a bit more. It sometimes happens that the illumination turns off. Then you must orientate yourself in the dark and be able to work without light.

They spent some more time on improving Saira's echolocation skills until she could orientate herself even in complete darkness. The palpation and identification of objects also worked well in the end, so Cherou finished the training and showed Saira around in the permitted areas. Among other things, he showed her the place where the plopkelp was cultivated and cut. They took a short break there and appeased their hunger. Many Lingits who worked there gave Saira pitying looks when they found out that she would work in the mines, while Saira envied these Lingits their simple activity. She was glad when Cherou finally moved her on. At the end of the light phase Cherou brought Saira back to the room that had been her habitation until now.

"You should know some rules of behaviour and keep to them before you start your work tomorrow. This will avoid much needless trouble and pain for you." Cherou explained friendly but firmly. "We are not allowed to talk with each other while working. If you want to say something, say it in few short words and talk very quietly. The Draughs have very sensitive hearing and can hear you over quite long distances. So be careful, or you will be punished!"

Saira looked at him rattled, then nodded.

"Always try to work rhythmically and with concentration, otherwise it could happen that you'll hurt yourself or one of the other Lingits with your tool. If you can't continue to work, the other Lingits must work more because they have to dig your missing quantity of fire-stone too, and you are punished for your negligence," Cherou explained with a severe expression.

Saira just nodded again in resignation.

"Always behave submissively to Torg and the other Draughs, even if it's difficult for you at the beginning. They are high up in the hierarchy and therefore request the appropriate respect though they don't deserve it because most of the time they are mean and treat us very badly. If you don't, they can be extremely nasty and cruel, which has painful and degrading consequences for you," Cherou admonished her. "If you talk to Torg or answer a question then always call him Genjai Torg. That's a title that identifies him as a superior being. If you don't know the name of the Draugh who talks to you then just call him Genjai. Never forget this or you will soon regret it, that you can be sure of," Cherou promised seriously.

Fear gradually crawled up in Saira again. It became clear to her that every little mistake she made would have unpleasant consequences for her. She had to memorize so much in so short a time, had to observe so many things, that she seriously doubted she would be able to do everything properly from the start.

Cherou could clearly see how she felt and caressed her cheeks with one hand. "You don't need to be afraid. I will look out for you as well as I possibly can and protect you until you have settled in and get along on your own," he promised with a soothing voice. "For the moment, everything appears heavier and more complicated to you than it actually is, because you are still new, but you will settle in quickly. Anyway the days always pass the same. Working, eating, sleeping. I have already told you, if you do what they ask of you and follow the rules, that I have told you about, you have nothing to fear. Just always stay close to me and behave submissively, then nothing will harm you," he promised and gave her an encouraging smile. "Don't worry, other slaves have been less skilful than you and have still settled in without problems. You will get to know them tomorrow. And anyway, I'm always by your side, until I get on your nerves," Cherou grinned and winked at Saira.

She even managed a little smile. Although his words did not soothe Saira completely, behind Cherou's rough style she recognized much sympathy and helpfulness. She just hoped that he would protect her from the worst, at least over the next few days.

"Now it's time to sleep. Tomorrow we have to get up at the start of the light phase to reach the mine on time," Cherou explained seriously. "The first days are always very tiring, therefore you should make best use of the resting periods. There's also a longer break during the working time, so that we can eat enough of your beloved plopkelp," Cherou explained, grinning again, while Saira gave him a chastising look. Then he caressed her cheeks once more. "Now try to get some sleep and don't worry. I will look after you as much as possible, young fin!" he promised.

Slave

Although Saira was slightly nervous and scared, she got some sleep this night, not least because Cherou's presence gave her a certain confidence. She woke up much later, when she was shaken vigorously. As she opened her eyes, she looked straight into Cherou's friendly face.

"Wake up now, young fin!" he said smiling contentedly. It took a moment until Saira was completely awake. She looked around sleepily. The room was just dimly illuminated. Cherou had dimmed his luminous organs too, so he would not blind her. She rubbed the sleep out of her eyes and yawned heartily. Then Cherou handed her a bunch of plopkelp.

"Eat up quickly, so that we can leave in good time," Cherou challenged her.

Saira obediently bolted down the seaweed, this time without comment. Then they left the small room and set out for the mine.

"How are you?" Cherou asked kindly, while he swam beside her.

"A little bit nervous and scared," Saira admitted.

"Understandable," Cherou said. "But don't worry, I'm right here!" Then he winked at Saira encouragingly. She gave him a thankful look.

As they came close to the mine, Saira noticed a whole swarm of Lingits who swam along beneath them. There were so many of them, it made her shudder. "Those are all slaves?" she asked astonished.

"Sure!" Cherou confirmed bitterly. "All my people live here as slaves, some of them already in the third generation! There's not a single free Lingit anymore out there in the ocean. They all were caught by the Duumars and put into slavery," he explained sadly.

Saira looked at him, horrified, but kept quiet, so she would not cause Cherou even more grief. Instead, she watched how the sheer endless stream of slaves gradually divided and moved off in different directions, while they swam above it. She threw a short glance at Cherou, but he just swam beside her, his face blank. However, she could feel how this sight hurt him. There had to be thousands of slaves who lived and worked here. She could well imagine how he felt inside but had no more time to think about it because the Sergon mine came into view. Saira's nervousness rapidly increased as she sank deeper with Cherou. Many Lingits had already gathered on the well-illuminated plateau. Most of them just waited with apathetic expressions. Only a few of them noticed their arrival. Some of them cast a short glance up to them, but then turned away again, uninterested. Aside from some reproachful looks, Saira barely notice any reaction to her arrival. The whole scene seemed spooky because none of the Lingits said anything. The silence lay on Saira like a heavy cloak, while they finally reached the bottom of the mine. She did not dare to speak either, for fear of making a bad impression. Saira gave Cherou a helpless look and he answered with a soothing nod of his head and gestured for her just to wait quietly. Saira looked around with a fair degree of discomfort. The lethargy of the Lingits confused her more and more. What had been done to these creatures to make them behave like that? Fear crawled up in her again, and she moved closer to Cherou without being aware of it. He was the only being that was at least a bit familiar to her. From whom she could hope for some protection. She suddenly heard a faint stomping that quickly grew louder. The silhouette of a Draugh came into view; it hurried into the mine a short time later. As the long-legged creature entered the mine, Saira shivered from the frightening look that it gave her. The Draugh seemed to be ten times her size. The dark armour that enclosed the whole creature, was studded with countless protuberances. The huge shears on the first pair of extremities seemed as threatening as the mighty jaw claws that seemingly never stood still. The group of Lingits suddenly began to move. As if driven by an invisible command they swam to their working places and started to dig fire-stone. Only Cherou did not stir. The Draugh paused and looked around with its crystalline shining stalk-eyes. His gaze finally settled on Saira and Cherou. He pounded over to them and rose up in front of the two Lingits.

"Is the new slave ready for work?" his rough voice roared.

Cherou bowed down briefly. "Sure, Genjai Torg, as you desire it," he said in a friendly voice.

The Draugh now mustered Saira with a cold look. "What's your name, slave?"

"My name is Saira, Genjai Torg," the Lingit girl answered politely and quickly bowed down.

The Draugh laughed harshly. "As it seems, you have again done a really good job, Cherou!"

Cherou bowed down with unsurpassable elegance. "Just as you would expect from me," he said.

Saira noticed the mockery in Cherou's voice but did not let it show. The Draught did not react to it either. Maybe he did not notice it, or maybe he just let it pass.

"Then I'm sure you know that you're forbidden to speak during the working time, unless you have to report something, or I ask you a question," Torg turned again to Saira.

"That I know, Genjai Torg," Saira agreed as calmly as she could.

"Well then, move to your places and start working," Torg yelled at the two Lingits.

Cherou gave Saira a sign to follow him. He slid into a gap between the other Lingits. Saira took the place next to him. She greeted the Lingit beside her with a friendly smile, but he just gave her a reproachful look and did not take any further notice. Slightly confused she took her tool and began digging. She really did not feel good between the doggedly working Lingits and being constantly watched by Torg. It was difficult at first for her to concentrate on the work. Leastwise Cherou sometimes gave her a friendly smile, which soothed her a little. When her collection bin was filled with fire-stone for the first time, she heard Torg pounding up to her from behind and got really nervous. The Draugh quickly inspected the filled box. "You are doing a good job, carry on!" he ordered

Saira and replaced the full box with an empty one. Then he pounded away with the filled container and put it down at the edge of the mine, where it was later taken away by another Draugh.

"At least he is in good mood today," Cherou whispered and winked at Saira, who smiled with relief and relaxed a little. The Lingit next to Saira gave her a condescending look. Saira clearly felt the aversion he displayed towards her. The disdainful behaviour from most of the Lingits seemed very disturbing to her and made her feel extremely uncomfortable, since she did not know the reason for it. Maybe Cherou could later give her an answer. The whole atmosphere in the mine, the desperate silence of the Lingits, and the constant observation by the Draugh put more and more strain on Saira. Her arms started to hurt from the tiring work too, while the hours seemed to drag along endlessly. She was startled by an extremely loud howling sound that suddenly reverberated through the mine. The next moment the Lingits dropped their tools and swam to the rear part of the mine.

"Come, it's mealtime," Cherou explained and dropped his tool too. Saira did the same and followed Cherou to the other Lingits. A large container was standing there. An older Lingit distributed the plopkelp it contained to the workers. When it was Saira's turn, the old Lingit briefly hesitated, but then handed her a portion with a friendly smile. Saira thanked him with a brief nod and smiled back at him. Then she moved with Cherou to the edge of the mine and ate her seaweed.

"How are you?" Cherou asked quietly.

"Completely exhausted and my arms hurt" Saira answered tiredly.

"Then take a rest now. You have already completed half of the working time," Cherou remarked encouraging. "If it's getting too tiring for you, then just work a bit slower. I will support you as well as I can, then Torg won't notice."

Saira gave him a thankful smile and looked around uncertainly. "Why are they all so stand-offish?" she asked as quietly as she could.

"I'll explain later, after work," Cherou whispered. "You'd better get some rest until we have to get back to work."

Saira had to make do with this reply, so she tried to relax a little. The break was over much too soon anyway, and she had to return to work. Today, time seemed to expand endlessly, and Saira was really not sure if she had enough strength to last to the end of the working period. Later she just hammered and dug without thinking, every muscle of her arms hurting and every movement turning to torment. Cherou had told her to cut smaller pieces, which were not so heavy, but after some time this did not help anymore either. She would never have managed the required quantity if Cherou had not helped her. Later still, she barely noticed her surroundings anymore, did not even hear the signal that announced the end of the working period. Only when Cherou carefully stopped her working, she woke up from her trance. At first, she looked at him without comprehension, until his voice reached her.

"It's over, you've made it!" he said urgently.

It took a moment until she realized what he had said and finally, she dropped her tool, relieved.

"Come on, I'll now guide you to the communal place where the other Lingits have their resting place too," Cherou explained and told her to follow him.

"Is it far away?" Saira asked completely exhausted.

"No, just a short way from here," Cherou said. "There I'll look after you, so keep up, we'll soon be there."

Saira again resigned herself to her fate and followed Cherou as best she could, but the distance seemed endless to her. What she had observed in the morning now repeated itself the other way around. Huge swarms of Lingits left the mines and gathered to swim to their resting places. Saira and Cherou were part of a big group too until they finally arrived at their destination. Cherou led Saira into a huge, well-illuminated cave where many Lingits had already assembled. Most of them had simply settled comfortably on the smooth sandy ground. Some few of them talked quietly

46

together. Cherou finally stopped and let himself sink to the ground a little away from the others at the edge of the cave, followed by Saira, who was glad to take a rest at last. Cherou asked her to lay flat on her face so he could help her with the pain. Saira willingly complied, and Cherou began to systematically massage particular areas on her back. The effect was amazing. After a short time her cramping muscles relaxed and the pain eased quickly.

"Are you feeling better now?" Cherou asked after the treatment.

"Oh yes! Much better!" Saira answered eagerly and stretched out contentedly in the sand. "How have you done this?" she asked inquisitively.

"I also work as a healer, therefore I'm quite well versed in this field," Cherou answered. "Now rest up, you had a very hard day. But you have done well," he praised her.

"I thought the day would never end!" Saira sighed tiredly.

"That happens to everyone at first, but soon you'll become accustomed to the work," Cherou said.

"Maybe you can explain to me now why the Lingits are so rejecting towards me?" Saira whispered.

"In their eyes you are a so called Thae'Kor, some type of weird being," Cherou explained after a short while. "You are neither a Lingit, nor what you have been before your transformation. All Thae'Kors are from another world and originate from another culture. A culture that often seems strange or even bizarre to us. Often they behave very strangely as a result, which mostly seems really repulsive to the Lingits. Many of us also have had some bad experiences. Admittedly, all kind of rumours are going around about you people, which mostly don't comply with reality. But many of us give credit to these stories, therefore most of the Lingits don't like you." As he caught her worried look he added soothingly: "Don't worry, you don't need to fear them. At first, just keep away from them. And eventually, they will accept you."

"Hopefully!" Saira replied. "I really feel very uncomfortable among the other Lingits at the moment."

"That's understandable," Cherou replied. "But if you behave inconspicuously and work well, your origin soon won't disturb them any longer."

Saira stretched out in the sand again. "I suppose I can fall asleep right now. I'm so tired, I can barely keep my eyes open."

"Then you should better lie on your back," Cherou advised her. "Otherwise you'll inhale sand tonight, which may be very unpleasant. Then you'll have a coughing fit and wake up the other Lingits, which will make you quite unpopular. "

"As you like ...," Saira replied, yawned and turned on her back. A short time later her deep, regular breathing proved that she had fallen asleep.

Cherou made himself comfortable beside her and looked at her pensively. For the first time in a long while, he was not quite sure of his feelings. Before, he had never felt anything for the abducted slaves other than compassion, but with Saira it was different. Her gentle, funny, and sometimes still childlike manner seemed very attractive to him and made her extremely likeable. He felt a certain affection, which he had not felt for a very long time. He actually could not afford such feelings, for he had to do his duty and would certainly have to take care of and train up many more slaves. She was not even a real Lingit, but for some reason that did not matter. The long loneliness and the dull, harsh life was gradually taking its toll. He did not know how to handle his feelings for the moment, but to start with, he would take care of Saira as much as possible, stay close to her and protect her as well as he could, until he was more certain of the situation. He finally fell asleep contentedly beside her with this thought in his mind.

*

Torem was nearly driven to despair. The morning had already gone and still he had found no trace of Saira. The spell that created the portal was so complex that not even the Sunstone could determine its origin. The inextricable mesh of magic was constructed with a tremendous number of traps, false tracks, deceptive and defensive spells. Only a very strong magician with enormous knowledge could create such a spell. But what type of character was this magician? Did they have to fear further attacks? How could they defend themselves against him? The Sunstone had immediately placed a very strong shield around the planet, but that did not ensure full protection against new attacks. No further abductions had happened so far. Although all the magicians of Wuun were watching their surroundings with utmost attention, they had not been able to detect any unusual activity so far. The demons attempts to discover a trace of Saira were in vain too. The deception of the portal was so perfect that all the traces got lost somewhere in the higher dimensions. Though all of them did their best, the probability of finding the Velbe girl rapidly decreased.

*

Saira hacked, dug and shovelled as fast as she could, but the huge hill of fire-stone that rose up in front of her seemed to grow even higher with every strike of her tool. She did not know how long she had already been working. Her whole body just consisted of pain, but she tried with all her strength to work even faster. She hacked more and more fiercely at the fire-stone, cut bigger and bigger pieces out of it and threw them in the collection bin beside her, which seemed to grow in parallel with the hill, too. Her strength faded very quickly now, her tool grew heavier with every strike, but with the power of desperation she continued hacking. She suddenly struck too hard, and the fire-stone very quickly went up in flames. She desperately tried to extinguish the flames, but the whole hill was already on fire. Saira watched with horror as the burning pieces that came away from the hill rumbled downwards. The hill became more and more unstable. Bigger and bigger pieces came away and crashed to the ground around her. Saira seemed to be paralyzed and could not move, as the whole hill finally collapsed.

It plunged down with a tremendous noise and buried her beneath tons of burning debris ...

Saira shot up and sucked in a whole lot of water. It took her a moment to realize that it had all just been a bad dream. Shivering and confused she looked around. Although the lights of the hall had been extinguished, she could see very well. All around her, Lingits lay in deep slumber, only their luminous organs glowed or flickered slightly. Saira noticed with relief that she had not woken anybody up. Cherou slept beside her, breathing deeply and calmly. She sank back and made herself comfortable again, but the dream had upset her so much that at first she could not relax. Only when she cuddled up to Cherou and felt his closeness, she relaxed again and finally fell into a peaceful sleep.

*

Suddenly Saira was fiercely shaken awake. A bit confused she opened her eyes slightly and hazily saw Cherou's smiling face. "What's the matter, why are you waking me up already?" she grumbled sleepily. "I have only just fallen asleep!"

"Surely not!" Cherou answered amused. "Open your eyes, and you will see that the light phase has already begun."

Saira complied with his demand hesitatingly and squinted into the light. "But I'm still so tired ..."

"I know," Cherou said understandingly. "That's why I let you sleep as long as possible, but now we have to start for the mine, otherwise we won't get anything to eat."

Saira had woken up completely and noticed that the big cave was almost empty. She got up a bit clumsily and followed Cherou to the mine. A short time later they reached the brightly illuminated plateau where the old Lingit from the day before was already handing out fresh seaweed to the workers. Cherou and Saira lined up with the waiting Lingits. When it was Saira's turn, the old Lingit hesitated again.

"Ah, one of our new ones!" he said smilingly and pulled out a big bunch of plopkelp. "For you I have reserved a special portion." He bowed slightly forward and whispered "But don't tell anyone about it," while he winked at her mischievously.

Saira at first looked down with embarrassment, but then gave him a big smile and, after a short pause, said: "I promise!" She nodded at him thankfully, while the old Lingit winked at her again with a conspiratorial expression.

Cherou had watched the whole scene with amusement. When it finally was his turn, the old Lingit gave him a portion of seaweed.

"Take good care of her, she is still so young!" he whispered kindly and a little bit worried.

"Sure, old friend!" Cherou answered in a whisper and nodded at him gratefully. Then he joined Saira at the edge of the mine.

"At least the Lingit at the food supply is nice to me," Saira said quietly.

"Old Flemm is nice to everyone. He is also one of the oldest Lingits and has experienced quite a lot," Cherou said.

"So you two have known each other quite well for a long time," Saira said inquisitively.

"Indeed!" Cherou replied. "He has trained me up, and many other Lingits in the mines, and taught me nearly everything I know today. One day he got too old for the hard work. So they assigned him to the food supply. He was lucky. If somebody is no longer able to work, he normally gets ..." He wrapped a seaweed-stalk around his hand and tore it with a rip, while Saira looked at him, horrified. "But Old Flemm has just too much experience for them to simply get rid of him. Nobody knows more about seaweed cultivation, and he is better versed than anyone else in the medical arts."

"You want to tell me you're ..." Saira searched for words, "... simply killed when you're too weak or old?" she whispered.

Cherou did not answer, but the look he gave her seemed to confirm her statement. At that moment, Torg entered the mine and immediately went straight up to some Lingits who had gotten up too late.

"Will you start working, you rotten parasites, or shall I cut your fins?" the Draugh snorted loudly and crushed his big shears together menacingly, while the Lingits hurried to take their places.

"Be careful, today he's in a bad mood!" Cherou whispered to Saira. She cast a short glance over her shoulder and saw the Draugh rising up menacingly behind them. Once more fear crawled up inside her, and although she had not recovered from the previous day, she tried to work as quickly and with as much concentration as possible, though her arms again started to hurt after a short while. The other Lingits worked more grimly too, and the fearful silence that lay over the mine seemed extremely oppressive to Saira. But her suffering got even worse later when Torg, completely without reason, shouted at one of the Lingits and accused him of working too slowly. Then he grasped the Lingit with his big shears and dragged him brutally backwards. The Lingit vainly begged for mercy as Torg pressed him in the sand right in front and tormented him with extremely loud sonar pulses. His victim writhed screaming and whining in the sand, while Torg kept tormenting him mercilessly. The cries of the Lingit were hard to bear for Saira. The sonar pulses were painfully loud even for her, how bad must they be for the poor Lingit. While Saira paused shortly, Cherou hissed at her: "Carry on!" Saira gave him a desperate look, but continued working as well as she could. Torg never seemed to finish his punishment, but tormented the Lingit further with his sonar.

"Why doesn't he stop?" Saira whispered on the verge of tears.

"Don't care about him and continue working, or you are next!" the Lingit beside her hissed threateningly. His look left no doubt how serious he was.

At that moment Torg at last finished torturing his victim and let him go. The Lingit swam totteringly back to his place. He shook so much that he could barely hold his tool.

"Let that be a lesson to you! This will happen to everyone who doesn't work properly!" Torg shouted threateningly and rose up again behind the Lingits.

Saira was relieved, but the cruel punishment, which was completely unjustified, had upset her so much that she could barely concentrate on her work. Every time the Draugh came close to her, she winced and expected to be punished next. She still made an effort to dig as much fire-stone as possible, although her arms hurt terribly. The signal that initiated mealtime finally seemed like salvation. She wordlessly took her seaweed and sat down in the sand somewhere apart from the other slaves. Old Flemm had just given her a pitying look this time. Cherou sat down beside her. When Saira chewed on her seaweed mutely, with a blank face, he asked anxiously:

"Are you all right?"

Saira just gave him a quick look and nodded. Over and over again, the terrible incident of the Lingit's punishment went through her mind. Again and again she heard the terrible cries of the tormented victim. She felt real fear for the first time in her life. She really did not know how to handle this, but then she felt Cherou's hand on her shoulder.

"I know how you feel," he said gently. "All of us felt that way at first. We too had to learn to live with the unfairness and the cruelty of our masters. Just try to distract yourself from your feelings by working." Then he gave her an encouraging look. "One day it won't bother you any more!"

Saira was not really convinced, but she gave Cherou a thankful look anyway. Then the break was over.

*

The rest of the day passed without further incidents, so Saira did not have to witness any more punishments. She tried to follow Cherou's advice and concentrated on her work as well as possible, but she just could not ignore the leaden atmosphere in the mine. The other Lingits did not seem to feel better either. They hacked, dug and shovelled, their blank faces even grimmer than usual, while Torg patrolled behind them with menacingly open shears and seemed to control their every move. Time appeared to extend endlessly, and for the first time in her life Saira yearned for the end of the day. She rather felt her arms, as well as the rest of her body, refused to obey. Never before had she been so exhausted and at the end of her strength, when at last the signal announced the end of the working time. Tired as she was, she just dropped her tool and hurried to leave the mine as quickly as possible. A short time later Cherou came up and swam quietly beside her. He was also wrapped in his thoughts. Although he had witnessed many punishments before, he was still horrified every time one of the Lingits had to endure the torture. Even today, the brutal and unfair behaviour of the Draughs sometimes made him furious because the Lingits were defencelessly at their mercy. He had hoped that Saira would not be confronted with this dark chapter of their existence so soon. However, she now realized what she had to expect if she did not resign herself to her fate. It remained to be seen how she would cope with it.

*

Thurgun looked with obvious contentment at the current information concerning the quantity of fire-stone his slaves had dug today in the Sergon mine. The result clearly surpassed the quantity achieved by the Gilgoia mine. Torg's little punitive action had definitely not missed its target and had pushed the Lingits to even greater efficiency. He could count on this Draugh, as usual! Thurgun would soon express his thanks to him with a small Lingit, which the Draugh could tear apart and eat up with gusto. "These Lingits are of no use for anything else," Thurgun thought snidely. At least the new slave was doing a good job. He had at first refused to take a Thae'Kor into his group, but no real Lingit could be obtained at the moment. So he had of necessity agreed to replace the missing slave as quickly as possible and so far, he had not regretted his decision. Pegrell, the leader of the Gilgoia mine, would surely now wriggle his eight arms furiously because the quantity of fire-stone mined by him was lower, Thurgun thought to himself with malicious delight and rubbed four of his arms together. That had to be celebrated, he thought good-humouredly and went to the entertainment centre.

*

Saira sank onto the floor at the edge of the huge sleeping cave, a bit apart from the other Lingits, and made herself as comfortable as possible in the soft sand. Her whole body hurt, and today's terrible experiences still worried her. She just wanted to be left alone. Again and again she witnessed the Lingit's cruel punishment in her mind. Saw how Torg brutally grasped and dragged him away, then tormented him with his sonar, heard the terrible cries of the defenceless victim, felt the fear of the remaining Lingits. Slowly, panic crept up on her, and she began to shiver uncontrollably while she stared into space, her eyes wide with dread. Cherou noticed this, carefully laid an arm around her shoulder and asked anxiously: "What's the matter with you?"

"Oh Cherou, this terrible punishment, I just can't ..." the rest was lost in quiet sobbing as her strain finally dissolved in a violent crying fit. Cherou gently held her tight while she hugged him shakily. He had not expected that this experience would horrify her this much. She must have come from a carefree life without fear and violence, or such events would not upset her so much, he thought.

Saira had indeed enjoyed an easy-going childhood until now, and had never experienced or been witness to any type of violence or cruelty. On Wuun, her world of origin, everyone lived a peaceful life. Once there had been a bad time in the past, while the power of darkness had spread terror and fear on their planet. But that had happened long before Saira's birth. The wounds of this terrible period had healed long ago, and the inhabitants of Wuun lived a calm and harmonious life again. They helped and respected each other. So Saira had grown up well protected, with all the love and compassion one could hope for. No wonder the cruel behaviour on Turoon frightened her so much and shook her deeply. It took a long time until Saira had calmed down again and loosened her grip. Cherou let go of her, gently caressed her cheeks and asked cautiously: "Are you feeling better now?"

Saira lifted her face and looked at him, her eyes veiled with tears, but nodded wordless.

"I can understand very well that Torg's brutal behaviour shocks you. We all had to learn to cope with it. Most of us simply try not to think about it, we just concentrate on the work. There's nothing else we can do, and otherwise we would all go mad with fear." Cherou explained understandingly.

Saira swallowed hard a few times and then asked uncertainly: "Have you never fought against it?"

"Oh yes, there have even been real rebellions," Cherou stated. "But the Duumars and their helpers stopped them with brutal force and punished the leaders in such a cruel way that we haven't dared to rise up since then. It would just cause more bloodshed."

Saira looked at him horrified again. "Why is everybody so cruel and unfair in this world?" she finally asked uncomprehendingly.

"The Duumars and their helpers have their own idea of fairness. As long as they are stronger than us, nothing will change," Cherou explained. "Don't think about it. We all have asked ourselves the same question, and haven't found a solution yet. We just have to accept it, although it is very difficult for us. We have no other choice." Cherou decided to keep to himself that some of the Lingits had already committed suicide in the magic traps, because they could not stand the cruelty any longer. He did not want to shock Saira even more. "But don't worry, new slaves are always spared by Torg, because they first have to get used to the hard work. So you have nothing to fear for the moment," Cherou stated. "Now try to relax. You have worked a lot today and must recover now."

Saira nodded and looked at him a bit embarrassed. "Would you just hold me tight for a little while?" she finally asked quietly.

Cherou gave her an understanding smile and said: "With pleasure, if it feels good to you." Then he settled down next to Saira, laid an arm around her and held her softly and tightly, while Saira cuddled up to him. "Is this okay?" he asked kindly.

"Yes, thank you," Saira replied quietly. Cherou's closeness felt good and seemed soothing to Saira. She gradually relaxed, and her fear faded.

Cherou also enjoyed the smooth touch of her body. It was a long time since he had last held a Lingit girl in his arms. It felt good to experience the closeness of another being, although Saira was no real Lingit. To feel her so close beside him was more than pleasant, and for the first time in ages, Cherou experienced a feeling of affection again. He gently caressed her head and a short time later noticed that she had fallen asleep in his arms.

*

The next morning Saira woke with a start to the sound of the waking-up signal and immediately sank back groaning. Her whole body hurt, all her muscles seemed to rebel at every movement.

"Stay put and don't move," Cherou advised her and held some strange looking leaves in front of her. "Eat that, then you will soon feel better and the pain will ease."

Saira obediently stuffed the leaves into her mouth and a short time later pulled a disgusted face.

"I thought right away that the leaves would taste good to you," Cherou said with a wide grin. "You could really get used to them!"

57

Saira choked down the leaves and gulped some water to get rid of the gross taste. "Yuck, that really tastes disgusting!" she scolded.

"You young fins just don't know, what's good for you," Cherou teased her.

"Not true!" Saira grumbled. "This makes even your plopkelp taste delicious!"

"As I can see, you're slowly acquiring a taste for it," Cherou teased her further.

"You are quite outrageous!" Saira scolded in feigned annoyance.

"And you look sweet when you're angry," Cherou retaliated.

Saira shot up and put her hands on her hips. "My father always says that, when he teases mother or me with his jokes!"

"Well, he's right!" Cherou said, grinning. "It seems you're feeling all right again," he remarked after a brief pause.

The pain had indeed eased and Saira could move again much more easily. "That hideous herb has really helped!"

"I can happily get you more of it, if you like it so much," Cherou said as casually as possible.

Saira glared at him. "You really are outrageous!"

"And I'm hungry, so let's swim to the mine," Cherou said with a challenging gesture. "To your beloved plopkelp," which earned him another hard stare from Saira.

"Cheeky fellow!" she growled pretending to be annoyed. When Cherou wanted to swim off, Saira stopped him and looked down, a little embarrassed. "By the way, thanks for being so nice and understanding yesterday."

Cherou gave her an amicable smile. "You're welcome young fin," he answered kindly. Then they swam out together. "The effect of the leaves will fade with time. Try to keep going until mealtime. I have asked Flemm to give you some more of the leaves with the seaweed, for you to last through the day."

"Thanks, you're really nice," Saira answered touched. "Though this stuff really does taste hideous!"

58

*

The next few working days passed without further incidents, so Saira did not have to witness more punishments, which was quite a relief for her. She also gradually got used to the hard work and the monotonous existence.

Thurgun however could not at all get used to the fact that, once again, at the Gilgoia mine markedly more fire-stone had been extracted than in his Sergon mine. That sneaky Pegrell had simply acquired another slave, and now he drove his workers to the limit. He really stopped at nothing to achieve success, but his triumph would not last long. If his masters had approved another worker for Pegrell, that slave-driver, they would have to allocate more slaves to him, too. Thurgun immediately started to put his plan into action. He would show that slave-driver Pegrell!

*

Just two light phases later Cherou was sent to Thurgun after work. Saira could already imagine what he would have to tell her when he returned to the sleeping cave a short time later.

"Unfortunately I have to train another slave," Cherou explained regretfully. "They'll bring him or her over during the next light phase."

"That quickly?" Saira called astonished.

"I'm surprised myself that Thurgun has requested a slave again," Cherou replied.

"Then you're not in the mine with me tomorrow ," Saira said disappointedly. She felt quite uneasy. She had hoped that more time would pass before she had to work in the mine on her own.

"It will take just a few light phases until I have familiarized the new slave," Cherou tried to comfort her. "Don't worry, you will get along fine on your own. I don't even have to wake you up on time anymore, dream-swimmer!"

59

A brief smile flitted across Saira's face. She had certainly settled down some, but Cherou's closeness still gave her much-needed support. She also did not have to fear the other Lingits, who still excluded her but left her alone. The idea of being completely on her own made her feel very uneasy. "I suppose I will miss you quite a lot," she admitted slightly embarrassed.

"Don't worry, you will be just fine!" Cherou said. "As I told you, it will take just a few light phases. If you have any problems, you can always ask Flemm. He will certainly help you." I will miss you too, he added in his thoughts, but did not tell her. Although at first he did not want to admit it, he had become very fond of this warm-hearted, sometimes a little naive Thae'Kor and felt more than just sympathy for her. "Furthermore, you don't have to put up with me annoying you for the next few light phases!" he joked, to hide his feelings.

"I don't anyway," Saira replied quietly. "Although sometimes you are outrageous," she said and winked at him.

"Who ... me?" Cherou asked with feigned disgust and pulled his most harmless face.

"Yes, you!" Saira confirmed.

"And you are the most naughty young fin I ever met!" Cherou retaliated and pinched her in the belly, which made Saira wince giggle. Then they made themselves comfortable next to one another in the soft sand and Cherou stroked her cheek. "Don't worry, you'll get along fine on your own. Nothing can harm you as long as you work and aren't conspicuous."

"I hope so," Saira said uncertainly.

"And I hope that the new slave learns as quickly as you did," Cherou confessed. "Even though I don't have to work in the mine during that time, it often isn't easy to train the new slaves for their new life here."

"It's cruel enough just to be abducted to this place from your own world," Saira said angrily. "But then to learn that you have to work here as a slave for the rest of your life, that's almost unbearable."

60

"That's the worst moment for me too, you can be sure of that," Cherou said and lowered his gaze.

Saira just looked at him with pity. "I can imagine. I think I would feel the same," she said understandingly. "Do you want to talk about it?"

"Maybe some other time," he replied evasively. "We'd better just enjoy this dark phase together."

"As you like," Saira answered and gave him a lovely smile. Then she cuddled up to Cherou and they both enjoyed being close to each other.

*

Next Morning, the farewell was hard for both of them and Saira felt distinctly uncomfortable as she swam out to the mine on her own for the first time. But the day passed as usual. She only missed Cherou during the break, because the other Lingits just ignored her and she was completely alone during that time. After work, Saira first used her time to take a closer look around near the sleeping cave. She moved as inconspicuously as possible within the permitted areas and examined the magic barriers and traps that surrounded her. Many spells were still unknown to her, others much too strong to overcome. She finally returned to the sleeping cave without having found a suitable place because the dark phase began. Saira hoped to have better luck in one of the other areas. Somewhere, there must be a spell she could overcome. She just had to be patient and keep looking around inconspicuously. She would surely find a place from where she could escape. Once outside, maybe there was a possibility to get in contact with the Sunstone or the demons, so that she could finally return home. Memories of her former home planet Wuun came flooding back to her. Memories that she had pushed far away until now, because they were too painful. She thought about her parents again. They would be completely desperate, for they had lost their only daughter whom they had raised so lovingly and with so much kindness, on Wuun, where Saira had spent such a carefree childhood. In her imagination, she saw her village again, surrounded by the beautiful forests of her world of origin. Saw its inhabitants who would surely all mourn her, especially the children and young people who had grown up with her ... No! She must not think about! It hurt too much! She swallowed hard as tears rose into her eyes. Whichever way she would manage it, she had to return home again, somehow! This terrible place full of cruelty and brutality would never be her home. The other poor victims did not belong to this place either. Maybe Saira could also help them to finally return to their home. But first she had to get away from here. She decided, while Cherou was away, to search intensively for a place that would enable her to escape. There must be a possibility to flee from here! There must be a place somewhere in the magic wall that she could pass through with her magic powers. She must not surrender, but she also had to be careful not to draw attention to herself. The possibility of getting away from this terrible place was soothing to Saira. She finally fell asleep contentedly with this thought in her mind.

*

They had again brought a land-dweller to him! Why did they not abduct creatures from other waterworlds? That would make his job so much easier. Again, it was a female being, actually much too young and delicate to work in the mines. Cherou predicted that this would be another hard task. He didn't know how adept she would turn out to be and how quickly she would learn, provided she would ever overcome the shock. He just hoped that she would settle down as quickly as Saira had. But considering her delicate shape, it did not seem likely that she was particularly suited for digging fire-stone. That meant a longer learning period, which would surely annoy Thurgun very much. Torg would not be amused by this tender creature, either. So, a great deal of displeasure and difficulties were in store again for Cherou. Well, it was not the first time that he had to face such problems. As ever, he would fulfil his duty as well as possible. His thoughts briefly wandered to the mine in which Saira now was, for the first time, completely on her own. He hoped that she was well and getting along all right. He finally had to admit that he really missed her. He had not known this feeling for such a long time, but it was pleasing to feel a certain affection for a female being once more. At that moment, the new slave moved, and Cherou had to concentrate fully on his impending duty again. He had to make it clear to yet another creature that it had been deprived of its future. Then the young slave opened her eyes for the first time in her new life.

*

The next working day also passed uneventfully. Although Torg forced the Lingits to even more efficiency to compensate for Cherou's absence, after work Saira found enough strength to continue her search for a suitable place to escape. She moved again along the magic barriers as carefully as possible, ensuring that she was not observed by anybody. For her safety she weaved a protective spell around herself, which would warn her about the approach of other creatures. Her search was unsuccessful for a long period again this time. She was just about to give up for today and swim back to the sleeping cave, when she suddenly felt the signature of a spell she knew. She carefully went nearer to the place and looked around. The terrain was completely exposed here, and no creature could sneak up on her unnoticed. Saira was also highly visible, but she had never yet met any large creature this far from the sleeping cave. She carefully studied the spell, checked its function and borders. It was complicated, but Saira was definitely able to constrict it to leave an open gap through which she could slip away, undetected. She rubbed her hands together triumphantly. At long last she had found a way to escape! She was just about to concentrate on the spell to constrict it enough so she could slip through it, when suddenly her protective spell went off to tell her about the approach of another creature. Startled, Saira looked around, at first she could not detect anything. But when she lifted her head, she saw a big Galanx swimming directly towards her from above. He must not have seen her yet because he swam along so leisurely, but he might discover her soon! Panic rose up in her. There was no place to hide in this open terrain. She could expect some unpleasant consequences if this guardian detected her, for she was not allowed to enter this area. The Galanx came ever nearer. What should she do? She looked around desperately, but there was really no possibility to hide. The Galanx was almost close enough, he would detect her any moment now. So Saira did the only thing possible. She sank down onto the sand and weaved a spell to make herself invisible. But this spell required much strength and she could not keep it up for long. She also could not control it completely. Everything was all right as long as she did not move. But every little movement would at least show her outline, because at the edge of the spell small irregularities occurred which only an accomplished magician could prevent. Every little flickering of her luminous organs would also shine through the spell and show her presence. The Galanx was now right above Saira. She even felt the streams of water caused by his body. She tried to keep calm despite of her fear. No movement and no emitting of light right now! The Galanx must not have detected her, because he just examined the surroundings, looking bored. But then he gazed straight at her. Had he detected her outline? He focused on her for a long time. Saira hardly dared to breathe. Then she remembered that the spell just protected her optically. He would discover her immediately if he used his sonar right now. The guardian still focused on her. Saira could barely stop herself from shivering. The spell also drained more and more of her strength, so that soon she would not be able to keep it going any longer, but the Galanx still did not move. She let out a quick prayer that he should finally swim away, but not until Saira was about to faint did the Galanx finally move on, moving very slowly. Saira dissolved the spell. She was completely exhausted and lay in the sand breathing heavily. That was close! She lifted her head and looked around carefully, but nobody was there. Even this movement took a tremendous effort, but she had to swim back before the dark phase began, otherwise they would notice her absence. So she finally summoned all her strength and dragged herself back to the sleeping cave. The way back seemed to be never-ending. Even her sight gradually grew hazy. She saw the entrance of the big cave as an indistinctly glowing contour, and hoped not to collide with another Lingit while she swam through it. At the nearest possible place she sank onto the sand, where she collapsed, unconscious.

*

The new slave had overcome the first shock quite well. But she had some difficulties with controlling her new body. The coordination of her movements was quite clumsy, but Cherou had to concede that she tried her best. It took her a long time to be able to swim moderately well, and the controlling of her luminous organs was difficult for her, too. At the end of the light phase, it was clear that her training would take a lot longer than Saira's development. So Cherou swam to Thurgun, feeling uneasy. He knew that the Duumar would not be pleased with his report. The leader of the mine reacted very angrily indeed to Cherou's news. Once more he cursed all Lingits and of course his opponent Pegrell, whose output was again much higher than Thurgun's. Cherou was glad when the furious Duumar finally let him go. The training of the new slave would be very exhausting for her and for Cherou, but it was not the first time he was confronted with such difficulties. She too would soon be able to take up her work in the mines, though Cherou did not believe she would last long. She needed just a bit more time and some more intensive training. His superiors should not make such a fuss. So far, he had always managed to turn every abducted being into a good slave.

*

Saira was startled out of her sleep when again she was roughly shaken.

"Hey, don't you want to work today, Thae'Kor?" somebody asked crossly and shook her until Saira finally opened her eyes.

It took a moment until she was fully awake and recognized the Lingit. It was the slave who worked directly beside her.

"Come on, get up now, dream-swimmer!" the Lingit said surprisingly gently. "You won't get anything to eat if you are late." Then he gave her a pitying look and swam away.

Saira was still completely exhausted from her experience of the day before. She would have arrived late at work if the Lingit had not woken her up. He had prevented her from being punished, but why? Before, he had always been so dismissive and unfriendly. Confused, Saira got up and swam to the mine as well as she could. Flemm was appalled when he saw her.

"Well, young fin, you are looking rather exhausted!" he said anxiously. "You seem to have overstrained yourself a bit in the last few days." Then he gave her an extra big bunch of plopkelp and mixed the tendrils of another plant with it. "Here, this will give you back some strength!" he said and winked at her. Saira thanked him, then settled down on the soft sand to eat her meal. The other plant tasted surprisingly good, and after a short time she felt a lot stronger. One could always count on Flemm in times of trouble. A little later, her work started. When Saira took her place beside the Lingit who had so kindly woken her, she gave him an embarrassed smile and whispered her thanks. The Lingit gave her another pitying look and growled sullenly, but then something approaching a smile flitted briefly across his face. Everything was just as normal for a while, but suddenly it got dark! Saira jumped with fright when the illumination of the mine went out. Instinctively the Lingits let their luminous organs flare up. It took Saira a bit longer to do the same. A brief murmur went through the group while Torg's strong voice sounded: "Continue working! The illumination has gone out again. The lights will soon start shining!" Some of the Lingits were already starting to work again, they now orientated themselves with the help of their light and their sonar. They appeared to be used to such blackouts, not like Saira, who first had to familiarize herself with the new situation, which really was not easy for her. The Lingits were used to moving in complete darkness, as they lived in the deep sea. But Saira had spent the greatest part of her life in daylight, and now felt very uncomfortable in the darkness. The orientation was also difficult for her because of the strange flickers of the luminous organs. The whole scene seemed absolutely ghostly to her. The shining Lingits, working in one line, and behind them the Draugh, whose whole body, with its long extremities, emitted a red, diffuse light, as though he was glowing from the inside. The sight was almost hypnotic for her, and it was difficult for her to keep from looking at it. But it was even more difficult for her to work under such bad light conditions. She tried to emit as much light as possible to see better, but realized soon that she dissipated a lot more energy than usual in this way. She was already debilitated today, and now this! She really was spared nothing!

"Better use your click sonar. That helps conserve your strength," the Lingit beside her whispered and looked at her with pity.

Saira gave him a thankful look and nodded at him. Admittedly, her first tries were unsuccessful because the clicking sounds of the other Lingits blurred the "picture" that she received through her sonar. But in due course, the images got sharper and were soon as clear as the pictures she perceived with her eyes. Finally. she was able to dim the light of her luminous organs, but could still see her surroundings quite clearly. The Lingit was right. Saira noticed with relief that the work really was less tiring this way. She was however very exhausted by break time, because it took ages until the illumination was switched on again. Saira hoped that at least the rest of the day would pass without further incidents.

*

Thurgun stared furiously at his current information. The long blackout had resulted in even less fire-stone being mined in this light phase than before! By comparison, Pegrell had again delivered a remarkable quantity. This could not be allowed to continue! Torg was just too good-natured and did not force the slaves sufficiently. The time had come to give them a lecture again, so they would finally deliver enough fire-stone. Well, this should be no problem, because Thurgun knew very well how to entice the Draugh. He would also cause some trouble to that old rascal Pegrell in future. Sometimes, bigger accidents were simply unavoidable ...

A brief friendship

Saira woke up in time at the start of the next light phase. This time, she had immediately returned to the sleeping cave after work and retired so that she could recover at least a little bit. The experiences of the last few days had taken much of her strength, but now she knew that a real opportunity for escaping existed! She had already found the right place. Now she just had to find the right time, so she would not be swimming right into the fins of one of the guardians again. Therefore she first had to recover her strength, because for this attempt she needed keen senses and a clear mind. The expectation of leaving this terrible place in the near future raised her spirits appreciably. So she swam to the mine and took a big bunch of seaweed from Flemm, which she ate up in a good mood. But her good humour paled quite quickly when Torg entered the mine. One only had to see how he stomped in to know that once again he was in a very bad mood, and he really made no secret of it. He went straight up to some Lingits and chased them to their places, while he uttered vile swearwords. Then he drove them on mercilessly and checked the accumulation bins for the fire-stone over and over again. The Lingits worked as hard and fast as they could, but that seemed not to be enough for the Draugh. After only a short time, he grabbed hold of one of the slaves and pulled him backwards. Saira knew exactly what would happen now, and it filled her with the same horror as the first time. Once more, she heard the screaming and whimpering of the tortured Lingit, and again she could barely take it. With a bitter expression on her face and her hands shaking, she worked on as well as she could and tried not to listen, but she just could not ignore the pain of the tormented Lingit. The punishment seemed to last forever. Once more, tears rose up in her eyes and she quietly prayed that Torg should stop. After a seemingly endless period of time, the Draugh finally let go of his victim and again uttered some wild threats and insults, while he merciless continued to harass the slaves.

But that was not enough! Before the break another punishment followed, and after the break one of the Lingits was in for it again. Never before in her entire life had Saira yearned that strongly for the day to end. Fear was written in the faces of the Lingits, and the tension was unbearable. Never before in her entire life had Saira experienced as much fear as she did today. She really did not know how long she could take it. After a seemingly endless period, the signal finally and mercifully sounded to announce the end of the working day. Saira left the mine, this place of horror, as fast as possible and returned to the sleeping cave. This time she was completely distraught. The cruelty and brutality she had to experience today was nearly unbearable for her. How good and peacefully was life on her world of origin compared to this place! Now another feeling came to her, too, which she had repressed for so long: homesickness! This was more than she could endure. Saira retreated to the wall of the cave and started to cry bitterly, overcome by all the memories of her previous life. She wished Cherou was beside her now. He had always comforted her at such times and given her some support, but he was far away, and she was all alone with her pain. So she lay huddled up against the wall, while the rising despair made her pain worse, and the force of her crying made her shake again and again. At some point she felt how somebody gently stroked her hair. When she lifted her head, she saw through her tears a female Lingit who looked at her kindly.

"What's the matter, dear? Why you are crying so hard?" she asked kindly. But Saira could not answer, was again shaken by tears. The Lingit woman tenderly took her in her arms, which Saira let happen gratefully. It just felt good to have somebody by her side, whom she could snuggle up to at such a moment. Saira continued crying for some time, while the Lingit woman held and stroked her gently. Finally her tears dried up, and the pain gradually became bearable. Saira raised herself up a little and looked thankfully at the Lingit woman, who gave her a lovely smile.

"Are you better now?" she asked in a friendly voice.

Saira nodded and swallowed hard. "Yes, thank you," she whispered hoarsely. Then she wiped the last of her tears from her eyes.

"What happened that made you cry so hard?" the Lingit woman asked.

And so Saira told her about today's experiences, about Torg's cruel punishment, and the fear she had experienced. The Lingit woman listened patiently while she stroked Saira. Finally she said: "I can well understand that all this grieves you very much and horrifies you. You are quite young and seemingly have never experienced such brutality in your life. Many of us felt the same at first, because the Lingits are a peaceful tribe. Even today, it is still difficult for us to live with the brutality and unfairness, but we have no choice. All we can do is support each other, so the hard fate that we share made us even closer. We just help one another as best we can. That also applies to you!"

"But I'm a Thae'Kor, and the other Lingits don't like me much!" Saira disagreed.

"That's only what it looks like. We don't abandon anybody. You maybe don't fully belong to our community yet, but we care for everyone among us and for each other," the Lingit woman answered. "Oh, I have not introduced myself yet, please excuse me! My name is Genvin."

"And I'm called Saira" She sat up and looked into the face of her benefactress, who gave Saira a lovely smile. Genvin was nearly as tall as Cherou and of a sturdy shape. She was obviously younger than he was, but seemed to have experienced a lot, too. "Thank you for being so kind to me!" Saira finally said and looked down embarrassed.

"You're welcome, dear," Genvin answered pleasantly and gently caressed her cheek. "You work in the Sergon mine under Torg?" she asked a short while later, and Saira nodded. "Well, then we are neighbours. I work in the Gilgoia mine."

"That's the mine next to ours!" Saira said, surprised.

"That's right," Genvin agreed.

71

"Is your overseer as brutal and mean?" Saira wanted to know.

"All the Draughs are brutal and mean. In their eyes, we are just scum," Genvin grumbled.

"Why do they punish you so often without any reason?" Saira asked uncomprehendingly.

"That we don't know. Maybe it's just fun for them to torment us," Genvin answered, and Saira looked at her in horror. "I suppose you will experience a lot more of such unpleasant things in this world," Genvin said with resignation. "But don't surrender. We Lingits help each other, even if we are sometimes a bit sullen." She pulled a face, which made Saira smile. "Don't be frightened, I'm sure you will be all right," Genvin finally said encouragingly.

Saira gave her a thankful look. Now it became clear to her why the Lingit, who worked beside her, recently had been so helpful and had even saved her from being punished.The chilly attitude of the Lingits was really just superficial. Compared with the inhabitants of Wuun, it took them a bit longer to accept novices among them. But in case of emergency, they assisted them too. That gave Saira hope for finding more friends among the Lingits, in time. So she was after all not as alone as it had first seemed. Genvin's closeness seemed pleasing and soothing to Saira, so she finally asked, a bit embarrassed: "Genvin, would you stay near me tonight?"

"With pleasure, if it feels good to you!" she answered kindly.

And Saira gave her such an imploring look that Genvin hugged her, moved. "Don't be afraid, I'm here!"

*

Meanwhile, Thurgun had received the result of this light phase. Although Torg had driven the slaves quite hard this time, the quantity of fire-stone had not increased by much. The output of the Gilgoia mine was again markedly higher today. The time had come to put that slave-driver Pegrell in his place. Thurgun sent out a short magic command, which was directed at his most loyal helper. He was just the right one for this type of dirty little mission. Thurgun could rely on him, and he would surely not fail this time. It took a while, then the breathing-water supply grate was lifted. A little Ganva slid out through it and sank on the tabletop in front of Thurgun. The creature, barely larger than a Lingit's hand, looked like a terrestrial swimming crab. Its strongly armoured body was studded with numerous spiky lumps. Luminous organs on the armour and the strong shears characterized it as a deep-sea dweller.

"Ah, there you are, my nasty friend!" Thurgun remarked delightedly.

"What do you want?" the Ganva asked a bit surly.

"I have a wicked little job for you," Thurgun said with a grin and laid down a tiny sack in front of the Ganva.

"What's that?" the Ganva asked.

"A small amount of Kalyss-powder," Thurgun explained. "When fire-stone comes in contact with, it quickly starts to burn."

"And what am I supposed to do with it?" the Ganva asked, seemly bored.

"You just take this powder to the Gilgoia mine and pour it out at a suitable place, so that a nice little fire starts by accident, if you know what I mean," Thurgun remarked as harmlessly as possible.

"Could that nice little fire perhaps be a bit bigger?" the Ganva asked maliciously.

"Well, in principle I wouldn't be against that," Thurgun answered, grinning. "I see we understand each other."

"I suppose you'll ensure a suitable reward again this time," the Ganva remarked casually.

"Have I ever disappointed you?" Thurgun asked with feigned disgust.

The Ganva made no reply. Instead, he grasped the sack with the Kalyss-powder and disappeared the way he had come.

*

Genvins farewell from Saira the next morning had been very affectionate, and Saira was glad to have finally found a friend among the Lingits. For the first time in a long while, she had experienced something like safety next to Genvin, and for that she was truly grateful. With new courage, Saira went to the mine. In future, she did not want to be intimidated by Torg's brutality any more. Should he try to punish her unjustly, she would simply give him an appropriate lecture with her magic. But this day, the Draugh seemed to be in a much better mood. He still continued to harass the Lingits with his threats and insults, but he left them alone. As it seemed, this would be just another regular working day for Saira and the other slaves, but it should soon become worse ...

*

Meanwhile, the little Ganva had reached the Gilgoia mine, and sneaked along its boundary to where the Lingits were working in line. His small size and the dark colour of his armoured body made him nearly invisible on the surrounding rocks. Thus, he managed to approach the Lingit working on the edge without being detected. Now the most difficult moment came, because the Ganva had to leave the cover of the rocks and crawl onto the bright sand, where he could easily be seen. The end result should look like an accident, which one of the slaves had caused. Therefore, he had to move as close as possible to the Lingit, and empty the sack with the Kalyss powder at the right moment, without being noticed by the slave. That was truly not easy, and not entirely without danger. If the Lingit moved aside at the wrong moment, he could simply squash the Ganva. So the Ganva climbed carefully down the rocks and sneaked cautiously from behind towards the Lingit, who was completely involved in his work and focused on his tools. The Ganva now dug himself into the sand to hide, then carefully slid closer beneath the sand, until he had nearly reached the Lingit. He briefly hesitated to check the situation, but nobody seemed to have noticed him so far. So he completed the last bit of the way as carefully as possible, until he sat directly beside the Lingit towering next to him, and the Ganva could feel his every movement through the vibration of the sand. He quickly opened the sack with the powder. When the Lingit hit the fire-stone again with his tool, the Ganva hurled the powder over the sand. The fire-stone immediately started to burn just as Thurgun had promised. At that moment, the Lingit jerked to the side with a frightened outcry, and jammed one of the Ganva's legs beneath him. The Ganva desperately tried to get free, but did not succeed. None of those present could have guessed that the fire-stone beneath the mine had nearly dissolved completely from the warming of the rocks. A huge gas bubble had developed, which was only covered by a thin layer of fire-stone forming the bottom of the mine. The fire burned through this layer in a few moments and reached the gas bubble. Before the Lingits ever really noticed the fire, the whole mine was torn apart by a giant explosion, which none of those present survived.

*

Cherou and Jir, the new slave, had started out late to the training-mine this morning, which is what saved their lives. The closeness of the explosion and the powerful pressure wave would have been their end had they been inside the open mine. But they were still above the city when the giant explosion occurred. Cherou was first to recognize the approaching pressure wave and pulled Jir downwards as fast as he could, to seek protection between the buildings. They held on to a lamppost, and Cherou tried to protect Jir with his body as well as he could when the pressure wave raced across above them. But even the offshoots caused extremely strong whirls between the buildings. The two Lingits were thrown to and fro, while masses of sand were whirled up and impeded their breathing. A sudden metallic shriek could be heard as one of the roof constructions directly above them crashed down. Cherou saw it just in time. He let go of the lamppost at the last moment and was whirled out onto the street with Jir. Then the falling pieces crashed down on the ground with a massive noise. By now they were defencelessly at the mercy of the furious mass of water and were whirled around and around. Cherou held on to Jir as tightly as he could, and just hoped that they would not get hurt too badly, while they were being driven faster and faster through the gorges between the buildings. Then, with great force, the water hurled them against a wall.

*

The Lingits in the Sergon mine jumped with fright as they heard the giant explosion. The illumination extinguished again almost immediately, which made the incident even scarier. Then the pressure wave raced across above them. As the mine lay in a hollow, large amounts of sand were whirled up, but the offshoots of the pressure wave caused no actual damage. The illumination flickered again and stabilized a short time later. At that moment, several things fell into the sand in front of Saira. When she looked closer at them, she recognized that they were pieces torn off the corpses of Lingits! She jumped up with a horrified outcry.

"What's the matter?" Torg shouted angrily and stomped up to her. When he noticed what had frightened Saira so much, he turned to her and said tersely: "What are you getting so upset about, these are just some torn Lingits." Then he grasped the body parts with his shears and took them away, while Saira watched him, horrified. "Come on, continue working!" the Draugh shouted at her. Saira followed the command hesitatingly and moved again in between the other Lingits. A short time later, she suddenly heard a loud crack and crunch behind her. She carefully turned her head and could not believe her eyes. The Draugh was eating the body parts! Horrified, she could not stop watching the repulsive scene. Then she felt sick and turned away, full of loathing. She swallowed hard a few times to ease the urge to throw up. Then she checked once more to ensure that she was not dreaming, that it was really true. What she saw was real! The sickness came up again. The Lingit beside her just gave her a pitying look when he noticed that she again swallowed hard.

*

Cherou slid to the floor, dazed. The noise and the wild water-whirls finally decreased. He carefully tried to move, and succeeded without problems or pain. As it seemed he was not injured, which appeared like a miracle to him because of the hard impact. But where was Jir? Cherou shot upwards and a strong flash of pain zoomed through his body. Apparently, he had not come through completely unhurt after all. He looked around quickly. He could not see the slave anywhere at first, but then he saw her head poking out between some debris. As fast as his maltreated body allowed, he swam over to her. She had been lucky. The debris above her was only small and not sharp-edged. Cherou quickly freed her, and could see immediately that she had no visible injuries aside from some slight scratches. When Cherou gently lifted her up, she opened her eyes and looked around in surprise.

"What ... happened?" she asked confused.

"The flood wave separated us, and you were hurled aside," Cherou explained mildly. "But you seem to be uninjured. Can you move?"

Jir raised herself up a bit cumbersomely and moved her arms and fins. "Seems like nothing's broken," she finally answered confidently. Then she saw a movement some distance away and told Cherou.

He immediately recognized the octopus-like silhouette of the approaching Duumars. "Come on, we have to leave this place. We'll get trouble if they find us here!" He took Jir by the hand and swam upwards with her. The magnitude of the destruction was clearly visible from that position. The flood wave had just slightly damaged the surrounding buildings, but at the edge of the city, nearer to the mines, some of the buildings were completely destroyed. A massive curtain of sand obstructed the view in this direction. The disaster must have happened somewhere there. Cherou was relieved to see that the flood wave had not come from the direction of the Sergon mine. They could not get there anyway for the moment, but had to wait, until the sand had dropped again. Cherou was just about to turn around when he suddenly heard a deep, low rumbling and thudding, followed by a great whooshing noise, which dissipated quickly. Then the sound faded just as fast as it had begun. Only the wall of sand some distance away was once again whirled around violently.

*

At a nearby slope, the intense vibrations of the explosion induced a huge avalanche of stones and scree to plunge down into the depth. This caused enormous flood waves, which moved away from the city of the Duumars at high speed. These flood waves barely damaged the deep areas of the ocean, but were extremely dangerous for a high reef located just beneath the water's surface. After the explosion, the flood waves took many hours to reach the distant reef. The seabed ascended steeply a short distance before the reef, so that the first flood wave had already risen up like an enormous mountain of water. The water first retracted from the reef and drained a large area. Then the first giant wave raced up to the reef and collapsed directly above it. Unimaginable masses of water shot across with brute force and caused indescribable damage. The coral's sensitive lime skeletons were literally smashed to pieces by the wave, the inhabitants either crushed or torn to shreds by the sharp-edged lime shells. This first wave had already caused disastrous damage, but the flood waves that followed caused the complete destruction of the entire region. In the end, all that was left of the once so beautiful reef was a vast desert of debris and rubble.

*

It was mealtime in the Sergon mine and as usual Saira sat a bit offside and chewed without appetite on her seaweed. She was still shocked about the heavy explosion, and the memory of the Draugh eating the Lingit body parts horrified her deeply. She gave a start as one of the Lingits talked to her.

"Hey, Thae'Kor, maybe Cherou hasn't told you yet, we are fed to the Draughs when we are no longer of use for working!"

Horrified, Saira looked at the Lingit. It was her neighbour who had woken her up some days before, so she would not be late for work. "W ... What!" she stuttered unbelievingly.

"Ask the other Lingits if you don't believe me," he said roughly. "They will confirm it. Everybody here knows this, so you better get your head around it soon!" Then he sank to the ground beside her. His expression showed Saira that he certainly was not making fun of her. He was really serious! "I know, it's not easy to take," the Lingit now said a little conciliatory. "I realized that you were not acquainted with this fact when I noticed your horror at Torg's behaviour just now. But you should know the truth."

At first, Saira gave him a terrified look, but then she thanked him for his candour.

"You are welcome, Thae'Kor, just take it as an inducement to staying alive for as long as possible," the Lingit advised her.

Saira looked at him with a bitter expression, then a certain decisiveness returned to her eyes and she said defiantly: "By the way, my name is Saira, not Thae'Kor."

The Lingit glanced at her ironically. "And my name is Gorv," he introduced himself.

In that very moment Torg stomped back into the mine, but surprisingly he did not chase the Lingits back to their working place. Instead he asked for attention. "To prevent any speculation I have enquired what caused the explosion today. A terrible accident has happened in the Gilgoia mine. It has been completely destroyed!"

A frightened rustle went through the lines of the Lingits. "Oh no!" Saira whispered horrified. Genvin! What had happened to

Genvin? Was she still alive? "Has anyone survived?" Saira asked desperately. She completely forgot the usual designation of honour for the Draugh, but he did not seem to notice.

"No, there are no survivors!" Torg said despondently. The death of the overseer of the Gilgoia mine seemed to upset even him.

The reaction of the Lingits was much stronger this time. Aside from Saira, many more burst into tears while they heard about the death of their family and friends. Torg just let them be, he too was shocked by the severity of this accident. But his masters still demanded their toll to be taken from his slaves, so he finally made them work again. Most of them had difficulties concentrating on the work after this bitter news, but Torg let them be this time. He was glad that the Lingits continued working at all. The quantity of fire-stone mined today would certainly be less than usual, but that should not bother Thurgun any more, now that he had ruined his biggest opponent.

*

Saira had retreated to the edge of the sleeping cave after work, where she was now lying sadly, her eyes filled with tears, while she bewailed Genvin's death. The other Lingits also sat there with gloomy faces or cried for their lost family and friends. Saira wished Cherou could be there right now. Like during the days before, she missed him badly. Then someone timidly touched her shoulder. Saira looked up and recognized Gorv, the Lingit who worked beside her. He looked sad too, his face had none of the harshness it usually showed. "The Lingits want to mourn the dead together. I want to invite you because you are one of us now," he said to her, sounding friendly.

Saira rubbed the tears out of her eyes and answered with a raspy voice: "Thank you, that's very kind of you!"

"Then come with me." Gorv invited her and reached out his hand.

Saira got up a little stiffly, took his hand gratefully and let Gorv guide her to the centre of the hall. Several Lingits had already sat down there in a big circle. Gorv and Saira joined them and waited until all the Lingits had taken their places. Then it suddenly grew quiet. Saira looked at Gorv, a little uncertain, but he just made a becalming gesture. Then the Lingits started to sing, but they sang without words. They intoned a drawn-out melody that seemed ancient. The unity of their voices and the strange melody expressed sorrow and resignation to their fate. It had an almost hypnotic effect on Saira, so her voice soon joined the great choir. The Lingits swayed together in the rhythm of the melody, and sometimes even uttered short sonar pulses, which were in harmony with the song. Saira seemed to merge with the other Lingits as they were all joined together to express their pain and sorrow. They shared the grief all of them endured, and gave mutual strength to each other to gradually overcome the hardship and the pain. Her spirit seemed to swim in an ocean of feelings and dreams, an ocean made up from the souls of all those present, gently swaying her back and forth in the swell. The feeling was intoxicating, but also it induced a restful calmness, which lay comfortingly over the vastness of sorrow and fear everybody carried inside, and finally covered it like a soft cloth. The pain gradually faded and was replaced by a feeling of contented safety. So they blessed their deceased and released their souls, who now peacefully left the ocean and rose to a higher level, where the living could not follow them.

*

Thurgun was rather angry. What had that damned Ganva done? He was just supposed to spread a fire. Nobody had told him to blast the whole mine. Was there nobody he could rely on any more? He was still pondering when the door opened, and Pegrells massive body filled the frame. The Duumar trembled with rage, his face was distorted into a fierce grimace. "You son of a Dorgon

81

have ruined me!" he roared furiously. Then he jumped forward and wanted to rush at Thurgun, who stepped aside at the last moment, and Pegrell missed him and crashed against the console. But evidently the old Duumar did not feel the pain at all, because he turned around immediately. This time he got hold of Thurgun. He beat him up furiously until his enemy recovered from the fright and smashed Pegrell heavily against the wall.

"You have lost your senses, Pegrell. I have no part in the destruction of your mine!" Thurgun shouted angrily.

"You damn liar!" Pegrell shrieked furiously and rushed again at his enemy, but this time Thurgun was prepared for it. He dodged as quick as a flash, got hold of one of Pegrell's arms and smashed him once more against the wall. Dazed, the old Duumar shook himself. That gave Thurgun a short break. Old Pegrell must have gone completely mad, Thurgun thought to himself. The time had come to remove this maniac! At that very moment, Pegrell roared and jumped up again, and Thurgun hurled a magic energy disc at him. The old Duumar was not at all prepared for this attack and jumped directly into the disc's way. The lightning killed him immediately, and his body sank lifelessly to the ground.

Thurgun breathed a sigh of relief. He was finally rid of his biggest opponent. Now he had to remove the corpse, but that was no problem. This was not the first corpse he let vanish in secret. He had to move some opponent or other out of his way before, or he would never have become manager of this mine so quickly. The cadaver of the old Duumar would be a welcome feast for the Draughs.

*

That night, Saira slept among the Lingits for the first time. Their closeness was pleasant, and she finally felt a little safer again. Most of the Lingits had let go of their chilly attitude and treated her now as one of their own. The next morning, Saira swam to the mine with a completely new feeling. The Lingits had finally accepted her among them. Her joy grew even larger when she saw Cherou swimming up to the mine with the new slave. She swam a short way towards them and welcomed Cherou happily. She would have flung her arms around his neck, but the other Lingits didn't have to know just yet what she felt for him. Cherou also greeted her happily, but discreetly. Then he introduced the new slave to Saira, who welcomed her, while Jir greeted Saira a bit shyly. Saira saw that Jir was a little younger and smaller than herself. Jir seemed quite fragile because of her delicate body, and Saira wondered how she would ever accomplish the hard work in the mine. But she kept her doubts to herself for the moment and accompanied Cherou and Jir to the mine. A short time later, Torg appeared and Saira started to work with the other Lingits, while Cherou winked at her once more. When the Draugh saw the new slave, his face darkened.

"What kind of a shrimp are you bringing to me?" he growled angrily.

"I'm not responsible for the selection of the slaves," Cherou countered. "You'll have to take this up with the Duumars, Genjai."

Torg uttered a deep, menacing grumble and stared furiously at Cherou, who effortlessly resisted the look. "All right, then start working now!" Torg snorted.

Jir had shrunk under the threatening look of the Draugh and was glad to be allowed to withdraw. Cherou led her to the other slaves and fit her between Saira and himself. Saira could clearly see the fear in her eyes, and gave her an encouraging smile. Jir answered with a short, thankful look. She behaved surprisingly skilfully and worked quite well initially. But as expected, she tired fast, and she was quite exhausted at break time. Saira certainly knew how the poor, young creature felt, and, together with Cherou, took good care of Jir. The work became more and more difficult for Jir after the break. Cherou supported her with all his might, and Saira helped out too, so that she would reach the required quantity of fire-stone. They even had to help her while swimming back after work. She was so exhausted, she closed her eyes almost immediately after reaching the sleeping cave. Saira pitied the dainty creature. How could the Duumars ever choose such a young girl for such hard work? Saira and Cherou finally had some time for each other because Jir had fallen asleep. They retreated to the edge of the cave and Saira told Cherou all that had happened during his absence, but prudently concealed her secret excursions for finding a possible escape route, and her experience with the Galanx. Cherou let her talk and listened, enchanted, while he enjoyed her closeness. Saira finally admitted to him how much she had missed him during this time. Cherou had felt the same and he was glad to be by her side again. They both now enjoyed their time together and hoped not to be separated again so quickly. The time soon had come to go to sleep, and both Lingits settled down next to Jir. Saira cuddled up to Cherou and they both enjoyed being close to each other until they finally fell asleep together.

*

Thurgun was very angry when he heard Torg's report about the new slave. He would hardly be able to increase his production with this shrimp. He had indeed eliminated his biggest opponent, but he would certainly not risk losing his reputation because of this slave. So he had ordered Torg to use some persuasive power again. He knew that he could rely on the Draugh. He would teach this shrimpy thing to dig enough fire-stone, or she would enrich his menu after an awful accident.

*

Cherou had some problems waking up Jir the next morning. He had to shake her hard a few times until she finally woke up because she slept so deeply. She was still exhausted from the day before, but she quickly found her strength again after Flemm offered her an opulent meal of seaweed. She initially kept up very well, not least because Saira and Cherou secretly supplied her with the odd piece of fire-stone. So she continued until mealtime, but then her strength faded visibly. Her accumulation bin was not adequately filled when Torg checked it next time, so the Draugh first yelled insults at her, then he grasped her and dragged her brutally backwards. Saira turned around, terrified. She could not believe that Torg would actually punish her on her second working day, but he really did! While Jir whimpered and screamed in horror, the Draugh threw her in the sand in front of him, pressed her on the ground and then assaulted her with his sonar. Imploringly, Saira turned to Cherou.

"Please, do something!" she whispered desperately.

But Cherou just looked down with a bitter expression. "I'm sorry, I can't help her," he whispered helplessly.

"But ... he can't do that!" Saira whispered terrified and turned back to Jir, who writhed helplessly screaming and whimpering beneath the Draugh.

Gorv put a hand on her shoulder. His eyes had their usual harshness again as he told her: "Nobody can help her. Just continue working, or you are the next to get punished!" His forceful voice gave his words the appropriate effect.

Saira looked at him simultaneously horrified and desperate, but Gorv just shook his head regretfully. She finally followed his order hesitatingly, but Jirs cries were unbearable for her. Somebody had to help this poor creature! She just could not watch helplessly while this young being was tortured senselessly. Tears of desperation rose up again in Saira's eyes. Why wouldn't Torg stop? Finally Saira could not stand it any longer. If none of the Lingits wanted to help then she just had to do it! Saira looked briefly over her shoulder to determine direction and distance, then, with a short, barely visible motion of her hand, she weaved a magic shock wave. This shock wave would simply have bowled the Draugh over in a normal atmosphere, but here, the effect of the shock wave was stronger because of the significantly higher density of the water. Torg was not just bowled over but smashed against the rocks behind him with an intense force. There he collapsed, with a terrified outcry. The Lingits turned around in surprise and were rather astonished when they saw Torg lying some distance away between the rocks. They stopped working and moved carefully closer to him, while Saira just looked on in surprise.

"How did you do that?" Cherou asked astonished.

"Do what?" Saira asked as innocently as possible.

"You know exactly what I mean!" Cherou replied, irritated.

"You better go and take care of Jir, she needs your help now," Saira retorted defiantly.

Cherou gave her a furious look. "We will talk about this later!" Then he swam over to Jir and examined her. The delicate being was nearly unconscious and gave a start when Cherou touched her, but he managed to quickly calm her down. She would not be able to continue working in this condition, so Cherou gently lifted her in his arms and took her back to the sleeping cave, while the other Lingits gathered around Torg at a respectful distance.

"Is he dead?" one of the slaves asked.

"No, just unconscious." He said this with a certain degree of regret and pointed at the breathing openings inside the armour of the Draugh, where water came out in regular intervals.

"Then we had better continue working," another Lingit said. "When he wakes up and sees that we are not at work, he might punish even more of us!"

That convinced the other Lingits and they quickly started to work again. Meanwhile, Cherou had returned and joined them next to Saira. "I have taken her back to the sleeping cave and given her a soothing extract. She's asleep now and will not wake up before tomorrow morning," he explained briefly. Then he turned to his work again. Saira could feel his anger, especially as he took no further notice of her, but she was sure to have done the right thing. At least she had given that monster of a Draugh a lecture. The spell should not have such an intense effect, but now it had happened this way and she could not change it any more. She just had to remember that she was surrounded by water and not by air. She had become so used to it, she did not think about it any more. Other conditions prevailed in these surroundings, which she would do well to remember when using magic. Only this way could she prevent even more mishaps.

Torg started to move again and finally shook himself out of his daze. Then he sat back on his legs and tried all his limbs. His strong armour had protected him from being injured. What had happened? Where had the shock wave come from that had smashed into him? Torg looked around but could not discover anything that might have caused the shock wave. His slaves were just carrying on as though nothing had happened. Something strange was going on here! He quickly noticed that the slave he had punished before was missing. "Where has that shrimp gone?" he growled angrily.

Cherou turned around and answered as pleasantly as he could: "Your punishment has distressed her too much, Genjai. She was no longer able to work, therefore I have taken her back to the sleeping cave and attended to her, but she can work again tomorrow."

"That shrimp really can't cope with anything!" Torg shouted angrily. "Then all of you will just have to work for her too, or I'll snip your fins!" he threatened angrily.

"Certainly, Genjai," Cherou answered submissively and started to work again.

*

After work, Saira and Cherou swam silently side by side back to the sleeping cave. Shortly before the entry, Cherou changed direction and asked Saira to follow him. He led her to a group of rocks some distance away where they were undisturbed and no one could listen to their conversation.

"What did you do in the mine to smash Torg against the rocks?" Cherou immediately came to the point.

"What do you mean?" Saira asked as innocently as possible.

"Saira, please don't make a fool of me!" Cherou could hardly restrain himself. "I watched you before Torg crashed against the rocks. How did you do that? Do you maybe have magic powers?"

"And what if I do?" Saira grumbled back angrily. "That cruel creep just got his well-deserved penalty!"

"This is not a game, Saira!" Cherou erupted. "You are practically dead if the Duumars discover that you really have magic powers!"

Saira first glanced at him in astonishment because he reacted so harshly, then she looked down, offended.

"Please understand!" Cherou now said almost pleadingly. "If the Duumars discover that you have magic powers, you become much too dangerous for them. Their whole might is based solely on their magic powers. If they realize that you are a match for them, they will kill you for sure!"

Saira looked up briefly, then turned away from him wordlessly.

Cherou rolled his eyes. She drew back from him while he wanted to touch her, which finally made him furious. He angrily grasped one of her arms and pressed her against the rock face.

"Ouch, you are hurting me!" Saira yelled frightened.

"Then stop behaving so foolishly and answer my question!" Cherou shouted enraged. "I really don't want you to be killed!" He paused and released his grip. "I like you too much for that ...," he said quietly, keeping his eyes averted.

Saira looked at him in surprise, then looked down, embarrassed. "I'm sorry, I didn't mean to annoy you," she said apologetically. After a short pause she finally admitted: "Yes, I have magic powers, but I'm not a fully trained magician, just an apprentice."

Cherou nodded understandingly. "Then listen to me now, and listen good. You mustn't show your powers so openly. If we are lucky, nobody else has noticed. Otherwise, you are in great danger, do you understand?" Cherou asked urgently.

Saira nodded with concern.

"Well then, we'll behave as inconspicuously as possible, hoping that the incident will soon be forgotten," Cherou said.

"I will try my best," Saira promised dejectedly. Cherou was about to return to the sleeping cave when she stopped him once more. He looked at her inquiringly.

"There ... is ... another thing I have to tell you." Saira started to speak hesitatingly. "I ... don't know how long I can take all of this. First Torg punished the three Lingits for no reason at all, then Genvin died, and now Torg is so cruel to Jir. I can't stand it any more." She paused again. "Cherou, I want to get away from here, and I have already found the right place!"

Cherou's eyes widened. "You want to flee?" he asked, surprised.

Saira nodded resolutely.

"I have secretly checked the protection spells while you were gone, and found a place from where I can escape without being caught," Saira now confessed.

Cherou exhaled noisily. "I feared that one day it would come to this, but I never thought it would happen so quickly," he said pensively. "But that's not so easy! You don't know our world at all, and countless enemies lie in wait for us out there in the open ocean. We taste quite good to some of them, and the ocean itself is often malicious and can quickly turn into a deadly trap if you don't know it. You wouldn't survive two light phases out there all alone!"

"You forget my magic powers," Saira said self-confidently.

"They won't be of any use to you if you don't know the dangers and how you should behave in certain situations. Believe me, I know what I'm talking about. I know this world better than most of the other Lingits!" Cherou argued.

"I will manage out there somehow," Saira replied confidently. "Even if not, I'd rather die in freedom than let myself be tortured here by the Draughs for no reason and finally end up being eaten by them! I just can't stand this life in captivity any longer, and this perpetual fear!" Her voice almost cracked.

Cherou looked at her in surprise. "So they have told you about that already?"

"Indeed," Saira answered bitterly.

Cherou looked down regretfully and seemed deep in thought. "Even if you stay alive out there, where would you want to swim to then?" he asked after a while.

" To start with, as far away from here as possible," Saira replied.

"How will you manage that? You don't know this world at all!" Cherou said, slightly annoyed. "If you just swim out, after a short time you'll end up as a meal for a Dorgon or a Peltai."

"Then come with me!" was Saira's surprising answer. "With your experience and my magic powers we'll surely be able to manage to stay alive out there!"

Stunned, Cherou looked at her. "You want us to flee together?"

Saira nodded fiercely. She would feel much safer with Cherou by her side out there in the unknown deep of the ocean. The idea of just leaving him behind here was almost unbearable. She liked Cherou and had always felt safe when she was close to him. To separate from him now would be really painful, and Saira hoped very much that he would escape with her.

Cherou did not like the idea of leaving Saira to her fate in this huge dangerous ocean with its countless perils, he liked her far too much. But to just get up and escape with her now, without any idea of where they were headed, did not seem like a good idea to him. Certainly, the idea of finally escaping from the enslavement of the Duumars was appealing, and with Saira's magic powers, this possibility seemed tangibly close for the very first time. But what would happen afterwards? The Duumars would chase them across the ocean. A successful escape of two Lingits was the last thing they wanted! If he and Saira wanted to safely get through this, they would need allies who would grant them asylum and assist them in the fight against their persecutors. But who out there would be ready to defy the mighty Duumars? He caught Saira's pleading look while he was still thinking. So he included her in his deliberations and asked her for a little patience, for he had to think over the situation carefully. The time had come to return to the sleeping cave, as the dark phase would begin soon. Saira finally agreed, although she was a bit disappointed, because she certainly understood his motives. But she asked him not to ponder for too long. Then she followed Cherou to the sleeping cave.

*

All night long, Cherou tried to work out where they should flee to and who might assist them against the Duumars and their helpers. But no reasonable solution came to his mind until he remembered a conversation with Flemm a long time ago. Flemm had once told him how, when the Duumars had seized power, the Qails had put up fierce resistance. The Qails, this legendary tribe, had tried with all their might to stop the Duumars and to prevent the enslavement of the Lingits. But the Duumars were already too strong and ferociously quashed their resistance, so that their only option was to flee. Many legends were told about this tribe, which was presumed to live in exile somewhere in the wideness of the ocean. Many stories told about the wondrous capabilities those creatures could call their own, and how they were the only hope to deprive the Duumars of power. But where should one search for them? Some rumours existed about where they might be, but they described the place rather vaguely. At least it was a first point of reference, an idea in which direction the escape should aim. Under the circumstances, it was quite understandable that the Qails tried to keep their whereabouts a secret. If the stories were to be believed, they would appear to be quite a serious threat to the Duumars. Admittedly, they had no magic powers, but could produce nearly every type of energy, and naturally use it as weapons, too. Why they were once defeated by the Duumars remained a riddle to this day. The only certainty was that these beings still existed some-where out there. Right then, a daring plan took shape in Cherou's mind. He would have to find out more about the whereabouts of the Qails. Flemm would help him with his comprehensive knowledge. He would ask him tomorrow, early in the morning. The old Lingit would surely be able to give him the information he needed. Then nothing would prevent a successful escape any more. This could change the history of Turoon. It would completely rearrange the balance of power in this world and give it a new countenance.

Escape

Cherou visited Flemm the next morning as he had intended. His early morning visits were nothing exceptional since it was the only time the two Lingits could talk together and discuss their experiences without being disturbed. Flemm was quite surprised by the sudden interest his former protégé displayed for the Qails, but willingly gave him the information. And so, this morning, Cherou learned all he needed to know for the escape. It was perfectly clear to him that he could not fool his instructor, and indeed Flemm soon realized why Cherou needed the information. But Cherou also knew he could trust Flemm absolutely. So they said a heart-felt good-bye to each other, but not without an admonition from Flemm that Cherou should take good care of himself and his companion. Surprised, Cherou looked at Flemm as the old Lingit jokingly grumbled: "Do you think I haven't seen the looks you two exchange all the time? I may be old, but there's nothing wrong with my eye sight!"

"Nothing really stays hidden from you," Cherou replied, a bit embarrassed.

"Somebody has to take care of you young fins!" Flemm retorted with a grin. "Now hurry up, so you are back before the two girls wake up."

So, after a final salute, Cherou quickly swam back to the sleeping cave where Saira and Jir were still sleeping. Only very few Lingits were already awake at this time, but they just ignored him.

*

When Jir woke up and realized that this was the day she had to return to the mine, she was rather frightened. However, Cherou and Saira assured her that they would help her with the work, and that she had nothing to fear. It took a while until she had calmed down enough for them to be able to swim to the mine together.

Even so, Jir began to shiver when she saw Torg and behaved rather clumsily while working, because she was so scared. But Saira and Cherou supported her as best they could, and even Gorv helped when he realized how very afraid the girl was. So her accumulation bin was always well filled, which Torg registered with contentment. Jir finally had calmed down by break time, and she worked better for the rest of the day. She was even proud that she was able to keep up with the other workers in the end; Cherou and Saira met this with an amused smile. The fear Jir had experienced during this day and all her hard work finally took their toll and she quickly fell asleep in the evening. This enabled Cherou and Saira to find some time to work on their plans for the escape. Cherou led Saira back to the place where they had talked together the previous day.

"Listen Saira, now I know where we can flee to!" Cherou quickly came to the point, while Saira looked at him anxiously. Then Cherou told her about the Qails, how they had once resisted the Duumars and what he knew from Flemm about their current location. Although he had only expressed an assumption, Qails had been seen many times at the location in question, so it was fairly certain that they could be found there. Saira was immediately taken with the idea, but was told to slow down by Cherou, who said: "I will lead you there, but only if you do exactly as I tell you out there. It is very far and very dangerous. You barely know our world, and arbitrary actions can soon have deadly consequences. That's why you have to promise to stay close to me and to obey me. Only then will I accompany you, do you understand?" he asked emphatically.

Saira nodded after a short pause.

"Well then, the time has come to tell you about the greatest dangers out there, and to show you how to behave properly when faced with them," Cherou said. "There's no time left for explanations once we're under attack. Then you'll have to know what to do, or you're lost. Which is why I will teach you the most important rules and skills of how to survive in the open ocean, during the light phases after work. But I can't prepare you for everything that'll be waiting for us out there. In case of emergency, you'll have to trust your feelings, or just do the same as I do." Then Cherou started to explain about all the many natural enemies to Saira, their way of hunting and their strong and weak points. He taught her what she had to do to fight them, to hide from them, or to get out of their way. In no time, Saira's head was buzzing from all the information, but she tried to remember as much as she possibly could, and willingly allowed herself to be instructed by Cherou. She finally confessed that she had never expected escaping to be so difficult.

That's understandable, you barely know our world," Cherou replied kindly. "Life in your world is probably not as dangerous as it is here."

"That's for sure," Saira confessed. "We don't have to be afraid all the time in case something wants to eat us."

"Maybe you don't taste so good," Cherou remarked, grinning, and promptly took a punitive look from Saira.

"Well, should we take Jir along with us?" she asked after a while. "I fear she will not survive here for long on her own."

"No way!" Cherou answered sternly. "She is much too weak and would just hold us back. Here, she's safe at least. The other Lingits will look after her." When he saw Saira's sceptical look he added understandingly: "Believe me, it's better this way. Out there she has no chance of survival. Even for us it will be difficult enough, but for her, it would be hopeless. I would rather take her along too, but she really would not survive out there."

"Maybe you're right," Saira gave in after a while. "But I do feel bad about it."

"I understand," Cherou said. "But we have no choice, or our objective is doomed to failure right from the start."

Saira finally realized he was right and nodded.

"Well then, let's return to the cave, otherwise we'll attract attention," Cherou said in a friendly manner.

*

Cherou taught Saira all she needed to know during the course of the next two evenings. On the second evening, Cherou asked Saira to show him the place where she intended to overcome the magic barrier. After they had been hiding behind some rocks, Saira finally pointed in a particular direction of the open area in front of them. Cherou was sceptical at first because there was no cover, but Saira assured him this was the only place where she could get through the magic wall. "This is the only spell I know. I can use it without being noticed," she stated.

"Are you absolutely sure you can do it?" Cherou asked uncertainly. "I don't want our escape to be finished right here."

"Absolutely certain!" Saira said. "I have tried it once before," she then admitted a little reluctantly.

Cherou turned around quickly and snarled at her: "You've done what ...? How could you be so careless?"

"I just had to be sure it works," Saira defended herself. "Don't worry, I know what I'm doing, or do you think I'm not capable of it?" she asked provocatively.

Cherou gave her an angry look. "Sure you are capable, but it was careless anyway!"

"That's not true!" Saira countered angrily. "I'm sure to know a bit more about magic than you do!" She looked at him defiantly.

Cherou did not know why, but Saira's defiant reaction amused him, and a smile appeared on his face. "All right, you've got me," he finally admitted. "You're exceptionally better at this than I am!"

"I should say so!" Saira scolded halfway seriously. "What's to laugh about?"

"Because you look so sweet when you're angry!" Cherou replied with a grin.

Saira punched him on the shoulder. "You are quite outrageous!" she scolded in fake annoyance.

"Watch out!" Cherou suddenly hissed and pulled Saira deeper into the cover of the rocks. Saira looked at him inquiringly and he pointed forward to where a Galanx was leisurely swimming along in the distance. "They are the ones that concern me the most. We're as good as dead if one of them sees us," Cherou whispered worriedly.

"Do they regularly cruise around this area?" Saira asked in a low voice.

"Not at all. They patrol as they please. You can never be sure when they'll appear," Cherou answered.

Saira had already experienced that too, but did not tell Cherou about her encounter with the Galanx. "Then we'll just hope that none of them will detect us while we're escaping. At least I can take care of it with a protective spell, so we'll notice him in time before he sees us," she explained soothingly.

"Let's hope that your spell really protects us from detection," Cherou remarked uncertainly. "All right, the time to disappear is during this coming dark phase. We'll sneak out and try to escape from here when all are asleep."

Saira just nodded. It was not easy for her to suppress her excitement. At long last the time had come to leave this awful place!

"Well, let's swim back now. I know you are excited, but try to sleep a little anyway until it's time. All our senses must be alert if we want to be successful," Cherou advised her.

"I'll try to get some sleep," Saira promised, but she was sure she would not be able to.

Later, in the sleeping cave, Saira snuggled up to Cherou. His closeness felt good and seemed to calm her. She had started to feel somewhat precarious. She had indeed yearned for this moment for such a long time, but escaping from this place for real was completely different from thinking about it. She was very glad that Cherou was coming with her. She felt safer with him, and his great experience would surely be extremely useful. Now that Cherou had told her so much about this world, she realized that she would never be able to manage on her own out there, and would soon be getting into deadly danger. Her thoughts circled around this subject for quite a while, until she finally fell into a gentle sleep.

Cherou was also lost in his thoughts. He was certainly happy that he would be free again soon. But he knew that they would have to be constantly on the lookout for their pursuers in the open ocean. It would be a long and dangerous journey to the Qails, and he had to take good care of this young fin too, who had become so attached to him. Her magic powers would only be of limited use to them, although they were a great advantage for his longer-term plans. But first they had to escape from here and survive the long journey to the Qails. Cherou was confident they would be able to manage it. Then, hopefully, better times would come for his tribe.

*

Saira was startled when somebody gave her a slight push. Cherou hovered in front of her, his luminous organs glowing dimly, and gestured for her to be quiet. She shook off her disorientation and briefly looked around. All the Lingits were fast asleep and nobody would notice their disappearance. Cherou gestured for Saira to follow him. She hesitated for a moment and gave Jir a regretful look. She would have liked to caress her as a farewell, but did not, for fear of waking her up by mistake. In her thoughts, she promised Jir to return and free her from captivity. Then she followed Cherou out of the cave. Outside, they moved as carefully as they could to avoid any chance of being detected. Saira weaved her protective spell again, which would warn her at the approach of other beings. They finally reached the group of rocks close to the open area where the magic barrier was located. Cherou carefully looked out from behind the rocks, but could not detect any movement. Saira's protective spell also gave no warning, so it seemed that crossing the open area to the barrier was safe.

"Are you ready?" Cherou asked expectantly.

Saira nodded resolutely.

"Well, then let's get out of here," Cherou whispered.

They started to swim while carefully monitoring their surroundings. A short time later, they had reached the barrier without any problems and sank to the ground. Cherou kept monitoring the surroundings while Saira began to delimit the spell in front of them. It seemed to take forever until it was possible to get through the barrier. He would have liked to hurry her along, but he knew he must not disturb her now. She was doing her best to enable them to get out of here as quickly as possible. After a seemingly endless time, she turned to him with a beaming smile.

"I succeeded, we can go!" she proclaimed proudly. "The opening is not big enough for both of us side by side, that's why you must stay right behind me, or they'll detect us."

"All right then, swim ahead," Cherou replied with great relief and got ready to follow Saira.

She started to swim. Cherou followed right behind her until Saira sank to the ground again a little further on.

"We're through!" she said excitedly. " Now I'll just have to expand the spell again."

"Well hurry up then," Cherou said. He did not feel at all happy, out there in the open ocean. He kept a lookout for danger again while simultaneously searching for a hiding place for both of them. He noticed a group of rocks some distance away, which would offer them sufficient cover. Not a moment too soon, because Saira's protective spell suddenly alerted her. She turned around quickly and could make out the silhouette of a Galanx in the distance, who was slowly coming nearer. Cherou had noticed her reaction and detected the guardian at the same time. "Let's get out of here!" he hissed and pointed at the Galanx.

"I can't, not until I have restored the spell, or they'll discover us immediately," Saira replied.

"But the Galanx will notice us if we don't disappear," Cherou said, getting more panicky.

"Go and hide, while I finish up here," she said, and when he hesitated, she added: "Don't worry, I know how to look out for myself."

"I can't leave you behind all alone!" Cherou said desperately.

"Will you just go!" Saira hissed urgently. "I'll be done soon!"

Cherou still hesitated while the Galanx had already come hazardously close.

"Now get out of here and find a safe place," Saira ordered him sternly. "I'll be fine!"

Cherou started to move hesitatingly while the Galanx was nearly within visual range. With a last desperate glance at Saira, he finally hurried to reach the cover of the rocks while she continued her work, relieved that he was safe. Just some more magic procedures and then the job was done. But the Galanx was faster! Saira glanced over her shoulder and saw him coming right towards her. She panicked instantly while Cherou had no choice but to watch the scene unfold, completely helpless, from his cover. He was amazed when Saira suddenly became invisible right in front of his eyes. The next moment the Galanx was really close. His mighty shadow fell on Cherou who drew back, frightened, further into the relative safety of the cover.

Meanwhile, Saira had sunk to the ground and tried not to move, while working hard to complete the defensive spell and staying invisible at the same time. The Galanx was hovering right above her and she felt the drag caused by his momentum. He kept moving his head to and fro, and for a short time he was directly above Saira, slowly sinking down. His giant body came closer and closer, and Saira realized with horror the absolutely enormous size of these guardians. The Galanx was still sinking down, and Saira was able to see just about every detail of his smooth skin. He would detect her immediately if he touched her, and their escape would end right here. The edge of his lower fin was only just an arm's width away and Saira wanted to yell in sheer panic. Slowly, he sank down even further. Saira was almost ready to jump aside, so she would not be buried beneath the giant body, when the guardian finally moved on. The bottom edge of his fin briefly touched her body, and Saira was sure that he would discover her now. But the Galanx did not seem to notice. He whirled up a huge amount of sand when he moved and finally swam away at a leisurely pace. When he was out of sight at last, Saira dissolved the invisibility-spell and rose up, shivering, while she quickly restored the protective spell. Then she hurried to reach Cherou, who took her joyfully in his arms and hugged her with great relief.

"I thought the Galanx had detected you for sure," he whispered anxiously.

"He even briefly touched me once, but luckily he didn't seem to notice," Saira answered excitedly and let herself sink to the ground. She was exhausted.

"Did you close the magic barrier?" Cherou asked after a short pause.

Saira nodded and tried to calm herself.

"Then you should take a rest and recover," Cherou recommended, and Saira looked at him gratefully. Cherou turned around and glanced out from the protective cover. He could not see any movement and the Galanx had not returned. But they needed to move away from here quickly. They were still much too close to the city of the Duumars and could be discovered at any time. Cherou waited for a while and continued watching their surroundings, but everything remained calm. Then he turned back to Saira.

"How are you doing? Do you think you are ready to swim on?" he asked.

"I'll be fine," Saira said and got up.

"Well then, follow me!" he told Saira and they left the cover together. They cautiously swam along the ground so that they would not be detected. The light that shone from the city gradually faded and gave way to the endless night of the deep ocean. In the diffuse penumbra of the last light, Cherou noticed a group of caves inside a big reef and turned towards it. The light there was very dim, so the two Lingits had to use their luminous organs to see. Saira was utterly amazed by the variety of creatures that populated the reef down here in the deepest darkness. For the first time in her life, she saw the bizarre shapes of all the different corals and admired the delicate tentacles of the polyps that lived within them. Strangely shaped creatures continuously scurried and crept around between them, creatures she had never seen before. It took her breath away, and she couldn't get enough of the amazing variety of life all around here. Cherou had to actually pull her along, while Saira's eyes were still held captive by the beauty of the reef. He finally manoeuvred her into the safety of a cave, and Saira was sorry at not being able to watch the creatures go about their business anymore.

"You will have enough opportunities to get to know this world," Cherou promised her smilingly. We are safe here for the time being. The light phase will soon begin, and it's better that we hide here."

"How do you know that the light phase is about to begin?" Saira asked, astonished. "You can't see it from here."

"Believe me, I'm right," Cherou stated. "I've lived down here long enough, and I can feel when it starts."

Saira had to be satisfied with that. She could not compete with his experience and just had to trust that he was right. She could not think about it any further because at that very moment both Lingits heard a menacing voice: "Don't move, or you're dead!"

*

Jir woke up this morning quite early and wondered why Cherou and Saira did not lie beside her. She rubbed the sleep from her eyes and looked around, but could not find the two Lingits any-where. "Has someone seen Cherou or Saira?" she asked the Lingits near her. But they shook their heads.

"Don't worry," one of the Lingits said. "Cherou often disappears early in the morning, but he is always back in time for work.

Nobody knows where he goes, but I'm sure he will be back soon. Maybe Saira has gone with him this time," he explained soothingly.

"You can swim to the mine with us," another Lingit offered. "Then at least you'll get enough to eat, otherwise you'll have to make do with the left-overs."

"You'll meet them at the mine," another Lingit promised.

Jir finally agreed after a short deliberation. Cherou and Saira would not mind if she joined another group of Lingits this one time. That way, she would at least become better acquainted with some other Lingits. She would surely meet both of them again later. So Jir started to swim with the other Lingits in direction of the mine.

*

A very sharp spike poked into Saira's and Cherou's back. Cherou cautiously glanced back over his shoulder, while Saira stiffened in terror. He recognized a familiar silhouette out of the corner of his eye. "Are you Hingais?" he asked carefully.

"That's right!" their leader confirmed. "How did you get here and what you are looking for?" he asked menacingly.

"We have escaped from the city of the Duumars and are looking for protection," Cherou answered truthfully.

"That's not possible!" the leader of the Hingais growled and pushed the spike even harder into Cherou's back. "No one can get through the magic barriers of the Duumars alive. So how did you come here? Maybe you are Duumar spies?"

"He's telling the truth!" Saira said. "I have some magic powers myself and I was able to overcome the barriers with their help. We are slaves of the Duumars and we just want to find a place to hide."

Now the Hingai behind Saira pressed the spike harder into her back. "That's impossible! No Lingit has magic powers!" he growled menacingly.

"I'm not a real Lingit, I've been abducted to this world," Saira replied as calmly as possible.

"That's true, she's a Thae'Kor," Cherou confirmed. "Just look at her and you'll see that she's no real Lingit!"

The Hingai behind Saira exchanged a short glance with the leader, who nodded at him. Then he drew back a short way and bellowed: "Turn around slowly!"

Saira followed the command and turned around carefully, while the Hingai menacingly pointed a spike at her. He enhanced the light of his luminous organs to be able to see Saira better. Her slender face, her long hair and her pointy ears were markedly different from Cherou, whose head was roundish and completely hairless. He also had no auricles, just small openings at both sides of his head.

Now Saira could see the Hingai more clearly too. He was just about half her size, and instead of just one big pair of wing fins, he carried a bigger pair in front and a smaller pair at the back. The outer edge of both pairs of fins was also a luminous organ. The head was not clearly distinguished from the body and tapered off. A long and very sharp spike rose out of one of the two arms, at the base of the hand.

The Hingai still pointed menacingly towards Saira with his spike. He looked at her sceptically. "She's not a real Lingit," he finally agreed.

"Please, believe us!" Saira begged emphatically. "We don't mean you any harm. We've fled from the Duumar mines and will not go back there!" She put her head down and said softly after a short pause: "I'd prefer to die here, rather than work as a slave again!"

"She's telling the truth!" Cherou said again. "Please believe us!"

The Hingais looked at each other again, then the leader finally eased the pressure of his spike on Cherou's back. "All right, if you really have escaped, then we don't want to refuse our help. You can stay with us for the moment, but be warned! If you deceive us, we will kill you!" Then he pulled in his spike, as did the other Hingais.

"Thank you very much! That's very kind of you!" Cherou thanked them with great relief. Saira bowed to them too.

"Follow us!" the leader of the Hingais commanded tersely.

*

By now, all the Lingits had arrived at the mine. Only Cherou and Saira were missing. Jir grew more and more nervous. Torg would most certainly be very angry if they did not arrive on time. She feared that once again, he would vent his rage on her, because she had been staying with them. A short time later, Torg entered the mine and the slaves moved to their places. Of course, Torg noticed the gap immediately and stomped up to Jir who crouched in fear. He rose up behind her and growled angrily: "Where's Cherou and this other Thae'Kor?"

"I ... I ... don't know ... Genjai!" Jir stuttered, scared to death.

The Draugh bent down to her. "What do you mean, you don't know?" he asked, perilously friendly. "Didn't you swim with them to the mine today?"

"N ... no ... G ... Genjai," Jir stuttered and shrunk even more.

"Will you stop stuttering while you talk to me!" Torg suddenly roared, while Jir winced and started to cry.

"G ... Genjai, I ... haven't seen them ... yet today," she stammered in a tearful voice.

"She's telling the truth," Gorv helped her. "None of us has seen them today."

"Who asked you?" Torg shouted at him. "You'll have to do their work too, until they reappear!" he yelled at the Lingits and stomped to the mine's exit where he ordered another Draugh to come up to him. "Search for these two parasites and bring them here. I myself will snip their fins!" he commanded with a growl. The other Draugh clapped his shears together to show that he had understood and started the search.

The Hingais led them through a labyrinth of caves and corridors, in which the Lingits soon lost their orientation. The water was markedly warmer here and had a strange taste. Also, breathing was suddenly more difficult. The Hingais finally stopped and the leader uttered a complex signal of whistling sounds and pulses of light. Suddenly, a rock in the ceiling crunchingly rolled aside, revealing an opening through which the Hingais swam quickly. Cherou and Saira had to squeeze through, and the opening was closed immediately behind them. Another extensive system of caves, serving as habitation for the Hingais, lay in front of them. The two Lingits were led into a bigger cave, where they were ordered to wait. Then the leader of the Hingais swam out again, but placed several guards in front of the cave's entrance.

Saira gave Cherou an uncertain look. He answered with a soothing gesture. Both Lingits felt obviously uneasy for the moment. Their pursuers would not find them here, but the Hingais had not proved quite as friendly as they'd hoped. The leader returned a short time later with a much older Hingai. The old Hingai scrutinized both the Lingits silently while sinking to the ground. Then he said with a rough voice: "I've been told that you have escaped from the Duumars, and one of you has magic powers. Is that correct?"

"That's true," Cherou confirmed, his voice as friendly as possible. "We are slaves from the mines of the Duumars. My partner Saira was abducted from another world and has some low-level magic powers. We were able to overcome the magic barriers with their help."

The old Hingai looked at them for a short while, then nodded. "I would gladly believe you, but I have to maintain the safety of my tribe. You can stay here for the moment and enjoy our protection, but you'll be under observation. The Duumars are wicked and an enduring danger to our people. Their careless behaviour makes our life more and more difficult. The fact that you've got magic powers can also be a peril for us. I hope you understand."

"I can understand your concerns, but they're unfounded. We don't wish you any harm," Saira assured him. "I would never hurt anyone with my magic powers. So you need not fear us. We just want to get away from this terrible place, where they keep us in slavery and constantly torment and humiliate us. We can't stand this life of captivity any longer and want to be free again!"

"That's perfectly understandable," the old Hingai said patiently. "But I have to be sure no further harm is done to our people. Too much sorrow has come over us in recent times, too much sacrifice has been required, we can't cope with any more," he said bitterly. When he saw the baffled looks on the faces of the two Lingits, he got up and asked them to follow. Flanked by several guards, he led them into a big cave. Its upright walls were completely overgrown by corals, but the coloured splendour of the reef they had seen outside was missing. Taking a closer look, they noticed that the corals were bleached and lifeless. Between them, algae grew rampantly and covered the reef with a maze of pale filaments and tufts, giving them a spooky appearance. "The current carries the water of the city of the Duumars right here. It's much too warm and contains too little breathable gas for the corals. Besides, it's full of toxic substances that encourage the growth of algae. That's why this reef is dead and is now gradually getting covered by algae, but the bad water has even worse consequences," the old Hingai explained and led them to another cave. There, lying on the soft sandy floor, were a large number of quite small Hingais. "The toxic substances in the water are more harmful to our children than to the adults, as you can see here. Most of them are very sick, and many have already died," the old Hingai explained bitterly. "We are unable to help them because our herbs are useless against this poison. We can only try to ease their suffering a little."

The sight of all those sick and whimpering children nearly broke Saira's heart. When she tried to get closer, one of the guards moved between them and, with a forceful gesture, ordered her to retreat. Frightened, Saira obeyed. Cherou, too, was appalled and horrified by the many sick children. They left the cave and the old Hingai led them through several more caves, where Hingais were involved in doing various kinds of work. All of them were thin, emaciated figures, who looked at them with empty eyes.

"You see, my tribe has been starving for a long time. The activity of the Duumars has not just poisoned the water, but also changed the currents. We have to swim out farther and farther to find food. The creatures we eat gradually move away from this area and often our hunters return empty-handed. Soon, we'll find nothing to eat here anymore at all, and we'll have to leave this place, too, to avoid dying of starvation," the old Hingai said sadly.

"Why have you not left this place before now?" Saira asked.

"Our sick children would not survive the journey. Lots of them are too ill to be moved," the Hingai explained bitterly.

Saira stared at him in dismay, then lowered her gaze. "That is quite terrible," she whispered quietly.

The old Hingai led them back to their cave. Other Hingais had laid out some food there for the Lingits. "Now you know our fate, and I hope you can understand why our people can't take any more! That's why we are so suspicious of everything that comes from the city of the Duumars. You can move freely now, but you will be constantly accompanied by our guards for the time being. Now get some rest."

Cherou blocked his way when he prepared to leave the cave.

"Would you please tell me your name?" he asked as kindly as he could.

"I'm called Seveg," the old Hingai answered soundlessly, and swam out without a further greeting.

*

The Draugh Torg had sent out to search for the missing Lingits returned after a long period and reported. "We have searched several times all the areas in which the Lingits are allowed to stay. They couldn't be found there. If you wish, we will expand our search now to cover the whole city."

Torg did not move while he briefly pondered the matter. If the two Lingits had not remained within the permitted areas, this could only mean that they had made an attempt to escape. Cherou knew the magic barriers, and he knew they were absolutely insurmountable. How could he be so silly and try to escape, when he knew very well that this was impossible. Well, the Draughs or the Galanx would detect them and then Torg would snip their fins. "All right, search the whole city and inform the Galanx too. They should watch the area with increased attention," he finally ordered. "And bring them uninjured, so that I can teach them a lesson!"

"Shall we inform Thurgun?" the other Draugh asked.

"No, they'll have searched for a place to hide inside of the city. We don't need to inform Thurgun right now. Just find them as quickly as possible," Torg answered.

The other Draugh again clapped his shears together, turned on the spot and left, while Torg went back to his slaves. It would cause a great deal of annoyance if Thurgun came to know about Cherou's attempted escape. The most judicious of his slaves making an attempt to escape! Torg could not believe it. Had the new young female slave leaned on him so much that he was no longer the master of his senses? Even though she was just a Thae'Kor? Well, he would teach these two fugitives not to cause any more trouble. He just hoped the guardians would find them soon, otherwise he would have to report it. Then even he would suffer for it. He knew the quick excitability of Thurgun and his unpredictable reactions, once he was in this state.

*

Meanwhile, Cherou and Saira had settled comfortably on the soft sandy floor and had eaten some of the food the Hingais had provided for them. Considering the Hingais were starving, it was not easy for them to eat anything at all. The Hingais were meat eaters and the Lingits fed solely on vegetation, so at least they were not taking any of their food. Saira looked sad and Cherou, too, was lost in his thoughts. Seveg and the other Hingais still mistrusted them, but at least they gave them protection. Even so, Cherou felt like a prisoner. It would be best if they did not stay here long. After some light phases had passed, the Duumars would not concentrate their search only on the immediate surroundings of the city anymore. Then he and Saira could slip away unrecognized. Until then, they had to convince the Hingais that they did not mean them any harm. There had to be a way to thank them for their help, somehow.

"I know how to help them!" Saira suddenly said in a muted voice.

Cherou looked baffled. "Can you even read my thoughts now?" he asked, astonished. "Just now, I was asking myself the same question."

Saira looked at him and smiled. "No, that's not something my magic powers allow me to do."

Cherou gave her a sceptical look. "You are starting to scare me," he said jokingly.

"During my training, I also learned to use magic to heal other beings," Saira explained quietly. "If they can't cure their children with their herbs, then maybe I could try with my magic. It would be worth a try."

"I don't believe Seveg would permit it. He would be afraid that you might harm the children even more," Cherou replied.

"I have seen enough dying children in there. If I can make him understand that they may have a chance of recovery through my help, he might agree to it. Some of the children look like they won't even survive the next few days." Saira argued.

"Are you really sure you can do it?" Cherou asked sceptically. "Don't get me wrong – I really have confidence in you, but if you fail, Seveg will hold you responsible for the death of a child. Then we are practically dead, too," Cherou expressed his doubts.

"I know, but I can't just sit around and watch these poor children suffer and die, when I might be able to help them," Saira said.

"If you are absolutely certain, it's worth a try," Cherou finally agreed.

"Then let's try it," Saira said hopefully and got up. They moved to the exit where the guardians immediately blocked their way. "Would you please lead us to Seveg," Saira asked in a friendly voice. "I may be able to help your sick children."

The guards exchanged a short glance then nodded. "Follow us," one of them ordered the Lingits. Soon they had reached a cave where Seveg and some other Hingais were staying. One of the guardians told the Lingits to wait, then reported to Seveg.

Seveg waved to them and got up. "How do you propose to help our children?" he asked.

Saira told him about her training as a healer and explained that she might be able to cure the children with her magic powers. Seveg did not seem to be very enthusiastic about the idea at first, but Saira received unexpected help from the other Hingais.

"Just let her at least try, Seveg," one of the Hingais in the cave begged. "You know just how sick our children are. Some of them may not even see the next light phase!"

"What if they cause more harm to them?" Seveg replied gruffly. "I don't trust these Lingits!"

"It would still be worth a try," another Hingai said. "Some of the children will die anyhow. They have nothing more to lose. At least give them a chance," the Hingai begged almost pleadingly.

A short, fierce discussion began, during the course of which Seveg was persuaded by the majority of the Hingais to allow Saira to try. Happily Saira followed them to the children. Cherou accompanied her as a precaution, so that at least he could comfort her. He knew he had no chance against the poisonous spikes of the Hingais, even though he was twice their size. When they reached the cave with the sick children, Saira was guided to the patients who were the most ill. The nurse led her to a child who was extremely weak.

"That's little Joleg. He is the most sick of all. If you can help him, we would be very grateful," the nurse said quietly.

"I will do my best," Saira promised. Then she sank down beside the child with the nurse, who took Joleg's hand and caressed it tenderly. The child opened its eyes hesitatingly and watched Saira and the male nurse with a tired look.

"Joleg, that's Saira, she wants to help you get well again," the nurse said.

Joleg watched Saira uncertainly.

"Don't be scared, I will not hurt you," Saira promised and smiled at the little patient. "But I need your assistance, or I can't help you. Keep lying very still. Even if my treatment may get a bit unpleasant, please don't resist. Let me continue, otherwise it's even more difficult for me to heal you. Will you promise me that?"

The child exchanged a short glance with the nurse, then nodded hesitatingly.

"Don't worry, I'm right beside you," the nurse said soothingly and again stroked the child's little hand.

"Well, then I will start now. Just relax and keep completely still, it won't hurt," Saira said as calmly as she could and gave the child another friendly smile, which Joleg returned briefly. Then she closed her eyes and laid a hand on the child's upper body. She carefully got in touch with Joleg's spirit and body. She felt a short resistance as the child got scared, but the nurse calmed it down and Joleg relaxed again. Saira's magic cautiously penetrated deeper into the body, got in touch with its subconscious, tried to detect what caused the sickness. Although the body of the Hingais differed markedly in shape and function from a land-dweller's body, Saira found enough similarities to enable her to continue. Step by step, her magic detected the damage to the organs, the metabolism, and the various energy streams in the child's body. The effect of the poison and the deficiency of breathable gas became more and more obvious. The body itself showed her the damaged areas through its own consciousness and showed her the criteria for healing. At last, Saira finished her examination and opened her eyes. "It's looking good," she said, full of hope. "He's weak, but I think I can neutralize the effect of the poison." Then she looked at Joleg and asked in a friendly voice: "Now, was that bad for you?"

"No, I didn't feel anything," the child said a bit surprised.

"That may change now. Please just keep calm, and I'll complete the healing as quickly as possible," Saira promised the child with a kind smile, while Joleg bravely nodded once more. Then Saira closed her eyes again, to better be able to concentrate. Her magic entered the child's body again, searching for the damaged areas, and began to weave healing spells there. She moved deeper and deeper, flowing through the little body, searching for the poison to neutralize it. This procedure also demanded strength from the child's body, and gradually the amount of living energy decreased worryingly. The breathing flattened and the metabolism seemed to crash. The child would likely die under her hands if Saira could not quickly counteract developments. The only possibility left to her was to transfer enough of her own living energy to the child so it could stabilize. Just in time, she allowed a part of her own strength to flow into Joleg's body, and slowly he stabilized. However, this procedure had weakened Saira so much that she began to flag. The nurse watched her with concern and Cherou wanted to go to her.

"What's the matter, are you feeling sick?" the nurse asked, worried.

Saira opened her eyes and steadied herself again. Breathing with great effort, she gasped: "I'm all right," and made a soothing gesture with her hand. She relaxed briefly, then concentrated again on her task. One last time her magic entered the child's body and weaved the last of the healing spells. The body itself had to accomplish the remaining healing. Saira finally withdrew her magic out of Joleg's body and opened her eyes. Tired but happy, she proclaimed the success of her intervention and commended Joleg again for his bravery. "Just relax, you will soon feel better," she promised the child and caressed his cheek. Then she got up arduously.

"Thank you very much!" the nurse said happily. "I'll let you know when his condition improves."

Saira smiled. "You're welcome. Maybe I can help the other children too, but first I'll have to rest."

"Certainly," the nurse said understandingly.

Then Saira and Cherou were taken back to their cave again.

*

Although the Draughs had searched every part of the city, and the Galanx had inspected the edges of town most painstakingly, Cherou and Saira remained missing. At last, Torg had to report the escape of the two Lingits to Thurgun. As expected, the Duumar threw a tantrum and nearly attacked Torg. But Thurgun quickly regained control and immediately ordered the search to be extended to encompass the areas around the city. He could not imagine how the two Lingits had overcome the magic barrier, because this time no tunnel was found that led beneath it, like during another attempt a long time ago. If they were not in the city, they must have found a way out. Maybe the interrogation of the Lingits would provide further information. Thurgun just regretted that he could not use force, because if he did, the Lingits would be unable to work, and he had to keep his production running. Why did it have to be slaves of his mine, and why his best instructor, the one he had treated preferentially. This Thae'Kor must have induced him to escape! He had always been against the idea of employing workers other than the Lingits. These foreign creatures always caused so many difficulties. If he could get her, he would show this useless creature the way he solved such problems. Then she certainly would not cause him any more troubles. He was sorry about Cherou, though. He had proved himself a capable and obedient instructor. It would not be easy to replace him. But first, it was important that both of them were found. A successful escape was about the last thing Thurgun needed. Right now, while his career was going so well, and his biggest opponent was eliminated! He still had no doubt that the two fugitives would be found quickly. He could definitely trust the Draughs and the Galanx. They had discovered and brought back every single fugitive so far.

*

Saira had recovered from the exhausting treatment of little Joleg.

"What actually happened?" Cherou asked worriedly. "First the child barely breathed, then, a short time later, you nearly collapsed."

"Joleg was already too weak. The treatment took too much strength. That's why I had to give him some of my own energy," Saira explained.

"Not just some, but quite a lot!" Cherou remarked with a slight rebuke.

"I had no choice, otherwise he would not have survived," Saira justified herself. "My master knows a ritual that obtains energy directly from the magic. But this ritual is complicated and I don't know it completely, so I only could give some ... some of my own energy to the child." She glanced at Cherou with embarrassment. "I'm not a fully trained magician yet."

"You have done a very good job!" Cherou praised her. "But please, be a bit more careful the next time you give somebody some of your energy."

"I promise," Saira answered and smiled. "You too can volunteer as an energy supplier," she teased Cherou, grinning.

"That would suit you!" he grumbled, pretending to be annoyed. "First you read my thoughts, then you want to drain my energy. You wait, you cheeky young fin!" Then he tweaked her belly several times, while Saira twitched and giggled.

Right then, Seveg swam into the cave. The two Lingits got up and looked at him, a bit embarrassed. "I came to tell you that

Joleg is slowly feeling better. He can eat solid food again and is getting visibly stronger," he told them with relief. His face had lost some of its harshness and now he showed more confidence. "I want to thank you in the name of all the Hingais, and want to ask you if Saira might be able to heal more of our children?"

"Oh, I would be glad to, but today I'm still too weak for further treatments," Saira answered eagerly.

"Joleg's treatment must have taken much of your strength," Seveg replied. "So, please recover first, then you can resume later. It's better if you hide here for the moment anyway, because it's quite unsettled outside. The Draughs and the Galanx are searching every little cave. But don't worry, you are safe here. The Duumars and their helpers don't know these caves. They don't know anything about our existence, either. They will turn their attention to another area in some light phases. Then you can easily escape."

"Thank you very much for assisting us," Cherou said to the old Hingai.

"You are welcome. And you are helping us too. Please excuse our great distrust, we didn't mean to offend you," Seveg replied. "You can now move freely without the guards."

"Thanks, that's very kind of you," Saira said, while Seveg bowed down slightly.

"So please, just come to me when you feel strong enough to treat the other children. I don't want to urge you, but you have seen yourself how sick most of them are."

"I'll come as soon as possible," Saira promised.

"Will you tell me your name too?" Seveg turned to Cherou.

"I'm called Cherou," the Lingit answered and bowed down with some semblance of formality.

Seveg also bowed down slightly again, then he left them and gave the guards a sign to follow him.

*

During the next three light phases, Saira healed all the sick children of the Hingais. The Hingais were more than happy that their grief had finally ended and that they would be able to leave this place soon. As the guardians of the Duumars now had turned to another area, there was nothing to prevent the continuation of the Lingits' journey any longer.

"Do you have a particular destination in mind for your journey?" Seveg asked them.

"We intend to swim to the Qails. A big colony of them is supposed to be somewhere in the Djaraun-Layer," Cherou answered.

"Then you still have a very long way to swim. The Djaraun-Layer is located many light phases from here," Seveg argued.

"I know. But only there we'll be safe from the guardians of the Duumars," Cherou explained.

Seveg deliberated briefly. "The fastest and most pleasant route would be the Santimag-Stream. Follow this stream until you see a mountain range that looks like a Dorgon tooth. That's where the great Curun-Stream flows into a deep abyss. It verges on the Djaraun-Layer, so you just follow this stream further. It will take you directly to your destination."

"That's a good suggestion. We don't have to strain so much within the stream, and can just drift along for a while. Thank you very much for this advice," Cherou said.

"I'm glad if we can help you. We will never forget that you have given us the opportunity to find a better future," Seveg replied. "In grateful recognition for the saving of our children, we'll escort you to the Santimag-Stream. It's located some distance from our caves. You can quickly leave this area from there."

"Thanks, that's very kind of you," Saira said. "I'm really glad I could heal your children, and I hope you will soon find a new place were you can live a better life."

"We certainly will," Seveg assured her. "Thank you again for all your help. But now you should rest up for a while until it is time for you to move on. Your journey will be very exhausting."

117

And so Saira and Cherou returned into their cave, where the Hingais had laid out an adequate amount of food.

"This tastes a lot better than that dull plopkelp," Saira pronounced happily.

Cherou gave her an amused look. "So at least I mustn't listen to your never-ending complaints about the food anymore," he teased her, grinning.

"That's not true at all!" Saira grumbled and pretended to be annoyed. "I haven't complained all that often!"

"Oh yes, you have," Cherou answered, still grinning.

"Not at all!" Saira said, playing at being offended.

"Yes!" Cherou insisted, amused.

"No!" Saira said.

"Yeees!" Cherou said with a long drawl.

"No, that's not true!" Saira scolded. "Take it back immediately!"

"No way!" Cherou said.

"Yes you will!" Saira insisted.

"No, I won't!" Cherou said, grinning broadly.

"You are really mean!" Saira said, seemingly offended.

"And you look so sweet when you're angry," Cherou teased her further.

Saira got tired of this. "You are quite outrageous!" she scolded and punched his chest with her fists. "Will you take it back, or I'll transform you into a ..." She searched for a suitable term, but did not find one.

"You want to transform me into a what?" Cherou asked, laughing.

"Oh, all I can think of is even worse than you!" Saira complained.

Now Cherou really had to laugh. "May I take this as a compliment?"

"Just take it as whatever you like!" Saira grumbled, pretending to be offended. Then she gave him an amused look. "Cheeky fellow!"

Dangerous encounters

After the two Lingits had rested for a while longer, the time had come for them to leave, but before they went, Saira insisted on looking in again on the sick children. When the children heard she would be leaving, the strongest of them got up and hugged Saira to thank her. She had to fight bursting into tears because she was so moved by the kindness of the children. The farewell from the adult Hingais was very amicable, too. After the guardians had made sure one last time that the area was safe, they accompanied the two Lingits right up to the edge of the Santimag-Stream. There, they said good-bye to Cherou and Saira with a final salute. The two Lingits dived into the stream and drifted again into the eternal night of the deep sea, using slight movements of their fins to stabilize. Saira felt for the first time the mighty power of the stream, which was accompanied by a constant deep noise. She also noticed another sound that she had never noticed before. Mighty deep reverberations, long drawn-out singing, trilling whistles and chirping clicks surrounded her, wherever she was.

"What are these strange sounds?" Saira asked. She felt a little frightened.

"We call it the song of the ocean," Cherou explained. "What you hear are the sounds of countless creatures that either orientate them-selves or communicate among themselves with these sounds. Here in the lightless deep ocean, sound is the best way of getting in contact over long distances or to explore one's surroundings. In the open water, sounds can be heard everywhere. In due course, you will learn to recognize the different creatures around you."

Fascinated, Saira listened and for a short time forgot they were on the run. The darkness had frightened her at first and it felt really good to have Cherou close-by. Gradually she got used to the absence of light and learned to rely more on her sonar than on her eyes. Soon, she could manage quite well and added her own sounds to the song of the ocean. The lightless depth lost its horror once she was able to orientate herself in absolute darkness. The two Lingits swam next to each other with their pale luminous organs glowing, so that they could at least have eye contact. Cherou had asked Saira not to produce too much light. Not only would it take unnecessary strength, but it would also attract the attention of potential marauders. Nearly all the hunters of the deep sea had very sensitive eyes, which could perceive even the slightest quantity of light. So they would easily alert pursuers this way. Again and again, Saira noticed the flashes and shiny silhouettes of other ocean dwellers. Cherou never tired of describing and explaining the different creatures to her and which beings were harmless and from whom she had better keep away. They had been swimming along without any problems for quite some time, when Saira suddenly perceived a shape through her sonar, a shape rushing up from beneath her. It just flashed up briefly in the image, so Saira could not recognize it. Instinctively she enhanced her light and, in the gleam of her luminous organs, could just about make out a long spike, which seemed to aim to pierce her! With a horrified outcry she shot upwards, which saved her life. The figure raced up just in front of her and the attack failed. Cherou reacted very quickly, pushed Saira aside and catapulted himself out of danger's way.

"Watch out, a Peltai!" Cherou shouted at her. At the same moment he heard the rattling sonar of the blind hunter searching for his prey. Now Cherou also uttered very loud sonar signals and clicks in rapid succession, to mislead the hunter. Then he quickly darted away to use his sonar again at another place. His clicks and whistles disturbed the Peltai's perception, who now rushed towards Cherou. He suddenly sped down from above, but because of Cherou's sound interference he just missed him, and his attack failed again. By then, Saira had recovered from her scare and did the same as Cherou. Both of them continuously uttered loud sonar signals. The echoes seemed to disturb the hunter, but a Peltai did not surrender so quickly. Instead of relying to his sonar, the Peltai now kept silent and tried to locate his victims by their own sounds. This time he concentrated on Saira. He rushed closer again. Saira detected him at the last moment and jumped aside, which saved her life once again, otherwise the Peltai would have pierced her with his pointy snout. By then Cherou had already come close and gestured for Saira to be quiet. Only the song of the ocean could be heard for a moment, then the rattling sonar of the Peltai sounded again. Saira and Cherou scattered and again sent out loud sonar signals in different directions. They kept in continuous movement, so the signals always came from another angle and were widespread. The resulting interference caused a cacophony, which disturbed the Peltai very much. Again and again he missed his prey and searched for them in vain with his sonar. Finally, they took the opportunity to escape upwards, and the hunter left off with a last furious growl. Cherou and Saira sped ahead, relieved to get away from the Peltai's hunting ground. Both were exhausted and out of breath when they finally found shelter in the safety of a small cave.

"He nearly caught me quite a few times," Saira said, still trembling from fear.

"Yes, I'm a bit out of practice too," Cherou admitted, breathing heavily.

"Are they always so persistent?" Saira wanted to know.

"Most of the time," Cherou replied tersely. The two Lingits sank to the ground to recover from the arduous escape. When they could breathe easily again, Cherou praised Saira: "Well done! You reacted absolutely correctly."

"I just tried to stay alive," Saira replied. "Your training was successful, otherwise I wouldn't have known what to do." She paused for a moment. "This Peltai attack has really frightened me. I don't think I've ever been so frightened before," Saira finally admitted.

"Everyone feels this way, when they are attacked for the first time and their life is in danger," Cherou said understandingly. "Eventually, you will learn to deal with it, because it is a part of your life." Then a smile came to his face. "Just look at it positively. It shows you are quite tasty, young fin!"

Saira gave him a punitive look. "You are quite outrageous!" she scolded. "And if you say how sweet I look now, you're going to get it in the neck!"

Cherou laughed, amused. "You are the first Lingit girl who's not happy about compliments," he said with a grin.

"I can do without such compliments," Saira grumbled.

"Well, maybe you don't taste all that good," Cherou countered, while Saira made a face at him. "My charm seems to be out of practice, too," Cherou admitted.

"Indeed!" Saira agreed with mock annoyance.

"Can you forgive me once more?" Cherou asked, hamming it up mightily.

"All right, just this once," Saira replied generously and snuggled up to him with an amused smile, while Cherou took her in his arms, looking relieved.

*

His closeness and his protective arms felt good and Saira fell into a light sleep a short while later. After some time, she was woken up by a strange noise. It clearly differed from the song of the ocean, which could also be heard faintly in the cave. No, this strange grinding and crunching could not originate from a living being. Cherou woke up too.

"What's that sound?" Saira asked, frightened.

"I don't know. I've never heard such a sound," Cherou replied quietly and got up. Carefully he glanced out of the cave's entrance, but could not detect anything unusual. Slowly the sound grew louder, and a pale red light became visible at some distance. It seemed to come out of a nearby canyon. Cherou sent out some sonar signals into the area. But they did not show any dangerous creatures nearby, so he and Saira finally left the cave and moved closer to the upper edge of the canyon. There, they sank down and darkened completely. The sight took their breath away! A group of Galanx was pulling a magic net across the bottom of the canyon, causing the strange noise. The red gleam illuminated the canyon and the big Galanx with a spooky light. Their strong sonar sounds mixed with the scratching and grinding of the net produced a scary atmosphere, making the Lingits shudder.

"What are they doing?" Saira asked, confused.

"They are collecting food for the Duumars," Cherou answered, thunderstruck. "I've always asked myself how they could gather up so much food in such a short time. Now I know! Look how many creatures they've already caught!" He pointed at the rear part of the trawl net, which now came into sight. It seemed to have a life of its own, at least it looked that way, because of the countless creatures who were caught inside, and now scrambled around in fear. But there was no escape from the magic net. "There must be thousands of them! No wonder the Hingais often can't find anything to eat. The Galanx are catching everything!"

Saira just watched with bewilderment how ruthlessly the Galanx pulled the net over the ground, while the number of captured creatures inside increased rapidly. As the strange crowd had passed, the destruction they left behind could be seen in the gleam of the net. The entire seabed was torn open, ploughed, rubbed off and left blank. No life would be possible in this place for a very long time!

"Just look at this!" Cherou said, devastated. "They don't only capture all the creatures and damage the whole of nature. No! They also destroy the entire environment and make it unliveable!"

"That's ... terrible!" Saira whispered hesitantly. She could not believe what she had witnessed just now. How could the Duumars and their helpers act so ruthlessly!

Cherou's luminous organs flickered excitedly, while he pulled Saira away from there. "Come with me. If other Galanx are around, they could dctcct us." He led her back into the secure cave and accumulated sand at the entrance, leaving just enough space for breathing water to enter.

"Here they can't detect us," he said. Then he sat down and leaned against the wall.

Saira snuggled up to him, appalled and disturbed. "How could anyone ever be so mean and ruthless?" she whispered hoarsely.

"They are just as mean and ruthless here as they are with the slaves," Cherou said with resignation. "I never realized they caused so much destruction and grief even all the way out here, but the Duumars seem to stop at nothing!" Then he stroked Saira as she looked at him desperately. "Maybe there will be a possibility to put an end to their terrible deeds one day," he comforted Saira. "If the Qails are ready to help us, there's at least a little chance to end the reign of the Duumars in time."

"Oh, that would be so good," Saira said tiredly.

Cherou gave her a hopeful smile and caressed her gently. After some time her deep breaths proved that she had fallen asleep in his arms. "Don't worry, the two of us will soon turn this world into a better and more peaceful place," Cherou whispered confidently.

*

The guardians of the Duumars had searched a large part of the area around the city. They had examined every little hole, but the two fugitives simply could not be found! It puzzled Thurgun, how the Lingits could possibly overcome the magic barriers. He had again ordered a thorough examination, but the barriers were complete. The other Duumars had noticed the activity of the guardians, so Thurgun now had to admit to his masters that two of his slaves had escaped. The Duumars extended the search. The interrogation of the slaves provided Thurgun with no further indications, although he had not exactly treated them gently. It simply made no sense. Only an experienced magician could overcome the magic barriers uninjured, but there were no beings with magic powers other than the Duumars. Suddenly a horrifying suspicion arose in Thurgun's mind. Maybe the Thae'Kor, who had fled with Cherou, possessed magic powers! This could be possible. These fools who kidnapped the slaves probably did not inquire exactly who it was they were going to abduct. If his assumptions were right, then this slave would be a serious risk for the guardians. Maybe the fugitives had not been found yet because she had also managed to deceive the patrols. If she possessed magic powers, she could easily get out of the reach of the guardians. It was just a suspicion, which Thurgun thought he would better keep to himself for the moment. But if it proved right, they had an extremely dangerous enemy to deal with, whose power they did not now. Thurgun hoped that his suspicion would not prove right, otherwise they all were in great danger!

*

"Did you sleep well, dream-swimmer?" Cherou greeted Saira after she had woken up in his arms. She shook away the last remnants of tiredness and stretched out contentedly.

"Yes, thank you," Saira replied.

"Then let's look for something to eat. I'm hungry," Cherou said and got up. After he had removed the sand from the cave's entrance, he sent out some brief sonar signals to make sure the surroundings were safe. He did not detect any danger, so he and Saira left the cave.

"We have to swim further upwards, where there's still some light. Down here, no plants can grow, because of the missing light," he explained. They carefully started their ascent. It led them along a mass of rocks. Where the stream was close-by and carried enough food and breathing gas, there was a great variety of life on the rock face, which Saira watched with fascination while they slowly climbed higher. But further up, outside of the Santimag-Stream, the rocks were a lot less populated. Also, breathing was more difficult here than in the stream. A short time later they reached the upper end of the rocky massif, where it turned into a sand-covered plateau. It was too dark here and food was scarce, so the ground was populated by only very few creatures. Saira and Cherou carefully moved further upwards. They saw another rocky massif at some distance. They went up higher along its sloped wall, until they finally saw light above them. Both Lingits swam close to the rocks and darkened themselves so they would not be detected. Soon there was enough light, and a rich assortment of plants grew on the rocks, with life swarming all around. Saira was overwhelmed by the beauty of this light-flooded habitat populated by countless creatures: corals, sponges, snails, starfish, jellyfish, crabs and fish in all kinds of different shapes and colours. She had never seen such a fantastic sight before! She could not get enough of this wonderful habitat and completely forgot why they had actually come here. Cherou smiled and let her enjoy herself, but made sure that the surroundings were safe, so they would not experience a nasty surprise. This apparent paradise also had its dark sides. Finally he swam close to her and said: "I see that you are impressed."

"This ... this ... is overwhelming!" she stuttered.

"My hunger is overwhelming too," Cherou remarked casually.

Saira looked at him, baffled, then she was embarrassed. "Sorry, but this has fascinated me so much, I completely forgot my hunger."

"That's all right!" Cherou said and laughed. "Everyone who sees this habitat for the first time is amazed by it. But let us eat something now. You can look around some more later." Then he showed Saira the tastiest plants, which appeased their hunger. Afterwards Cherou led Saira through the reef, and again she was completely lost in amazement.

"Can't we keep swimming around up here?" Saira asked disappointedly, after Cherou asked her to dive down again.

"That would be too dangerous, for we can be detected much easier here, and this reef only extends over a small area. The water gets deeper behind it, and we would be swimming in open waters, which is not a good idea, because danger lurks everywhere," Cherou explained.

So Saira left the beautiful reef behind, her heart heavy, and let Cherou lead her down again into the dark depth. Soon they had reached the twilight zone, where the light-flooded part of the ocean ended and turned into the eternal night of the deep sea. Saira looked up wistfully for one last time. Although she had learned to deal with the darkness, she felt so much better in the light. The last remains of light created an eerie atmosphere. A ghostly veil traversed the sea and generated a scary mood. It was quite difficult to escape from this effect. Although the water was clear, the veil restrained visibility and made orientation very difficult. Cherou also felt uneasy because he knew that a dreadful hunter lived down here. Again and again he carefully sent out brief sonar signals in different directions and tried to penetrate the veil with his eyes, while he hurried to pass this layer of water. They had nearly left the zone and Cherou was just about to breathe a sigh of relief, when he saw, out of the corner of his eye, something huge swimming towards them. He turned around, horrified, and saw the large head of a Dorgon coming right up to him. "Watch out!" he yelled to Saira and dragged her harshly aside, while he tried to reach a safe place himself, but it was already too late. The Dorgon threw open his giant mouth, which acted like a suction-trap. Cherou was grasped by the outflow of the swirl and hurled against the head of the hunter. The Dorgon turned around, growling, and snapped for Cherou, but the Lingit let his luminous organs flash up with utmost intensity and blinded the extremely sensitive eyes of the hunter. The Dorgon missed him and Cherou took his chance, made himself dark and fled. Then he saw Saira's luminous organs pulsing excitedly. At the same moment, the Dorgon saw the light too, and attacked! "Blind him!" Cherou shouted as loudly as he could, while Saira, frozen in panic, stared helplessly at the hunter. She managed to shake herself out of her panic at the last moment and let her luminous organs flash up brightly. Then she catapulted aside with a heavy stroke of her fins. The Dorgon roared, while his mighty jaws gaped apart in an instant. Saira was grasped by the suction and would have been hurtled into the mouth of the Dorgon, had Cherou not raced up and gripped her while swimming by, and pulled her along with him. "Darken yourself!" Cherou called to her, while he briefly stopped to release her. But the Dorgon had already started its pursuit. Cheated out of his prey, he was more furious than ever and attacked again. The two Lingits were prepared for him this time, blinding him together, then speeding off in different directions. The Dorgon hunted Cherou, came up to him and opened his big gaping mouth. But Cherou eluded skilfully, fired a bright flash at him and fled, leaving the Dorgon blinded for a short while. Just when he could see clearly again, the two Lingits suddenly hovered above his eyes and blinded him once more. The Dorgon snapped at them with a furious growl, but missed them and was promptly blinded again. He roared angrily, while Cherou and Saira hurried to reach the seabed. While the Dorgon was still snapping around blindly, they entrenched themselves into the smooth sand, until only the tips of their noses protruded. When the Dorgon finally could see clearly again, his two potential victims had vanished. He searched the area for some time and also moved across the ocean floor. But it was already too dark there, and he could not see the two Lingits anymore. He finally gave up and furiously swam away.

*

An expansion of the search had also proved unsuccessful. Now it was clear that the two Lingits had left the city. Searching for them now was pointless, because the area was just too enormous. Thurgun's suspicion that the Thae'Kor possessed magic powers had not yet been proven. Not one of the guardians had been attacked or had perceived any strange phenomena, which might suggest the use of magic. But they had to be careful. As long as they did not know what they were dealing with, and how strong their opponent was, they could not estimate what kind of danger they would have to deal with. Rumours of the escape had naturally spread everywhere, and the wildest ideas were circulating concerning how they had managed to escape. But the Duumars had nipped in the bud any further escape attempts by massively increasing the number of patrols. The patrols around the city had also been intensified, and all the guardians had been put on maximum alert. But the Duumars' possibilities for dealing with this matter were not yet exhausted. A wide network of informants existed across the ocean, who reported in regular intervals everything that happened in their surroundings. The Lingits could not escape this close network of scouts. It was just a question of time until they were observed. Then their insolent escape would soon come to an end.

*

Cherou got up first and shook the sand from his body, while he ensured that the surrounding area was safe. Saira too dared to get up again. She spit out the sand that had gotten into her mouth.

"No one said you should eat the sand," Cherou remarked, grinning, while Saira gave him a punitive look. Then he scanned the area once more for the Dorgon, but he could not be seen anywhere. "We're rid of him," Cherou finally said, relieved. "I was afraid he would catch you, the first time he attacked!"

"He would have caught me, if you hadn't saved me!" Saira answered, embarrassed. "I'm sorry, I just couldn't react quick enough."

"Don't worry," Cherou said understandingly. "It turned out all right. You will learn to react appropriately in due course."

"Hopefully before I'm eaten up!" Saira answered halfway seriously.

"Didn't I tell you that you taste well!" Cherou joked and once again was at the receiving end of a dark look from Saira. "Let's get away from here before the Dorgon returns. I have a feeling that he's still near-by."

He didn't have to tell Saira twice, and they dived down until they felt the Santimag-Stream again, which carried them gently along. The ground was rocky and offered no scope for hiding, so they did not have to fear a Peltai attack. The two Lingits stayed alert though, they did not want to be surprised by a hunter again. Later the canyon widened, and the stream flowed along more slowly. The ground here was covered with a thin layer of sand, which was still not thick enough to hide a Peltai. Then Saira suddenly felt a short pain at the edge of one of her wing fins. "Ouch!" she shouted and turned around. A little fish, barely bigger than her hand, had bitten out a small piece of her fin. Cherou also turned round and his eyes grew wide with fear at the same moment. "Oh no! Swim!" he shouted, horrified, sped up as fast as he could and pulled Saira with him, nearly tearing her arm out.

"What's the matter?" Saira asked, bewildered.

"Look back!" Cherou shouted.

Saira did. The sand seemed to explode behind them, and a giant swarm of little fish chased them with their mouths open wide! Saira yelled out in fright and swam as fast as she could.

"These are Tisters. If they catch us, they'll eat us alive!" Cherou shouted. Saira gave him a horrified look and tried to keep up with his speed. She briefly glanced over her shoulder, but the swarm was still pursuing them. The two Lingits swam for their lives, but the swarm would not be shaken off. Saira's strength gradually waned, and she had the impression that the swarm slowly got closer. She mobilized all her strength once more and swam as fast as she could, but it seemed like an eternity until the swarm finally gave up the pursuit. They swam on for some time to put as much distance as possible between them and the swarm. Coloured rings were dancing in front of Saira's eyes, and she could barely see clearly anymore when Cherou finally slowed down and sank to the ground. Breathing laboriously and completely exhausted, they lay next to each other for a long time, until they had recovered a little.

"That was a narrow escape," Cherou said.

"You never told me about these creatures," Saira said.

"I really hadn't thought about them at all," Cherou admitted. "I might have spent too much time in the mines." Then he got up wearily. "Let's look for a place to sleep, I'm completely exhausted and will have to recover before we can go on."

"Me too!" Saira agreed and got up too. After a short while they found a cave in a nearby rock wall that was big enough for them. Cherou piled up sand again to close the entrance, leaving just enough space for breathing water to enter. Then he lay down, groaning.

Saira looked at him, a little embarrassed. "Would you mind hold me tight for a while, tonight?"

"With pleasure!" Cherou replied, touched. He took her in his arms and realized that she was shivering. "Better now?" he asked kindly.

"A bit," Saira replied thankfully.

"A bit!" Cherou grumbled jokingly. "The Lingit girls used to be delighted if they dared to lie in my arms!"

Saira turned her head towards him and saw him blink his eyes. "Braggart!" she mumbled, smiling, and clung closer to him. It felt good to have him so close, and she gradually calmed down again. What a terrible thought, being eaten alive by those little beasts! Saira shook herself mentally and tried to suppress this thought, but not quite successfully, because later she even fled from the swarm in her dreams. At some point she woke up from her nightmares. It was completely dark in the cave and Saira briefly panicked. She didn't dare use her luminous organs, because she feared that the light might be seen outside the cave. She also did not want to use her sonar, for that would wake up Cherou. So she used her magic night vision, which enabled her to see clearly even in complete darkness. She realized with relief that the cave was empty, and even outside no suspicious sound could be heard, only the song of the ocean. She gradually calmed down again when she realized that it had just been a nightmare. Happily lying in Cherou's strong arms, she slowly relaxed. Sometimes he reminded her of her father Keh.

She smilingly remembered the funny pretend-fights she and her father used to have. Sometimes they lasted a long time, until her mother Hri had had quite enough and pulled the pointy ears of both opponents until they were even longer. As further memories of her home tried to rise up, Saira fought against them, for she knew only too well that she could not handle the homesickness that arrived with them. So she swallowed hard to clear her throat, and pushed away all thoughts of Wuun. Maybe she would return to her world one day. At least she was finally living a free life again, even if it offered her no safety at all. Because they still were on the run, and many creatures thought of them as a delicacy. But at least now she was not a slave anymore. Maybe all would turn out well in the end. She finally fell asleep with this hope in her heart.

*

Meanwhile on Wuun, it was noontime. All the magicians had been trying for hours to untwist the magic network of traps and wrong tracks that the pursuit of the magic portal had uncovered. Most of the tracks ended nowhere, but a few of them were heavily secured and attracted attention. They provided at least a first lead, which was worth following up. But they had to proceed with utmost care, because even the Guardians of the Light had never come across such a strong spell. They had to carefully examine it step by step, because a careless attempt might draw danger to their world, and the spell might retroactively affect Wuun. So the magic network exposed its secrets very slowly and supplied first references of the place that Saira had gone to. Step by step, further leads opened up and pointed to the way the portal had taken. For the first time, the magicians of Wuun were hopeful that maybe they would be able to find the girl. It was just a question of time now until the destination of the transport was found. But what would be waiting for them there, what kind of a world would they find, and would they ever be able to bring Saira back from there? These questions remained unanswered for the time being.

*

Saira and Cherou again followed the stream; they'd been doing this for quite a long time. The rest had been soothing for both of them after their exhausting escape from the Tister swarm. They had not been attacked since then. So the two Lingits let themselves drift in the stream, which slowly ascended and brought them again into higher water-layers.

"What I've been meaning to ask you for a longer time, Cherou: I've never seen any children in the mine and in the sleeping cave. You said that you've been living there for several generations. Where are your children?" she asked inquisitively.

"Well observed!" Cherou praised her. "I suppose the parents in your world probably raise their own children."

"Yes, of course!" Saira confirmed, astonished. "Don't you do that?"

"No. All our children are left with our juvenile attendants straight after birth. That's a special group of adult Lingits who take over the care, raising and education of our children. The parents can of course see their children anytime, but they stay with the juvenile attendants, until they can look after themselves," Cherou explained.

"Why would you do that?" Saira asked, surprised.

"As you have already determined, we live a very dangerous life. Out there in the ocean are a lot of dangers and many of us fall victim to them. If we would let our children be raised by their parents, many of them would soon be dead, because their parents would be killed out in the ocean, and so couldn't care for their children any more. Then other Lingits would have to take care of the children, who maybe would lose their life too. Our juvenile attendants always stay in their homes, safely protected by the group, so their survival is at least somewhat ensured. Naturally, there can sometimes be casualties amongst them too, like sickness or accidents, but ordinarily they grow older than most of the other Lingits. So the continuity of our race is ensured as best we can. This method of raising our children has proved successful over many generations, otherwise we might not exist anymore," Cherou answered.

"I never thought about it this way, but under the circumstances, that's a good solution," Saira admitted.

"There are special areas in the city of the Duumars where the juvenile attendants live with the children. We can visit them there any time. These areas are located away from the mines, that's why you have not seen the children," Cherou explained.

Saira nodded understandingly. "Do you have many children?"

"Oh you young fins always ask so many questions!" Cherou grumbled seemingly in despair. "And you are a particularly inquisitive specimen! But anyway, you won't give it a rest until I tell you. So listen up." And Cherou started to tell Saira about his people. How they had lived before the enslavement, which areas of the ocean they had populated, when they were captured and how they lived today. As they were above the twilight zone, they did not need their sonar anymore to orientate themselves, so Saira could follow Cherou's narration without interruptions. They could see adequately in the clear water to detect approaching dangers in time, so there was no risk of a surprise attack. Saira listened eagerly to Cherou's story, but kept monitoring their surroundings at the same time, until Cherou finally finished his tale. "So, now you know everything about us," he said. "But now you must tell me about your world, too."

"Maybe later," Saira said. "Otherwise I will feel homesick again, and that hurts too much at the moment."

"That I can understand," Cherou replied remorsefully. "I am sorry, I hadn't thought about that."

"It's all right," Saira answered. "As I told you, maybe another time. Let's search for something to eat. I'm hungry!"

Cherou felt the same, so he willingly helped her look for tasty aquatic plants. After they had finished eating, it was time to search for a place to spend the night. Unfortunately, no cave existed on this wide plain. The two Lingits searched for quite a long time, but did not find anything that would provide suitable shelter. They were still searching when dusk began. Now it really was high time to hide, for the hunters of the night would soon swarm out. Then it would be much too dangerous here, out in the open. In the end, the two Lingits came across a rock face with an entrance to a cave. The cave itself was enormous, but a swarm of Durkas had already retired inside. The skate-like creatures, who had two pairs of wing fins one behind the other, would not harm the Lingits, because they just ate small organisms. But the Durkas were not happy to share their habitat with other beings. However, this cave was the only one for miles around, so there was nothing left to do for Cherou and Saira than to beg for access. One of the Durkas next to the entrance of the cave swam up when he detected the two Lingits and blocked their way.

"Can't you see that this place is already occupied?" he mumbled sullenly.

"Please forgive us, but we are looking for a place to spend the night and this is the only cave around. Would you allow us to stay here for the night? We certainly won't disturb you," Cherou asked in his friendliest voice.

The Durka mumbled something incomprehensible and asked them to wait. He talked with some of his comrades inside the cave. Then he returned. "All right, you can stay here tonight," he mumbled again and let them pass. Cherou and Saira thanked him and searched for a place to sleep under the suspicious eyes of the Durkas. Saira did not feel good surrounded by these big creatures, who were about three times her size. She clearly felt that they were not welcome at all, but they had no choice, so they lay down on the smooth sand as far away from the Durkas as possible. Saira clung to Cherou, who lay down protectively in front of her. He felt Saira's uneasiness. He wasn't feeling too good about staying here either, but it was just this one dark phase they had to spend with the Durkas.

"Don't worry, they won't harm us," he whispered.

Saira gave him a sceptical look and tried to relax. Like all the times before, Cherou's closeness felt good this time, too, and after a short while she really did fall asleep. Neither of the two Lingits noticed that some time later one of the Durkas left the cave through another exit.

Betrayal

The cave had almost emptied when Saira and Cherou woke up the next morning. Only a few Durkas remained, but they took no notice of the two Lingits. So Cherou and Saira thanked the Durkas once more, then left the cave a short time later. Outside no danger seemed to lurk, at least nothing dangerous was in sight, but Saira kept feeling that something was not right. Cherou noticed her disquiet and was about to ask what was bothering her, when the sand around them seemed to explode. Saira yelled out and Cherou took her protectively in his arms. The two Lingits looked around in panic. The sight cleared and a moment later they were surrounded by a huge number of Draughs. At first, Saira wanted to use her magic against them, but realized that there were too many Draughs. She looked for a way to escape instead, but the Draughs had encircled them and there was no way out. The only escape route left seemed to be straight up. So, in panic, she freed herself from Cherou's arms with a short stroke of her fins and climbed up quickly. Up there she would be out of reach of the Draughs and would be better able to fight them.

"No, Saira, stay here!" Cherou called after her, but she did not listen and almost immediately found herself confronted with the giant snout of a Galanx. He fired a short but powerful sonar burst, which seemed to explode in Saira's head. Dazed and unable to move she sank back to the ground, where Cherou caught her. "You stupid girl, why don't you listen to me!" he asked desperately.

"That's right!" one of the Draughs growled. "You seriously believed you could escape from us? Don't put up any resistance, or we will eliminate you right here!"

Cherou soon recognized the Draugh who had spoken. It was Scang, the major guardian of the Draughs. He was infamous for his cruelty and therefore feared by all the Lingits. Any resistance against him was useless. He would not hesitate to kill them on the spot, even if the Duumars had forbidden him to do so, for Scang always made his own rules.

"I'm happy that you are at last reasonable!" the Draugh said with a rough voice. Then he commanded: "Get them right now!" The Draughs in the front row pounded up to the Lingits and were about to grasp them when the waters above them darkened. The Draughs hesitated, erected their stalk-eyes and lowered the rear part of their body, so they could better look up. The next moment one of them roared loudly: "Gamburas!" The giant swarm soon sank down on them, and the first of the rapid hunters shot towards the Draughs. Cherou ducked instinctively and tightly held on to Saira, who was still quite dazed. The Draughs scattered and raced away in all directions as quickly as their long legs would carry them. The Galanx sped up to their highest velocity and sought safety in flight. It got dark around Cherou when countless Gamburas swarmed around them, but they did not harm them. The gold coloured, gleaming, extremely fast hunters shot past the Lingits and rushed at the Draughs. The Draughs' strong armour protected at least their body, but the Gamburas went for the sensitive eyes and doggedly stuck to the limbs, so the Draughs could barely move anymore. They defended themselves as best they could with their shears, but against the enormous number of agile hunters they had no chance. The Galanx were not spared either. One of the Gamburas kept hovering in front of the Lingits and asked them to join their swarm, while the fight was still in progress. Cherou agreed immediately and pulled Saira along with him. She had by now recovered control of her senses. A short time later they had left the place of combat behind and, under protection of the swarm, fled from their pursuers, who still were massively attacked by the remaining Gamburas. They finally let off their victims and returned when the swarm had moved on far enough. Two Galanx were heavily wounded and several Draughs had lost some of their limbs, but all the guardians were alive.

Saira did not feel good among the Gamburas. They were her size, but their laterally flattened, golden gleaming body was more like the shape of a fish. Their deep-seated, dark eyes and the terrible teeth seemed very threatening to her.

"You don't need to fear them, they won't harm us!" Cherou said, but he saw Saira's sceptical look and knew that she did not want to believe him fully.

"Your partner's right, you don't have to fear us," said the Gambura who swam directly beside her. "Once we ate Lingits, too, but one day a huge swarm of us was trapped inside a cave, because the entry was barred by a quake. The Gamburas couldn't free themselves and would have suffocated or starved to death. But the Lingits had compassion for us and opened the entrance, so the whole swarm was saved. The Gamburas swore eternal friendship to thank the Lingits. Since then, no Lingit has ever been attacked or eaten by a Gambura. This oath is still valid today and for all times."

"Is that true?" Saira asked, surprised.

Cherou nodded. "Yes, that's the truth. That's why you don't have to fear them."

Saira was impressed with this story and felt a bit better, but some uneasiness remained, not least because of how threatening these extremely fast hunters looked.

"Have you fled from the Duumars?" one of the Gamburas next to Cherou asked. "We haven't seen any free Lingits for a long time."

"Yes, we are slaves from the mines of the Duumars," Cherou confirmed.

"Are you aiming for a particular destination in your escape?" the Gambura wanted to know.

"We are searching for the Curun-Stream," Cherou answered this question. "It is supposed to flow past a mountain that looks like a Dorgon tooth."

"That's right!" the Gambura confirmed. "This mountain is one light phase away. Please wait a moment."

After a short pause, he continued: "We agree and will accompany you to this place."

"How did you discuss that so quickly with all the other Gamburas?" Saira asked, surprised.

"We are many, but we are also one," the Gambura replied mysteriously. "We are an associate being and we are all linked with one another."

Saira looked at him uncomprehendingly and turned to Cherou for help. But he too just turned his palms up to show that he was as much at a loss as she.

"It's not easy to understand for single beings like you," the Gambura admitted.

"You don't need to make a detour for us," Cherou said.

"It doesn't matter which way we go," the Gambura replied. "We have no special destination."

"Thank you very much, that's very kind of you," Cherou said.

"That's what friends are for," the Gambura said.

They quietly swam for a while side by side, until the Gambura suddenly asked: "Aren't you hungry? You probably haven't eaten anything today."

"That's right," Saira replied and received an amused look from Cherou.

"Directly beneath us is a reef with plentiful vegetation. Eat as much as you want, meanwhile we'll make sure the surroundings are safe," said the Gambura. The huge swarm formed a ring around Saira and Cherou, while they all sank down together. Under the protection of the swarm, Cherou and Saira enjoyed a tasty meal. Then they rejoined the swarm and moved on with them.

*

Thurgun was beside himself when he learned that the Gamburas had attacked his guardians and had helped the Lingits to escape yet again. His guardians were heavily damaged and had to give up any thoughts of further pursuit for the time being. As long as the Lingits travelled with the Gamburas, every attempt at capturing them was doomed to failure. Well, at some point the Lingits would have to leave the protection of the swarm. The

140

scouts would most certainly report this in good time, and then they would pay.

*

"How did the Draughs discover us?" Saira asked, while she and Cherou swam on with the Gamburas. "How did they know we spent the night in the cave of the Durkas?"

"I don't know" Cherou admitted. " I would have noticed them if they'd been close to the cave before. There was nowhere large enough to hide them, and I would have certainly seen the Galanx in the open water!"

"Maybe they followed our sonar sounds?" Saira said.

"That's almost impossible. They too use their sonar to orientate themselves in complete darkness, and believe me, I'm quite familiar with the sonar sounds of the Draughs and Galanx! Their sonar is much louder than ours, that's why I'm sure I would have heard them before they could ever have noticed us," Cherou stated.

"Then maybe you were betrayed," the Gambura beside Cherou remarked to their surprise. "We have often noticed that the Galanx maintain good relationships to certain beings, and often supply them with food. Perhaps that's how the Duumars get information about the events in the ocean."

"That means that we won't be safe anywhere anymore!" Saira said, frightened. "Some scout could always lurk about somewhere and sell us out to the Duumars!"

"We don't know how big the influence of the Duumars is in the various areas of the ocean. I'm sure it decreases with the distance to their city, but you will have to be very careful and you can't trust anyone," the Gambura explained.

"I really hadn't expected that," Cherou admitted. "I'd never have imagined that their influence would reach this far. It means that we'll have to be a lot more careful and mustn't stay anywhere for long."

"That's right," the Gambura said. "We'll reach the Curun-Stream at the beginning of the next light phase. It's located inside a deep canyon where you'll be a great deal safer than up here in the illuminated area of the ocean," the Gambura explained soothingly.

So the two Lingits followed the swarm until it got dark. The Gamburas seemed to know this part of the ocean very well, because there was no long search for a cave of adequate size to shelter them for the night. The two Lingits spent the dark phase under the protection of the Gamburas, and started out again bright and early the next morning. As the Gamburas had promised, they reached the mountain that looked like the fang of a Dorgon after a short while. The swarm dived down and slid along for a while above the canyon through which the Curun-Stream flowed. The Lingits finally left the Gamburas under the cover of the swarm and dived down quickly. The darkness of the deep sea enclosed them again, but this time Saira felt much safer there than in the illuminated higher regions of the ocean. Cherou, too, was glad to be back in his usual environment. They relaxed and drifted along with the mighty stream.

*

The next day, hunger forced them to ascend again and search for food in the brighter regions of the sea. During their search, they reached the reef that had been destroyed some time before by the flood waves. Although some small plants and animals had colonized it again, the widespread devastation was still clearly visible. Saira was shocked by the destruction and asked Cherou what could have caused this.

"Such widespread destruction can only be caused by the water itself," he explained. After he caught Saira's inquisitive look, he continued: "The water sometimes creates disastrous force. You haven't experienced a storm yet, that's why you can't imagine how tremendous the power of the ocean is. But this destruction wasn't caused by a storm. It's too massive. A reef normally survives the strongest storms without much damage. This can only be caused by several gigantic flood waves, like those that some–times occur after a seaquake."

Saira looked around thunderstruck and could not believe what she was seeing, until Cherou asked her to move on since they would not find any food here. Later, they discovered some adequate vegetation deeper down and could appease their hunger. Afterwards, they returned again to the safety of the deep sea and once more drifted along with the stream. The canyon grew more and more narrow, causing the speed of the stream to increase greatly. The Lingits, too, went along faster, and had to be extremely careful to keep to the middle of the canyon, so they would not be smashed against the rock face, which was irregular and caused dangerous whirls with its overhanging rocks and deep cuts. If the Lingits lost control and smashed against the rocks, they would be doomed. Saira often only just managed to avoid the overhanging rocks because of Cherou's strength, experience and skilfulness. It was difficult for her to orientate herself with only her sonar at this high speed. In addition, the whirls of water falsified the echoes, so Saira received only blurred images of her surroundings. Her luminous organs were useless here, because their light did not reach far enough at this speed, and the whirling caused visual obstructions, which imposed further limitations. So she tried to let herself be guided by Cherou and stay as close to him as possible. The wild flight through the canyon with its narrow gaps and cuts seemed to take forever and took nearly all her strength. Several times Saira avoided crashing into overhanging, sharp-edged ledges by a hair's breadth. The force of the impact would have killed her, or at least caused severe injury. She felt extremely relieved when the water finally flowed more slowly, and she was able to change direction with slight moves of her fins again.

In the polar sea

The water was a lot colder now, and the stream gradually ascended to the surface of the sea. Cherou and Saira just drifted along; they were very tired. The extreme speed of their journey down the canyon had required all their strength and a great deal of concentration. The two Lingits were hoping to quickly find a cave for shelter, so that they could rest up and recover. But in the massive rock face no entrance could be found, so Cherou and Saira drifted on. The seabed had ascended so much that the two Lingits could see the surface shimmering high above them. Saira did not feel the cold, although the water was extremely chilly. But the coldness affected her mobility and made her sluggish. Saira again and again noticed small dark spots at the surface, their numbers increasing rapidly. "What are those strange spots up there?" she asked, astonished.

"That's ice," Cherou explained smilingly. "The water is so cold that it freezes in part, forming these blocks. Just wait! Later, you'll see complete mountains made up of ice."

Saira looked at him in disbelief, but soon saw that he was right. The objects grew larger very quickly, and soon the water was filled with the bizarre shapes of giant icebergs. Saira was lost in amazement as she swam through this strange world. Fantastic formations filled the water, created corridors and caves full of weird structures. The strange objects were in continuous movement, and everywhere the groaning of giant masses of ice could be heard. Saira reverently touched some of the almost transparent sculptures. At first, she drew back after touching them, surprised by their coldness, but then the smooth, shiny surfaces with their fascinating opalescence filled her with enthusiasm.

"Is there no ice in your world?" Cherou asked, surprised.

"Yes, of course there is," Saira said, still amazed by the fascinating view. "But not where I live. It's much too warm and sunny." Then she swam up to the edge of an iceberg. Cherou hurried to follow and attempted to pull her away from the shimmering giant. "What's the matter?" Saira asked, somewhat annoyed.

"I can understand your fascination, but these icebergs are dangerous. They have a habit of turning around suddenly. Then they lift you out of the water, and you immediately freeze to their surface, so that you can't get back into the water and you'll suffocate out there," Cherou explained emphatically. Saira looked at him again in disbelief. "Don't look at me this way! It has really happened to some Lingits. Especially to inquisitive, careless young fins like you," he said with a smile.

Saira pulled a face and mumbled something unintelligible, but still she swam away from the iceberg.

"Come on!" Cherou said conciliatorily. "There's quite a lot more to discover."

Saira followed him slowly. Sometimes she just didn't know whether Cherou really spoke the truth or was just kidding her. She slid after him, still slightly annoyed, but the overwhelming beauty of the landscape soon diverted her thoughts. She swam through a labyrinth of ice, amazed at the new, fantastic and bizarre objects that came into view. Suddenly, she picked up the still far away but increasing chatter of a strong sonar. It scared her at first, because she thought it was a Galanx coming closer, but Cherou swam on unperturbed, while diving down slowly. The strong sonar grew louder, until it hurt nearly her whole body. That's what the Lingits must feel like when Torg tormented them with his sonar. But these sounds were different, too deep for a Galanx or Draugh, and above all much too loud. The two Lingits had just reached the seabed, when a huge shadow appeared at some distance above them. The sonar sounds started again. Saira tried to cover her ears to keep out the loudness, but quickly recognized that it was useless. Every sound seemed like a small explosion. Even though she just felt the outflow, it still was strong enough to cause pain in her entire body. Meanwhile, the giant shadow was passing overhead. Saira saw a massive, long, stretched-out body with a barrel-shaped, big head that made up nearly one third of the entire torso. The rear part of the body tapered out in a long tail. Both sides of the body had enormous wing fins, which the giant used for swimming. Saira stared open-mouthed at the creature. It was at least four times the size of a Galanx!

"That's a Wra. They are the biggest creatures on Turoon," Cherou explained with awe. When he caught Saira's frighten look he said soothingly: "Don't worry, they won't harm us. They live on Dyx, very small creatures, barely the size of our fingers. You just have to mind their strong sonar!"

Saira followed the giant with a fascinated look. She waited until he was out of sight then turned to Cherou.

He smiled in amusement again. "I see you are impressed!"

"I've never seen such a big creature before," Saira admitted with admiration.

"They mostly live in the polar sea, because that's where most of the Dyx are," Cherou explained.

"What are Dyx?" Saira asked.

"Let's see if we can find any," Cherou replied. "They mostly hide in the niches and gaps of the ice during the light phase. They appear only in darkness, and they often shine most beautifully. Maybe we are lucky during this dark phase, and you can watch their dance. That's a fantastic sight you'll never forget!" They carefully went nearer to the edge of the ice again. After searching for a while, Cherou found some of the little crab-like creatures.

"The Wras feed on these small creatures?" Saira asked unbelievingly.

"Oh yes, indeed they do!" Cherou confirmed. "I know it seems absurd, but the Dyx appear in the darkness in huge swarms. The Wras stun great parts of the swarm with their sonar and eat them. Maybe you'll be able to see for yourself during the coming dark phase."

"I can't wait!" Saira said, still not quite sure what to believe.

Gradually dusk fell, so the two Lingits looked for a place to spend the night again. They settled comfortably in a cave until it had turned completely dark. Then, Cherou cautiously glanced out of the cave's entrance and made sure that the surroundings were safe. The first colourful flashes of the Dyx could already be seen above them. He waved for Saira to come nearer and pointed upwards. Both watched with fascination the spectacle that was silently unfolding above their heads. More and more of the small, crab-like creatures embarked on their excited dance, emitting bright signals of light. The waters above them finally became one large expanse of colourful glitter. The small bodies of the Dyx flashed up in shining colours and created a phosphorescence of the sea, so beautiful it took Saira's breath away. Saira was quite overwhelmed by the spectacle, and even Cherou was drawn under its spell. They reverently watched the wonderful performance of light and colours. Then, suddenly, they again heard the loud chatter of a Wra using his sonar. A short time later he appeared within the swarm of the Dyx, which shot apart. Their colourful light beams were reflected by the smooth skin of the giant and bathed him in a magical light. The two Lingits could clearly see how he raced forward and sucked a large number of his stunned prey into his giant mouth. This happened several times, and the swarm of the Dyx quickly became smaller. Cherou remembered that the swarms used to be much bigger, and even many Wras could not eat them all. The fact that just a single Wra hunted here was strange too, because they normally lived and hunted together in groups. It was not long before the giant Wra had eaten nearly the entire swarm. The remaining Dyx dispersed and rushed off to escape, and the spectacle ended as quickly as it had started. Again, the two Lingits settled comfortably in the cave, and in no time at all had fallen asleep.

*

The initial excitement concerning the escape of the two Lingits had cooled down in the city of the Duumars, and normal life resumed.

None of the scouts had seen the refugees lately, so the Duumars and their guardians were forced into inactivity. Thurgun was again angry, because the mined amount of fire-stone did not comply with his expectations. So he went to visit Torg.

"What's the matter, why don't you deliver more fire-stone to me?" he shouted at Torg.

"I can't drive the slaves further," Torg answered, completely unimpressed. "They already work as hard as they can. If I ask more from these weaklings, one after the other will break down. Then the output will decrease even more. The work of two good slaves can't be replaced like this."

"What about that new, weak Thae'Kor? Does she pull her weight at least?" Thurgun asked indignantly.

"You mean that shrimp?" Torg asked disparagingly. "My little punishment has definitely worked well. She works as much as she can, and she keeps up with the other slaves."

"Well at least that's one good thing," Thurgun grumbled crossly and was just about to leave, when Torg stopped him again.

"By the way, something strange happened during her punishment," Torg remarked off-handedly.

"What do you mean?" Thurgun asked.

"While I punished her with my sonar, I was suddenly thrown off my legs and briefly pushed against the rocks by a torrent," Torg answered.

"Why didn't you tell me about that before?" Thurgun flared up.

"Why should I bother you?" Torg asked laconically. "I can't explain how it happened, but it hasn't happened since. That's why I didn't see a meaning in it."

It was characteristic for the Draughs to regard such occurrences as trivial. What counted most was their prosperity, and that depended mostly on their food. They would do just about anything for a tasty and generous meal. Other things were barely of importance. Thurgun knew that too, and had often taken advantage of this attitude. But this time he was annoyed with Torg, although he knew a suitable rebuke was pointless, because Torg would not understand.

"Then at least do me a favour and don't tell the other Duumars," Thurgun asked with great restraint.

"As you wish," Torg answered tersely.

"No other strange things have happened?" Thurgun asked carefully.

Torg wagged his shear, implying "no".

"Well! Take care that your fire-stone mining won't drop even further. I will acquire two new slaves, because we definitely need to up the amounts," Thurgun promised and turned to leave. Now he had his proof at last, he thought while swimming out. This torrent, which had thrown Torg off his legs, could only have been a magic blast. The small Thae'Kor could not have done it, because she could surely not have woven the spell during punishment. The other Thae'Kor would surely have wanted to help her, and had thrown Torg off his legs. She must also have overcome the magic barrier with her magic. So much was finally clear. It would be more difficult to capture her under those circumstances. On the other hand, it was maybe better this way, because she would at least be no danger for the Duumars out there in the ocean. Admittedly, the successful escape would spoil his reputation, but after a while it would fall into oblivion. There was no danger for the Duumars, as long as the magician would not return. In this case, it would be better to gradually let the search for the fugitives peter out. Thurgun just hoped he would be able to convince the other Duumars of this, without having to tell them about the magic powers of the Thae'Kor. Well, this should not be very difficult, as he knew quite well how to juggle with words, and he could be very convincing if he had to!

*

When Cherou and Saira woke up the next day, the sun was already shining brightly. They left the cave and again swam through the bizarre environment of ice and water. Saira looked in vain for something to eat.

"Plants probably don't grow here, because it's too cold for them," she said.

"Yes, unfortunately that's true," Cherou agreed. "But there's something else to eat," he said and asked Saira to follow him. Cherou swam to the edge of an ice-floe with a greenish shimmer. "Come on, let's lick ice-algae!" he invited Saira, grinning. Then he lay on his back directly underneath the ice-floe and licked with his tongue over the greenish coating at the bottom of the icy surface. Saira hesitated, because she thought he was kidding her. "Come on, what you are waiting for, it tastes really nice!" Cherou called to her. Saira finally joined him, and found that the algae indeed tasted great. Saira could not get enough of them and in the end her tongue was almost numb.

"Faf taftes very goof," she lisped clumsily, making Cherou laugh.

"That's what happens when one's too greedy!" he said smilingly.

"If waf just fo fasty!" Saira defended herself.

"Fou can hear if," Cherou copied her and promptly received a hard stare. "Come, let's move on before somebody detects us and tells the Duumars!"

Saira just nodded, to avoid further mockery. They continued swimming through the wonderful environment. The terrain gradually decreased in height again, and the Curun-Stream pulled the two Lingits back into the lightless deep sea. There, they drifted for a while through a broad valley, which was part of a huge mountain chain, from which numerous wide canyons were branching off. Saira and Cherou suddenly heard a strange mournful sound, coming from of the canyons.

"What's that?" Saira whispered.

"I don't know," Cherou confessed "I've never heard anything like it."

They cautiously swam closer to the entry of the canyon from where the strange sound arose. Their sonar did not show any dangerous creatures around them. The weird noise grew clearer, a long mournful sound. There was no doubt that the creature making the sound was sick or heavily wounded. However, it could also be a trap. The Lingits swam closer, slowly and very carefully. Again and again they checked their surroundings, but their sonar revealed no danger. Then Cherou and Saira saw giant skeletons at the bottom of the canyon. As they cautiously swam closer, they recognized the skeletons of many Wras who had probably come here to die. They moved along the skeletons under the cover of the rocks, and for the first time saw just how enormous these creatures really were. The strange sound grew clearer and clearer. Here, amid the skeletons, the place seemed more sinister. The Lingits alternated between fear and helpfulness. This creature was clearly suffering. But where was the originator of this spooky sound? The two Lingits carefully swam on while keeping an eye on the safety aspect of their surroundings as best they could. More and more of the giant skeletons filled the bottom of the canyon, lying there in weird silence. Only the strange mournful sound carried across the water. The Lingits moved deeper into the canyon and at last found the one emitting the moans. An old Wra lay dying on the bottom of the canyon. Cherou and Saira cautiously came closer, once again ensuring the surroundings were safe. Then they let their luminous organs glow slightly, disclosing their identity to the Wra. This also allowed them to clearly see the head of the giant. He opened his weary eyes and looked at the Lingits apathetically. The Wra's skin was rough and wrinkly and splattered with numerous scars. He must be very old. The Lingits seemed tiny beside him.

"What are you doing here?" the old Wra asked in a faint voice, which still seemed quite loud to the Lingits.

"We heard your call and followed it, because we thought you maybe needed help. Please excuse us, we don't want to be intrusive," Cherou answered politely.

The old Wra uttered a contended growl, which shook the whole canyon. "That's very nice of you, but you can't help me anymore.

I'm old, and my end is near. That's why I swam to this place, which we call the ravine of silence. This is our final resting place.

"I understand," Cherou said. He felt quite sad.

"As you see, quite a lot of my brothers are assembled here. Once we were many, but our numbers are rapidly decreasing. We are a dying race, because the Duumars deprive us of our only food. They catch the Dyx in huge numbers and leave us to starve. We have often asked them to leave behind enough for us, but they don't care about our complaints. So we are doomed. I will soon follow my brothers like the few of us that are still alive." The Wra uttered again that mournful sound. "Please, let me die in peace ..." he breathed once more tiredly, then his eyes closed forever.

The two Lingits retreated respectfully. Saira had tears in her eyes, and Cherou had to swallow hard too. They left this place of sorrow and death as quickly as possible. The Duumars did not even stop their destruction for these majestic creatures, and had brought them to the verge of extinction. Cherou and Saira were deeply dismayed by what the old Wra had told them before he died, and swam on quietly for a long time. Both were wrapped in their thoughts and glad to have each other. The recklessness of the Duumars seemed to know no bounds. They destroyed entire habitats and exterminated one species after another in their unrestrained greediness. They contaminated the water and even diverted ocean-currents. What other dreadful things would they do to this world? How far would they go? Was this planet already doomed? Would the Duumars ever come to their senses? Existential questions for which there were no answers, but they would decide the fate of this world. The two Lingits continued to swim on thoughtfully while the canyon gradually became narrower. Giant vertically decreasing rock faces now loomed up at both sides. Right then, a loud rumble could be heard that increased more and more, turning to thunder. The whole of the ocean seemed to vibrate. The rock faces reverberated with the enormous noise and were shaken by the increasingly strong impact which moved out across the water.

The two Lingits were thrown to and fro, as one pressure wave after the other sped through the canyon. The rock faces seemed to dance wildly and were already starting to crumble, but the power of the impact increased further. Cherou and Saira could barely control how they moved and were in danger of being smashed against the rocks, while a massive seaquake shook the world around them. The thunder was so loud now that it hurt their whole body. The rock faces gradually became unstable, and the first heavy pieces were already shaking loose and crashing into the deep. But the quake carried on with undiminished violence. The canyon was shaken again and again by the heavy impact. Finally, the rock walls could no longer hold out against the charge. Giant pieces were breaking off directly above the Lingits, and there was no way for Cherou and Saira to escape them. Saira was the first to recognize the danger, while they were still being whirled around. Horrified, she looked for a means to escape the hail of giant rocks and scree. But the canyon was much too narrow and still more rocks and stones crumbled from the walls above them. With a powerful stroke of her fin she swam closer to Cherou, embraced him and held him tight with the strength of despair, while she built up a strong magic shield around them. Saira did not know if it would give them sufficient protection against the falling rocks, but at least they were not completely exposed to the hail of stones and scree. "Hold on to me tightly!" she shouted as loudly as possible. Cherou complied and hugged her close, looking terrified while the first mass of stones rained down on them. Then the world around them seemed to perish, as a tremendous mass of rocks crashed down and pulled them into the deep.

*

This time Thurgun had underestimated the stubbornness of the other Duumars. Because of their arrogance, they could not possibly tolerate being outfoxed by two simple slaves. They needed a victim to ensure their status, and therefore they would stop at nothing, even if it were senseless. They wanted to catch the slaves at any price. For good reason, Thurgun had kept it a secret that one of the two slaves was a magician, and that he even had proof of this. Naturally, there were rumours among the other Duumars, but none of them were keen to actually believe it. That suited Thurgun. If they found out that their suspicion was justified, it would cause panic, and this was certainly of no use to him at the moment. Not now, when everything was going so well for him. They had detected a new deposit of fire-stone a short while ago, and Thurgun had quickly staked his claim for the building of another mine. If the excavation rate in this mine was sufficient, he might even be able to restart the destroyed Gilgoia mine that used to belong to his previous opponent Pegrell. Then he would soon be the biggest mine owner of all times, which would quickly grant him even more wealth and power. But if the other Duumars were to panic because of this magician, the city would soon erupt in chaos. Nobody would make the required equipment and a sufficient number of slaves available to him, and Thurgun could bury his ambitious plans for a long time. That must not happen! Somehow he had to manage to lure the information of the scouts away. If the other Duumars received no information, they could not catch the slaves. At some point, they would stop their senseless undertaking. By then, Thurgun would have consolidated his power to the point where he had nothing to fear anymore. Well, he would have to use his connections once more, and would have to motivate his loyal dependants to report the arrival of each scout in good time. Accidents happened again and again, and a good many creatures were always getting lost in the wide ocean ...

In the dome of the sea-elves

There was light, bright light! But that could not be true. The last thing Saira could remember was the great avalanche of rocks that had pulled Cherou and her into the deep. She had lost control of the protective shield during the painful impact on the seabed, and they had been buried under enormous amounts of rubble and stones. But through her closed eyelids bright light was clearly visible. Saira opened her eyes carefully. She was indeed surrounded by light, but it did not blind her. Some contours became gradually visible once she had become accustomed to the brightness. She recognized Cherou who was lying directly beside her. His eyes were closed, but his chest rose and fell in the slow rhythm of his breathing. His body could be seen only indistinctly, because it was encased in some sort of shimmering cocoon. Only his head and arms lay outside the sheath. Saira looked down at her own body, which was also wrapped in a shimmering cocoon. She felt the signature of a healing spell emanating from the cocoons. Hers ensured that she could only move her head and arms, while the rest of her body was immobilized. Saira could have easily dissolved the spell, but she felt that it was there for their protection. She gradually saw some details of the surrounding area. They were inside a big irregularly formed room. Its walls, floor and ceiling were covered with shimmering crystals, some of which showed bizarre shapes. Many small, shiny spheres moved gently between them through the room. One of them hovered near Saira's face. Saira followed the figure with her eyes, when it suddenly stopped and cautiously moved closer. The little sphere was barely bigger than her hand. Directly above Saira's face it transformed into a tiny Lingit, who looked at her in a friendly manner.

"Oh, you are finally awake," the little creature called happily. "Don't have fear, we won't harm you. We found you buried under debris after a seaquake. You were heavily injured. That's why we brought you into our dome to heal you. You have not completely recovered, that's why you mustn't move. For that reason, we have encased your bodies with a healing sheath, which doesn't allow movement yet."

"Thank you, that's very kind!" Saira thanked the creature and looked around. "What is this place?" she asked, astonished.

"You are in the dome of the sea-elves, our home at the deepest point of the ocean," the shiny creature explained. "I took your shape so I would not frighten you. Sea-elves have no particular shape. We are creatures of pure energy. We can take on any shape we desire." The sea-elf paused briefly and hovered around Saira. "How are you?" he asked.

"Thanks, I'm fine," Saira said. "I have no pain, but am still feeling tired."

"That's normal during the healing process," the sea-elf said soothingly. "Oh, I haven't introduced myself yet. My name is Ajin."

"My name is Saira, and this is Cherou," Saira introduced herself and her partner.

"Then try to sleep a little, Saira," Ajin suggested. "The more you take care of yourself, the faster your injuries will heal. Are you hungry?"

"No," Saira replied and shook her head gently.

"Well, I'll let you sleep now and look in on you later again. If you need anything, just call me," Ajin said.

"Please wait!" Saira begged as Ajin wanted to swim on. The sea-elf stopped and turned to her again. "How long have we been here?"

"Five light phases," Ajin answered.

Saira was appalled. "What, that long?" she called out in surprise.

"As I told you, you were heavily injured. We are happy that your healing is making such good progress," Ajin explained patiently. "Don't worry, you will soon be completely healthy again." Then the sea-elf hovered away.

Saira tried to relax. If it were like Ajin had told her, the sea-elves had saved their lives. Otherwise, they would be dead by now, because of their heavy injuries. She looked again across to Cherou, but he still had his eyes closed and seemed to sleep deeply. They were at least safe here, and the sea-elves would heal them. She looked around for a while in the bizarre crystal world of the hall. The sea-elves moved about absolutely noiselessly. The pleasing silence and the feeling of safety finally made Saira even more tired and a short time later she had fallen asleep again.

*

"Damn! Why can't I get up? Saira, Saira!" she heard somebody yell beside her and shot up, still half asleep.

"There, you're finally awake!" Cherou grumbled when Saira opened her eyes. "What's going on here and why can't I move?"

"It's all right," Saira answered soothingly. "We are in the dome of the sea-elves. They found us buried under the rocks. Apparently, we were heavily injured. That's why they put a healing spell around our bodies. We mustn't move because we are not completely recovered. Don't worry, we are safe here. The sea-elves just want to help us."

"How do you know that?" Cherou asked, baffled.

So Saira told him about her short conversation with Ajin, after which Cherou calmed down quickly. "How are you?" Saira asked him.

"I'm fine and I have no pain," Cherou answered. "How are you?"

"I'm fine too, thanks!" Saira replied.

At that moment a small shiny sphere hovered nearer and transformed again to a Lingit. "It's nice that both of you are awake now!" said the shimmering creature and hovered closer to Cherou. "My name is Ajin," he introduced himself. "I suppose Saira has told you about our conversation. How are you?"

"Thanks, we are fine," Cherou answered.

"That's quite pleasing," Ajin said. "I have brought some food for you." Then he hovered between the two Lingits and let something flow into their hands. When Cherou and Saira took a closer look, there were just some bluish shiny grains. "I know, it doesn't look like much," Ajin remarked. "But it will nourish and heal you from the inside. It's magic food, which we produce ourselves. You just need to swallow it."

The two Lingits exchanged a short glance, then they ate the shimmering grains. They immediately felt completely sated. A warm and pleasing wave pulsated through their bodies.

"How do you feel now?" Ajin asked smilingly.

"Oh, that was quite soothing!" Saira answered. Cherou agreed with her. "Thank you very much. That felt good!"

"You're welcome!" Ajin replied. "If your healing continues this well, we can dissolve the healing spell in only two more light phases. Then you can move freely again, but you should be careful until you have recovered your full strength. I must ask you for some patience until then."

"We will try not to bother you," Saira promised smilingly.

"You don't bother us at all!" Ajin stated. "It's a pleasure for us to help you."

"Thanks, that's very kind of you!" Cherou said. "And thank you so very much for saving us. We surely wouldn't be alive right now without you!"

"You're welcome!" Ajin said once more. "Take a rest now. I will look in on again you later." Then he transformed into a small shiny sphere again and hovered away.

*

The two Lingits quickly regained their strength because of the good care of the sea-elves. Ajin visited them as often as he could, brought food and asked after their condition. He told them about his life to shorten the waiting time, explained how the sea-elves controlled the flow of energy of the planet. They often had to advance down to the planet's core, so their dome was built at the deepest point of the ocean to ensure the shortest way to the core. But the speed of energy consumption through the Duumars made it more and more difficult for the elves to control the power of the planet. Of late, they were losing control more often, which caused strong seaquakes and volcanic eruptions, which in turn shook huge areas of the planet and often caused terrible destruction. These areas remained uninhabitable for a long time, life could return to them only gradually. But the areas where the seaquakes and the volcanic eruptions happened grew larger, and their strength increased all the time. Not only the mechanical destruction through the force of the quakes and the devastation by the lava streams affected large parts of the ocean, but also the enormous amounts of toxic stuff and the great heat released by them caused a great deal of disturbance. The water was warming up more and more, and the toxic stuff often spread in high concentration over a wide area, so ever more habitats became uninhabitable. Not to mention the enormous number of victims caused by the natural disasters. It was just a question of time before Turoon's ocean reached a critical condition, which would lead to the extinction of countless individuals. The sea-elves did everything within their power to delay this moment, but they could only delay, not stop, the development. This world could only be saved if the Duumars finally stopped their ruthless exploitation of fire-stone and energy, but the chances of that happening were remote. The Duumars, greedy as they were, just did not want to recognize the consequences of their actions. They were only interested in the short-term acquisition of power. Whatever the result of their behaviour, it was of no importance to them. So it looked bad for Turoon's future, and it was only a question of time until a cataclysmic disaster would befall this world.

The Lingits were quite upset when they heard about the dreadful condition of their planet. They pitied the sea-elves, who had to witness more or less helplessly the slow perishing of this world. The sea-elves themselves felt responsible for the sorrow of the victims, which was why they had taken in Cherou and Saira to heal them. Never before had any creature seen the dome of the sea-elves. They were as old as the planet itself, and they had already been there at its genesis. But now it seemed as though they would soon have to witness the destruction of this world.

*

Ajin finally released the two Lingits from their healing cocoons after two more light phases, so they could move about freely again. The sea-elves had worked a small miracle, because their heavy injuries had indeed healed completely. Ajin led Cherou and Saira through the dome, which consisted of just one big cave. Its walls were covered with magic symbols made of shiny crystals, which gave the sea-elves new power for their hard work. Then Ajin led them outside. From there, the dome just looked like a gigantic, dark rocky peak inside a narrow high canyon. The two Lingits followed the sea-elf for a long while until Ajin stopped and asked them to stay put. Then he hovered further and increased his radiance. A weird sight was revealed to the Lingits. Dark clouds of boiling hot water were pulsating out of numerous rock chimneys. The entire surrounding area was shimmering because of the heat and was filled with the dark clouds roaring out of the funnels. When Saira wanted to swim nearer, Ajin said warningly: "Please stay where you are. The hot water and the poison would kill you within a very short time!" So Saira had to be contented with what she could see from her current position. Although the water was boiling hot and contained many poisonous substances, bright life existed even there: creatures that were seemingly immune against the heat and the poison. Cherou too was amazed at finding life at this place. Ajin left his position and returned to the Lingits.

"Unbelievable, that life exists in this boiling, poisonous broth," Cherou said, astonished.

"Life is very adaptable and always finds a way," Ajin explained. "Even worse conditions prevailed during the origination of this planet, but the richness of life still managed to develop in this world. This life is now in great danger. Our home is also in danger. More and more of these volcanic chimneys are growing ever closer to our dome. If they destroy it, we have no resting place any more. We could probably build a new dome someplace else, but it takes a lot of time and power to rebuild the magic ornaments. During this time, we would be unable to regulate the energy streams of the planet. You can imagine what would happen!"

The two Lingits nodded with concern. "Can you not stop the process?" Saira asked.

"No, we haven't enough power for that. We can only slow it down," Ajin explained.

"Have you never risen up against the Duumars?" Cherou wanted to know.

"We are a peaceful tribe and don't know how to fight. The Duumars are much too aggressive and obstinate. If we had tried to rise up against them, we would only have caused needless casualties. We are indeed made of energy, but we are not immortal. The Duumars can wipe us out with their strong magic powers," Ajin answered.

"You are right," Cherou said, feeling depressed.

"We can only hope that the Duumars will see sense before it's too late and this world is destroyed," Ajin said resignedly. "Let's go back. It's too dangerous for you so close to the chimneys."

So Ajin led the two Lingits back to the dome, where he left them, because he had to do some work. The two Lingits lay quietly next to each other, lost in their thoughts.

"Maybe we can help the sea-elves. I must confess something to you," Cherou said, a bit embarrassed.

"I'm anxious to know it!" Saira said with surprised.

"When I decided to escape with you, I'd not only planned to ask the Qails for asylum. I also hoped to persuade them to act against the Duumars once more, to finally free my tribe," Cherou explained.

Saira looked at him in astonishment. "Why haven't you told me this before?" she asked crossly.

"Well, you are so peace-loving and helpful," he started hesitatingly. "I feared you would escape on your own, because you would probably be against my plan. Your magic powers were the only chance I had to successfully escape captivity."

"In other words, you have used me to escape!" Saira said angrily.

"Yes and no," Cherou replied. "On the one hand, I thought about the rescue of my tribe. On the other hand, I just couldn't leave you on your own out there in the ocean, because you had no chance of survival. You have experienced yourself how dangerous the ocean can be." He paused. "And anyway, by that time I had already become quite fond of you, and I just didn't want to lose you," he admitted dejectedly and lowered his gaze bashfully.

Saira looked at him for a long time, while she fought with her feelings. She was angry, because he had not told her the truth. But she was also moved by his concern for her. She would have never come this far without his help and his protection. Her feelings for him had grown too. He had become a sort of father-substitute, a close and trusted friend. "Have you kept any more things from me?" she finally asked disappointedly.

"No, absolutely not!" Cherou said, almost in despair.

Saira fought again with her feelings. "This was really not fair," she said angrily. "But I understand your reasons very well." She paused. "Please don't ever lie to me again. I have trusted you the whole time, because you were the only one in this strange world who cared for me and understood me. I'd like to continue trusting you, but I can't if you don't tell me the truth!"

"I haven't lied to you!" Cherou defended himself. "I just haven't told you everything about my plan."

"That's the same!" Saira replied brusquely. "If you withhold such important things from me, I can't trust you anymore!"

"Yes, you are right!" Cherou admitted dejectedly. "I promise not to keep anything from you in future!"

Saira gave him a sceptical look. "I should hope not!" After a while she asked: "What's your idea then? What does your plan look like?"

"I have no perfect plan. I just know the Qails have defied the Duumars once before. Maybe they're ready to do it again, and maybe this time they'll succeed in depriving the Duumars of power," Cherou explained.

"But that would require open combat," Saira argued. "The Duumars have surely become even more powerful since the last uprising of the Qails. I can't see how the Qails would have any chance against such strong magicians!"

"You may be right, but the Qails are stronger than you can imagine," Cherou said. "Maybe there's another possibility. We will see how the Qails react to my request." He paused to think before he spoke again. "I suppose we can only prevent the Duumars from destroying our world by depriving them of their power."

"They will never give up without a fight. Believe me, it's very difficult to defeat such strong magicians. A terrible battle with many casualties will be the result!" Saira argued again.

"If they are not stopped, there soon will be many more casualties!" Cherou countered excitedly.

"Pardon me for interfering. I've overheard your conversation by chance," somebody suddenly said right next to the Lingits. Cherou and Saira turned around. A sea-elf hovered next to them. "My name is Sakev. Maybe I can tell you of a way to deprive the Duumars of power without a fight. First you must learn where they get their magic powers from."

"Continue!" Cherou invited Sakev.

The little sphere hovered nearer, then Sakev began to narrate: "Once the mighty Fire-Crystal ruled this world. It helped to create this planet and guarded it for a long time. At that time, the Duumars wanted to learn about the magic with good intentions, to help other beings. The Fire-Crystal did them the favour and instructed them in the magic skills. The Duumars learned quickly and for a long time used the magic only for good in this world. Because they were doing so well, the Fire-Crystal gave them a shard of itself to enhance their power. It all worked well at first, but then a

163

small group of Duumars was blinded by the power and eventually misused it for their own ends. In time, this group gained more and more power. It was already too late by the time the good Duumars realized what was going on. They were over–taken and sidelined by this small group, which quickly found more followers and within a short period of time had gained so much power that no one could stop them anymore. They drew so much power from the Fire-Crystal through the shard that it was no longer able to resist them. Now they were the real masters of Turoon. A dark time began, with the Duumars getting ever more powerful and greedy. They built a city, constructed machines, enslaved the Lingits and promised the Draughs and Galanx a protected life and plenty of food if they would work for and assist them. Both Draughs and Galanx agreed to a lazy life among the Duumars and enjoy it to this day. The shard of the Fire-Crystal is the source from which the Duumars receive their entire power. Their might is extinguished if you steal the shard from them and give it back to the Fire-Crystal. Then they will have no magic powers any more."

"Where is this shard kept these days?" Saira wanted to know.

"In the centre of the city of the Duumars, well concealed deep within the ocean floor in a secret chamber," Sakev answered. "Every creature with magic powers can feel it there if one knows what to look for. You already have enough power to find it," Sakev said to Saira.

"How do you know I've got magic powers?" Saira asked, baffled.

"We are magic creatures and can feel immediately when some-one else has this gift too," Sakev explained with amusement.

"Can you please show me how to recognize the aura of the Crystal Shard?" Saira asked politely.

"Just open your mind, then I will transfer my knowledge of it to you," Sakev told her.

"Be careful, Saira!" Cherou warned, but she made a soothing gesture.

"Don't worry, this is a normal method of transferring information between magicians. He can't harm me," she explained.

"Let's hope so!" Cherou said sceptically and watched Saira prepare for the transfer.

She closed her eyes so she could concentrate better, then opened the barrier around her mind and granted the sea-elf free access to her thoughts. That way, she too showed that she had nothing to hide. Saira was surprised about the intensity with which the small elf penetrated her mind. She had completely underestimated the strength of the elves. They had tremendous magic powers although they were quite small. But nothing bad was contained in that magic. It shone as brightly as the thoughts of the sea-elf. The transfer was finished quite quickly and Sakev withdrew completely from Saira's mind. Now she knew what she had to look for in order to localize the Crystal Shard.

"Thank you very much!" Saira said politely.

"May the magic lead and protect you!" Sakev said in a friendly voice. Now I must go about my duty again. Thank you for listening to me."

"We thank you for your help!" Saira answered. Then the sea-elf hovered away, while Saira turned to Cherou. "Now, what do you think about this idea?"

"You mean we should steal the Crystal Shard from the Duumars? That won't be easy, but it's much better than challenging the Duumars to open combat and risk so many lives," Cherou replied.

"Do you believe the Qails will support us?" Saira asked sceptically.

"Leave that to me. The important question is: are you ready to return to the city of the Duumars once more?" Cherou asked.

"I've no other choice. I'm the only one who can find the Crystal Shard," Saira answered.

"That's right," Cherou said. "But you risk a lot if you return. You may be killed, and I don't want to be responsible for your death."

"I'm clearly aware of that," Saira said. "But my decision is not completely unselfish."

"You hope that the Fire-Crystal might take you and the other abducted slaves back to your homes," Cherou said.

Saira just nodded and looked at him wistfully. "Cherou, I really like you, but I will never feel really comfortable in this world. I hope you can understand."

"I understand very well," Cherou answered with a friendly smile and softly caressed her cheek. "You are after all not a part of this world, but you have been abducted by force to this place, and now you have to live in a strange body in an unfamiliar environment. I wouldn't like that either!" He paused. "It will be difficult for me to let you go, because I have come to like you so very much. But the thought that you will never feel comfortable here is quite intolerable for me."

Saira gave him a slightly embarrassed but very happy smile. "Thanks for your understanding!"

"You're welcome, young fin," Cherou said kindly. "Until then you just have to scuffle along with me." Then he twinkled mischievously, which made Saira smile.

*

Some time later, Ajin returned again to the Lingits and let a bundle of algae and seaweed materialize in front of them. "As you don't need our magic food anymore, we have collected some aquatic plants for you. I hope they are tasty."

"Oh, thank you very much, that's very kind of you!" Cherou said. "Meanwhile, we have thought about how we can help you. There may be a possibility to finally stop the ruthless behaviour of the Duumars."

"I know, Sakev told me about it," Ajin said to the surprised Lingits. "He said you want to swim to the Qails and ask for their help in returning the Crystal Shard to its rightful owner."

"That's right!" said Cherou, baffled.

"A very hard and most dangerous undertaking. You risk your life doing this. It's asking too much from you," Ajin said.

"We're not doing it only for the sea-elves, but for all living beings on Turoon," Saira replied. "Because the Duumars won't be reasonable, we have no other choice than cutting them off from their power, so their destructive behaviour will come to an end soon. I can't and don't want to stand by and watch while they destroy this world!"

"Your attitude does you credit, but I'm not sure that you'll be a match for the Duumars. They are very powerful, and you are not a fully trained magician yet. Besides, you know as little about fighting as we do," Ajin argued.

"But the Qails are definitely able to cope with the Duumars," Cherou said excitedly.

"You forget that, once before, the Duumars have driven them away, and since then their power has become larger than ever," Ajin said.

"If we can be really smart, then maybe it won't come to fighting," Saira said. "There must be a possibility to steal the Crystal Shard without a fight."

"There may be, but the Duumars are clever and shrewd. Don't underestimate their capabilities, or it could be the last time you make a mistake!" Ajin warned.

"We'll see what's possible," Cherou said. "First we have to get to the Qails. Maybe they'll know what to do. At least they'll well remember the Duumars and their capabilities."

"I can help you with that. During the next light phase, I will show you a way of quickly getting to the Qails, if you like. Today it's already too late. It's not possible to make such a journey until the dark phase starts," Ajin suggested.

"That would be very helpful. The less time we lose, the better," Cherou said.

"Well, then stay with us once more this dark phase, take a rest and gain some more strength. You will need much of it for this arduous task!" Ajin said.

Cherou and Saira exchanged a short glance. "We agree!" Cherou confirmed and Saira nodded approvingly.

Natural forces

The next morning, the two Lingits said good-bye to the sea-elves, not without thanking them again for their rescue and for all the help they received. Ajin led them to the dome's exit where two Meyjoks, the fastest creatures in all of Turoon, were already waiting for them. These creatures could reach extreme speeds by sucking in water though their large mouths and ejecting it at high pressure through movable nozzles on both sides of their tail roots. They looked like sharks and were four times the size of a Lingit. Cherou stared at the two Meyjoks in fascination. Since they only inhabited the light-flooded layers of the ocean, he had never seen them close-up. Here in the deep sea they normally could not orientate themselves, because they had no sonar organs. So the sea-elves had led them to this place with their lights and now continued to provide sufficient illumination.

"Are you the two Lingits we are supposed to take to the Qails?" one of the Meyjoks asked politely.

"We are," Cherou confirmed. Then he introduced Saira and himself to the Meyjoks.

"I'm Mergos, and this is Gurin," the Meyjok said, introducing himself and his attendant.

"You best get on our backs and hold on tight to our dorsal fin," Gurin called to the two Lingits.

They followed his request and settled as comfortably as possible on their backs.

"Are you ready?" Mergos asked. The Lingits said, yes they were. "So we can leave now."

"Take good care of yourselves!" Ajin said. "May the magic lead and protect you." Then the Meyjoks started to move and followed a group of sea-elves who illuminated their path. Cherou and Saira waved and said thank you one last time. Then the Meyjoks swam faster, and the Lingits had to hold on tight so that they would not slip from their backs. A short time later they had reached brighter layers of water, where the sea-elves, who had led them this far, said good-bye and returned to the dome.

"Hold tight!" Gurin said and accelerated some more.

Saira, who had thought the Meyjoks were already swimming at maximum speed, yelled in fear: "Are you going to be swimming even faster?"

"Why of course!" Mergos confirmed, amused. Then a loud noise could be heard and the two Meyjoks were catapulted forward at incredible speed. Saira screamed and held on to Gurin's fin as best she could, clinging to his back. Cherou also had problems trying to stay on Mergo's back. At first it was quite difficult for the two Lingits to breathe at this high speed, until they had found an easier way of hanging on and staying safely in position. The surrounding area just sped past beside them, while the Meyjoks shot through the water with breathtaking speed. After some initial fear, the high speed gradually intoxicated Saira and she dared to lift her head a bit. The rapid flight through the water allowed fascinating views of the fast-changing surroundings. The two Meyjoks entered a narrow canyon and sped through a long valley. Despite of the high speed, they remained always precisely at the centre between the narrow walls and took the tight turns with elegance and astonishing assuredness. The view was breathtaking and the Lingits were lost in amazement. They had never before experienced racing through a canyon in such a way. The rock face sped along on both sides, and again and again their direction abruptly changed. They were often thrown to and fro in the narrow turns, but each emerging view intoxicated the two Lingits so much that they enjoyed even the wildest change of direction. Thunder suddenly could be heard, and directly in front of them the ground of the valley glowed and flared. Mighty curtains of gas bubbles climbed up and obstructed the sight. The Meyjoks immediately slowed down and swam up to the edge of the canyon, where they sped up again. For the first time, Saira witnessed the outbreak of a submarine volcano. The lava did not flow like a glowing ribbon through the canyon, but emerged simultaneously in several places, where it immediately caused strong steam explosions in the surrounding water. It hardened instantaneously and turned black, while more molten lava broke out of its rims as the whole process started anew. Like glowing fingers, more and more lava flowed out to solidify immediately. The heat let huge amounts of water vaporize and caused giant walls of gas bubbles. The uproar of the gas explosions and the noise of the boiling ocean were unbearably loud. The hot water glimmered and caused strong turbulence, making the Meyjoks slow down again. When they had reached the end of the lava-stream and were just about to accelerate again, Saira detected a Hingai settlement straight ahead on the bottom of the valley. Their caves were directly in the way of the lava! But the Hingais had not noticed the lava-stream, because of a bend in the valley a short way before their settlement. The lava was still hidden behind it right now. It would be too late by the time the lava had passed the bend. Then the colony would be buried beneath it!

"Stop, wait!" Saira shouted excitedly and pointed at the Hingai settlement they were just passing. "Look down there! The Hingais haven't yet noticed the lava-stream. It will overrun the settlement!"

The Meyjoks stopped abruptly. "You are right, we must warn them!" Mergos shouted.

From her position up high, Saira saw the lava-stream approaching quickly. Much too quickly! If they wanted to save the colony, only one possibility was left. "You swim down to the Hingais to warn them. I will try to halt the lava-stream!" Saira shouted to her attendants.

"Are you crazy? You can't halt a lava-stream!" Cherou said.

"My magic powers certainly can! We don't have time to argue about it. Go help the Hingais. I will be fine," Saira replied resolutely. "Please Gurin, take me to the edge of the lava-stream, quickly!"

The two Meyjoks exchanged a short glance. "As you wish," Gurin said and sped away.

"Damn you, Saira, stay here!" Cherou shouted after her, but she could not hear him anymore. Mergos moved on and sped down to the Hingai settlement.

*

Thurgun was secretly overjoyed. Since the incident with the Gamburas, there had been no further hints about the whereabouts of the two fugitives. Thurgun secretly hoped they had lost their lifes somewhere out there. If that had happened, then the wide ocean had again been kind to the Duumars and delivered them from great danger. But since there was no proof as yet that the two fugitives were indeed dead, it was important to continue to be watchful. But time would work in his favour. Every light phase brought Thurgun closer to his goal. He would soon open his new mine and supply the Duumars with even more fire-stone. He had received two new slaves who now worked in place of the two fugitives and the Sergon mine had finally regained its previous level of output. It would not take long until enough slaves for the new mine were available to him. This time he had ensured no Thae'Kors were among them, which would avoid many problems. He had already chosen an overseer for the new mine from among the Draughs who would drive the slaves properly, for the mine needed to make enough profit right from the start. If everything went well and these fugitives remained lost forever, a shining future was in store for Thurgun. He soon would be the mightiest mine-owner of all time. That would easily outweigh the small stain on his reputation caused by the escaped slaves. If he assembled the right helpers around him and eliminated some troublesome individuals, nothing would get in his way anymore and prevent his reign. Then he would lead the Duumars into a new era.

*

171

On the back of the Meyjok, Saira sped to the edge of the lava-stream. She saw a little plateau a short way up from the bottom of the canyon. "Gurin, can you drop me up there?" she shouted over the noise and pointed at the plateau. Instead of an answer, the Meyjok just changed his direction a little and sped to the plateau, slowed down just in front of it and came to a stop. Saira slid from his back and sat down on the plateau.

"Shall I wait here for you, so you can quickly escape in case of emergency?" Gurin asked worried.

"No, thanks. You'd better swim back to Mergos and the Hingais. They need your help. I'll be fine!" Saira said.

"Are you sure?" the Meyjok asked doubtingly.

"I am. Don't worry," Saira said soothingly. When Gurin still hesitated, she again asked him to swim to the Hingais.

"All right," Gurin replied. "But take good care of yourself!" Then he sped away.

Saira had reached the place just in time. The lava-stream was already making its way through the canyon in front of her. The canyon was very narrow at this point, so she would surely be able to halt the stream for some time with a strong shield. She weaved a massive magic barrier, and not a moment too soon, because the lava immediately surged against the shield. Saira was surprised at the force of the lava-stream. She strengthened the magic once more, so it would resist the stream for some time. But now she was sitting directly above the lava-stream. The steam explosions caused tremendous noise, and the whole plateau was enveloped in a wall of gas bubbles, so Saira could barely see a thing. The water temperature was rising at a horrifying speed and made it very difficult for her to breathe. Poisonous substances were released and were climbing up to where Saira was staying. The water soon took on a disgusting taste, and she had to fight against waves of nausea. Again and again she was shaken by fits of coughing and the increasing giddiness cause her a lot of trouble. But Saira stayed where she was and tried to keep up the magic shield to detain the lava-stream for as long as possible.

*

Cherou raced on Mergos' back to the settlement of the Hingais. As the Meyjok slowed down, Cherou swung from his back and let himself drift to the entrance to the colony. The Hingais drew out their poisonous spine and turned it menacingly towards Cherou.

"You must get away from here! A lava-stream is moving directly towards your settlement!" Cherou shouted to them and pointed agitatedly to the part of the canyon from where the lava-stream would be coming. Cherou became furious when the guards just looked at him uncomprehendingly. "We have seen it from above. A volcano has erupted in the canyon. A lava-stream is moving towards your settlement and will destroy everything. You must leave quickly!"

The guards finally woke up from their lethargy. One of them asked Cherou to follow him. He hurried him to a big cave with an old Hingai, where Cherou hastily repeated his warning. The old Hingai reacted quickly and ordered the immediate evacuation of the settlement. Cherou helped to move the sick and weak Hingais to safety. He had just reached the exit when he saw Gurin hovering next to Mergos. "What are you doing here? Why aren't you with Saira?" he asked crossly.

"Saira is doing fine on her own. I have come to help here," Gurin answered calmly.

"Oh, this reckless young fin!" Cherou remarked angrily. Then the two Meyjoks helped to move the Hingais to safety above the canyon as quickly as possible. Everyone who was able to do so helped to evacuate the settlement. The Meyjoks rushed up and down between the bottom and the upper edge of the canyon again and again, and so saved the lifes of many Hingais. But suddenly the rumble got louder and a terrified Cherou saw the lava-stream approach from the bend of the canyon. "Come on, move faster!" he roared as loudly as he could and helped evacuate a group of children. What had happened to Saira, he asked himself, panic-

173

stricken. As soon as he had moved the children to safety, he called for Gurin, who appeared a moment later in front of him. "Please, take me to Saira, I'm prepared for the worst!" he yelled in panic.

"Get on my back!" the Meyjok replied immediately.

"Mergos, stay here and help the Hingais. I'm going to look for Saira!" he called to the other Meyjok. "Come on!" he said to Gurin. The Meyjok accelerated to the limit and shot to the place where he had dropped Saira. But nothing could be seen there except for a glimmering wall of hot water and bubbles. The Meyjok moved closer at high speed, changed his course and tried to reach the place from up high. They finally caught a short glance of Saira, as the wall of bubbles opened for a moment. She was lying motionless on the plateau, right inside this chaos of fire, water, gas bubbles and heat. "There!" Cherou shouted, terrified, but Gurin was already moving directly towards the place. He broke through the curtain of gas bubbles and dived into the turbulent layers. They were thrown about wildly and the hot water scorched Cherou's skin, but he was concentrating so much on Saira that he barely noticed the pain. They finally reached the plateau, and Cherou pulled Saira up to him while he struggled not to lose consciousness inside the hot water. He held Saira tight with the last of his strength. "Let's get away from here!" he shouted to Gurin, who immediately accelerated and took them out of the canyon as fast as possible. A short time later, they reached the place where the Hingais had gathered in safety and were now caring for their wounded. Cherou slid down from Gurin, his breathing strained. "Thank you very much for your help!" he gasped.

"You're welcome," Gurin replied.

Cherou placed Saira on the floor and bent down to her. Her breathing was shallow but regular. There were burn marks all over her body, luckily they were not severe. Cherou gently shook Saira. She was suddenly shaken by a coughing attack, then she turned to the side and vomited. Cherou supported her as best he could and helped her lay down again afterwards. "You are lucky to be alive!"

he said with relief and stroked her head. At that moment, the Hingais' healer appeared by their side.

"What happened to your partner?" he asked anxiously and Cherou told him what Saira had been through. The healer pulled the root of a plant out of his bag and handed it to Saira. "Just chew this. It helps with decontamination and gives you strength." Saira thanked him in a low voice and took the root. Then the healer saw her burns and said: "I will get some Tengis leaves for your burns." He was just about to swim away, when a seaquake shook the whole canyon. The ground began to jolt with a thundering and rumbling. A short time later the first rocks broke out of the steep canyon wall and fell into the lava-stream, which had by now buried the Hingai settlement completely. The rocks crashed through the thin layer of hardened lava, so the glowing stream beneath came in direct contact with the water. Extreme explosions of steam followed, carrying liquid rock and hurling it far away. Often, it crashed new debris out of the rock face it hit, so the process kept repeating. The Hingais, now at the upper edge of the canyon, were spared, as they now were far above the lava-stream, but they were badly shaken by the seaquake. Again and again, parts of the rock face broke out and fell into the deep around them. This caused the Hingais to quickly retreat further from the rim of the canyon. Cherou picked Saira up and swam away from the edge, to where it appeared to be safer. He laid her down quickly, then helped the Hingais to save those who were too weak to swim. A short while later, the seaquake stopped as abruptly as it had started. When Cherou returned he found Saira lying there, looking terrible.

"How are you?" he asked, worried.

"A bit better, but the burns are very painful," Saira admitted in a low voice. "I'm too weak right now to weave a healing spell."

"I'm happy you're alive!" Cherou said. "When I suddenly saw the lava-stream approaching, I expected the worst!" He paused and put his hands on his hips. "How often do I have to save your life, you reckless young fin?" he asked, halfway seriously.

Saira looked at him in embarrassment. "I'm sorry, but what should I do? The lava-stream was just too fast. The Hingais would have been lost if I hadn't held it up."

"It's all right," Cherou said, laughing. "We're all proud of you! You risked your own life to save the Hingais." Then he became serious again. "It was very reckless of you, though! You had not got a clue just what you were taking on. I don't know how you managed to survive this boiling hell ..." He searched for the right words, then just said, with resignation: "Promise me at least to be a little more careful in future. Your helpfulness honours you, but you needn't risk your life all the time."

Saira dropped her eyes. "You're right, but this time I had no choice. I promise you to be more careful in the future."

"I should hope so!" Cherou grumbled and caressed her cheeks. At that moment, the healer returned with some big seaweed leaves. "Put this on your burns. The leaves will heal them and ease the pain."

"Thanks a lot!" Cherou replied and took the seaweed leaves. "What's going to happen with you now?" he asked the healer.

"The Meyjoks know a spacious valley with big caves not far from here. Kharn, our elder, is inspecting them now. If he finds a suitable place, we will build a new settlement there," the healer explained. "Please excuse me, but I have to look after some injured." Then he swam away. Kharn returned some time later and proclaimed with relief he had found a suitable cave. He invited Cherou and Saira to stay with them so they could wait for their injuries to heal, and the Hingais and the two Lingits moved into the new cave. The Meyjoks helped with the hunt to quickly acquire some food for the Hingais. They had settled down in their new home quite well. Saira also recovered quickly. During the next light phase, she was already strong enough to weave a healing spell, which made Cherou's and her own burns heal even faster. After two more light phases, they were already able to leave the Hingais. The Hingais were very grateful for the rescue and the assistance, realizing that most of their people would not be alive now without the help of the Lingits and the Meyjoks. After a fond farewell, the two Lingits again got on the Meyjoks' backs and let themselves be carried through the water at vast speed.

In the empire of the Qails

The remainder of the journey passed without further incidents, and the two Lingits finally reached their destination in the evening. The Meyjoks slowed down their rapid flight through the water and eventually came to a halt. "We've arrived," Mergos said. "Directly in front of us is the fortress of the Qails." Saira and Cherou slid from the Meyjoks' backs. A giant reef, full of bizarre shapes, unfolded in front of them and filled the entire horizon. It was populated by an immense number of colourful shiny creatures. The two Lingits cautiously swam closer when suddenly two big shadows left the reef and approached them quickly. "Watch out, these are Farkans, the feared guardians of the Qails!" Gurin warned them. Cherou and Saira sank down to the ground while the two shadows hovered closer and finally came to a stop directly in front of them. Saira got scared when she was able to see these deep-black creatures clearly. They were more than five times her size. Their longish flattened body was heavily armoured and ended in a long flexible tail carrying a red glowing sting. Each of the two forelimbs carried a huge pair of pliers. Several strong mouth-parts and eight red glowing ocelli gave these creatures a frightful and dangerous appearance. "What are you doing here?" one of the Farkans asked with a cutting voice.

"Be greeted," Cherou hurried to answer. "We have fled from the captivity of the Duumars and ask for help."

The two black creatures stared at them motionlessly, then they suddenly turned around jerkily. "Follow us!" they commanded. Then they drew several wing-like horn-shields out from their armour, and a loud noise could be heard. They seemed to use the same recoil propulsion as the Meyjoks, because in an instant they were already racing away with high acceleration. The two Lingits had a hard time following them, so the Meyjoks helped by carrying them again on their backs. Soon after, they passed through an opening, then down a wide corridor. The Farkans led them through a maze of further corridors, where the Lingits lost orientation very quickly. A big cave finally opened in front of them. At its centre hovered a jellyfish-like creature with many tentacles. Its entire body was covered with brilliant shiny spots, which constantly changed colour and caused a fantastic lightshow in the cave. The Farkans slowed down and sank to the ground at a respectful distance to the creature. The Meyjoks did the same, while Cherou and Saira slid from their backs. They looked with admiration at the shiny creature, which was approximately their size.

"Sembaja, these two Lingits have fled from the empire of the Duumars and are asking for help," one of the Farkans reported to the jellyfish-like creature.

"Thank you very much for your service," Sembaja replied while the Farkans drew back to the edge of the cave.

"Come nearer, nobody will harm you," Sembaja then turned to the Lingits, sounding friendly. They followed the request hesitantly.

"Be greeted, Sembaja!" Cherou spoke and bowed down slightly. "My name is Cherou and that's Saira," he introduced himself and his female attendant.

"Be greeted, Saira and Cherou!" Sembaja answered, stretched out one of his tentacles and touched Saira with it briefly. "You are not a real Lingit, but one of these unfortunate creatures that were abducted by the Duumars."

"That ... is right," Saira answered haltingly.

"You've certainly been a great help to them in their escape," Sembaja said to the Meyjoks.

"Well, we've just accompanied them for a short way to ensure a quicker journey," Gurin explained.

"We owe a lot to the Meyjoks," Saira said. "We wouldn't be here today without their help."

"The journey from the city of the Duumars to this place is very far and dangerous. You must have taken many risks and faced many dangers to get to us," Sembaja said admiringly. "How did you manage to escape? The magic barriers of the Duumars were always regarded as insurmountable."

"I have some magic powers. With their help, I was able to overcome the barrier," Saira admitted after a short hesitation.

"Oh, then the Duumars have abducted a magician, who now has slipped away. That serves them right!" Sembaja remarked, amused. "Haven't you been hunted?"

"Only at the beginning," Cherou explained. "Once they nearly caught us, but a swarm of Gamburas came to help us. After that we haven't detected any more hunters."

"Well, they wouldn't be able to follow the Meyjoks. That's for sure!" Sembaja agreed. "We haven't seen any Draughs or Galanx around, but that doesn't mean they aren't searching for you anymore. We just have to be a bit more watchful during the time to come. You can stay here anyhow, for now," Sembaja told the two Lingits.

"Thank you very much, that's very kind of you," Cherou said with relief. Saira also expressed her gratitude for granting them asylum.

"Do you need shelter, too?" Sembaja asked the two Meyjoks.

"No, thanks, our duty is done now. We're going to return," Mergos answered.

"Then we wish you all the best," Sembaja said in a friendly manner. "The Farkans will guide you to the outside."

Cherou and Saira said good-bye to the Meyjoks and thanked them again for their help. Then the rapid swimmers slid out and followed the Farkans.

"You must be exhausted from the long journey. First let us show you to your new quarters, so you can rest up and regain your strength," Sembaja said. "If you allow, I will visit you later, because I still have some questions, but that's not urgent."

Another Qail had appeared in the cave, who now introduced himself to them: "Be greeted, my name is Rijan. I will guide you to your quarters."

"Be greeted, Rijan," Cherou replied. "Thanks, that's very kind of you." Then Cherou turned back to Sembaja. "Thank you very much for your help!"

"Welcome in the empire of the Qails!" Sembaja replied.

Rijan led them again through a labyrinth of corridors, until he hovered to a stop in front of a cave. "That's your accommodation for the time being. I hope it's big enough for you."

Cherou and Saira moved through the entrance and found themselves in a spacious cave. The floor was covered with smooth sand. "Oh, thank you very much, it's larger than we would have expected," Cherou said.

"Then make yourselves at home," Rijan replied kindly. "I will find you something to eat. Take care you don't get lost when you leave your accommodation. The network of caves is quite big," he told the two Lingits before he swam away.

Cherou and Saira settled comfortably on the smooth sand. "Oh, finally we're safe!" Saira sighed with relief and clung to Cherou who hugged her, smiling. "At least we don't have to worry about being eaten here."

"You young fins are just not used to anything!" Cherou remarked grinningly.

"Now don't tell me you like always being in a state of alarm out there, and constantly fleeing creatures that might or might not want to eat you!" Saira scolded with pretence annoyance.

"Well, at least it gives some variety to our lives," Cherou answered with a grin and strengthened his grip around Saira, because she tried to punch him. She struggled in his grip but could not free herself.

"Let me go, you cheeky fellow!" she scolded.

"I wouldn't think of it!" Cherou said, laughing. She finally gave up her resistance and gave him a hard stare. He pinched her gently in the side as she took on an offended expression. Saira started giggling.

"Hey, stop!" she screamed, laughing. "That's unfair!"

"You still look so sweet when you're angry!" Cherou said, smiling, and eased his grip slightly, while Saira gave him a smack on the head.

"And you are still quite outrageous, you cheeky fellow!" she grumbled in feigned annoyance, but could not hide an amused smile.

*

At the beginning of the next light phase, Sembaja came to visit the two Lingits. "I hope you're comfortable in your new environment," he greeted them.

"Oh yes! Thanks for asking, it's very nice," Saira confirmed.

"May I ask what the situation is with your tribe, and what you know about the Duumars?" Sembaja came to the point immediately. Cherou told him about the sad fate of his people, who were still working as slaves, and about the infamous activity of the Duumars. How they polluted the water and stole the food of other beings. How they used more and more magic energy to cause ever worse natural disasters that were threatening the whole planet. Sembaja listened quietly. He did not show any feelings, but the flickering of his luminous organs showed how much this terrible news upset him. "These are quite disturbing facts!" he said after Cherou had finished his report.

"That's why we have come to consult you," Cherou now admitted. "We want to deprive the Duumars of power, but we will need your help."

"I assumed something like that. I suppose you already have a plan?" Sembaja said observantly.

"As you know, the Duumars owe their magic powers to a shard of the Fire-Crystal, which is well hidden in the centre of their city," Saira explained. "If we can manage to enter the city un-noticed, I am sure I can find the crystal, because I can feel its existence, and so will be able to determine its location. Then we'll just have to abduct it from there and take it back to the Fire-Crystal, and then the power of the Duumars will be gone forever!" Saira said euphorically.

"That sounds quite simple, but it's likely to be very difficult and dangerous," Sembaja remarked. "What's the job of the Qails?"

"Some of you should accompany us to help in case of emergency," Cherou explained. "Maybe you'll have to start a diversion that would help us to move the Crystal Shard out of the city unnoticed."

"Such a task needs intensive and careful preparation. We have once before risen up against the Duumars and have failed, as you know. Their power has since grown tremendously, so an open fight is doomed to failure from the start. We'll have to avoid direct confrontation, or we'll have many casualties. The Duumars are cruel and ruthless, but also very intelligent and shrewd. I'll first have to discuss this with the members of my clan. Your suggestion is truly excellent, but will have to be amended and tweaked quite a bit. I will call you once we have come to a decision," Sembaja promised.

"How long will that take?" Saira asked uncertainly.

"I can assure you that we will search for a solution as quickly as possible. As I told you, solid preparation is needed to keep the number of casualties as low as possible," Sembaja replied.

"Well, we'll wait," Cherou said. "Thank you for having listened to us."

"I thank you for your candour," Sembaja said. "Maybe we'll have a chance now to save this world and all its inhabitants. Meanwhile, try to recover from the strain of the escape. Here, you're safe for the moment." Then he said good-bye and swam away.

"Well, we're lucky Sembaja has reacted so rationally," Cherou said, most relieved. "I feared he would feed us to the Farkans once we told him our plan."

"Do you think he will help us?" Saira asked uncertainly.

"That's quite certain!" Cherou answered. "The Qails are the only creatures who can go up against the Duumars. It's just a question of time until their habitat is destroyed too. But the Qails will never let it come to that!"

"They look so dainty and fragile. I can't imagine how they could resist the Duumars," Saira remarked.

"Appearances are deceptive. They are fast and enduring swimmers, and they are heavily armed. Even the Draughs fear them," Cherou explained.

"I couldn't see any weapons on their body," Saira said.

"They don't carry weapons in the way the Farkans or the Draughs do. They are energy-transducers. They can create nearly any type of energy, and of course they can use it as a weapon. Also, many of their tentacles are very poisonous. The poison is so strong that it can kill even creatures quite a lot bigger than the Qails in a very short time." When Cherou noticed Saira's upset look, he said soothingly: "Don't worry, the Qails are normally very peaceful and very helpful. They only use their weapons when there is no other way. So we don't have anything to fear. You have to be careful with the Farkans, though. They are very excitable and completely fearless."

" I thought they looked quite scary anyway," Saira admitted.

"Don't worry," Cherou soothed her. "They are Sembaja's guardians of the fortress. They usually remain outside. We don't have to fear them inside."

"That sounds better," Saira admitted.

*

While Cherou and Saira enjoyed their freedom for the first time under the protection of the Qails, Sembaja held intensive discussions of the two Lingits' plan with the older Qails. They quickly agreed to it, so Saira and Cherou were included in the planning, too. In due course, a complex undertaking was designed, where Saira played a key part, for only she could find the shard of the Fire-Crystal. However, Farkans, Hingais, Gamburas and Wras would be required to help, if they were to succeed in depriving the Duumars of their power. So Sembaja sent out ambassadors, who contacted the various tribes to recruit them for this large-scale project. All of them finally agreed to support the plan, because its aim was nothing less than the rescue of the entire planet. In that way, an under-taking of tremendous scope came into existence, which would show Turoon in a different light.

Return

Saira could not sleep that night. She had barely found the time to recover from the strain of the escape, and now they were already caught up in the preparations to take the power away from the Duumars. Saira thought of the many endless hours they had spent with the Qails, discussing the procedure. She had been euphoric at the beginning, and had willingly promised her help and active support, but now she was not at all sure anymore whether she could actually meet all the requirements. She was supposed to take the major role in this plan. It mainly depended on her skills whether the undertaking would succeed or not. She was of course proud to play such an important part, but the responsibility seemed like a great burden on her young shoulders. Now it was too late to change her mind, because the next morning they would start their return to the city of the Duumars, this horrific place that she truly wanted to avoid forever, because so many terrible things happened there. Here and now she was free, but in the near future an environmental disaster of previously unknown dimensions would befall this world. So there was nothing left to her than to offer her help to prevent the worst, which was only possible if the Duumars were deprived of their power. They had of course taken other possibilities into consideration, but the Duumars would continue their selfish and destructive work until it was too late. So depriving them of their power finally was the only option left to avert the threatening disaster, and a magician was needed to accomplish this. Maybe there was even a possibility to get back home, if she gave back the shard to the Fire-Crystal and helped it to obtain its previous power. Memories of Wuun, her home planet, rose up again. Once more the homesickness threatened to overwhelm her. She had to fight with all her power not to break down in despair and tears. However, she could not suppress a stifled sob that caused Cherou to wake up. He saw the tears in her eyes.

"Hey, what's the matter, young fin?" he asked softly and caressed Saira's head.

"Oh, Cherou, I don't know whether I can do this," Saira said desperately.

Cherou tenderly held her, then said soothingly: "You don't need to be afraid. We will all stand by you. We are all in this together, that I'm quite sure of. Look, you've been through so many dangers already, you even halted a lava-stream and saved a great many Hingais. So I'm sure you'll be able to steal a simple Crystal Shard from the Duumars!" Then he smiled at her with confidence.

"I'm not so sure anymore," Saira admitted. "You can't imagine what a fully trained magician with the powers of the Duumars is capable of. They have after all managed to abduct me from my world of origin, and tremendous power is needed for that …"

"That may be true, but you forget the Qails are assisting us. They are certainly able to cope with a bunch of Duumars!" Cherou said forcefully. "We'll just have to be careful, and maybe there won't even be a fight."

"I don't know whether I can succeed," Saira said sceptically.

"You mustn't doubt your capabilities now. You have shown more than once what you can do, and I'm sure you will do fine this time!" Cherou said emphatically.

"Do you really believe so?" Saira asked uncertainly.

"With absolute certainty!" Cherou confirmed.

Saira briefly looked into his eyes. He was really serious.

Thank you," she said, somewhat embarrassed, and lowered her head.

Cherou gently grasped her chin and lifted her head up again. "Never lose your self-confidence! You are much stronger than you think, and you have demonstrated that more than enough already." Then he started to grin. "But you needn't get exuberant, all the same!"

Saira gave him a hard stare, but could not suppress an amused smile. "I will do my best!" she promised. Then she clung to Cherou and finally fell asleep a short while later.

*

At the beginning of the next light phase, the Qails distributed them-selves amongst the Farkans, who were to accompany them. Saira was surprised to see how calm and systematically everything proceeded. She was quite excited of course, and it was difficult for her to concentrate. Cherou's masterful confidence again proved a great help to the young girl. To start with, she was not happy at the thought of using one of the Farkans for transport. These creatures with their black armour and their red glowing ocelli just frightened her. Even the Qails telling her that she had nothing to worry about could not drive this fear away. But she had no choice, so she accepted her fate and lay down on the back of one of the scary creatures. Cherou was already lying diagonally in front of her and winked at her encouragingly, while four Qails settled on the rear part of the armour. Ravar, Silgai, Thorl and Mirgan would accompany Cherou and Saira later, in the city of the Duumars. All the members of the party had positioned themselves on the Farkans a short while later, and departure was imminent.

"Are you ready?" Tantaul asked. He was the Farkan carrying Cherou and Saira.

"Let's go!" Cherou replied impatiently.

The Farkan drew out the wing-like horn-shields on both sides of the armour. A loud whooshing noise could be heard as he started his recoil propulsion. Saira felt the flow of the water being sucked in at several places between the armour-plates, and then they were already moving up and sliding forward faster and faster. Saira was amazed that the Farkan could accelerate so fast, even though he carried such a heavy load. She looked around and saw the other Farkans now speeding away in different directions. The plan was that several small groups of Qails should get to the city of the Duumars by different routes, so they would not be noticed by the scouts, which the Duumars had distributed everywhere in the oceans. The Farkans could not quite reach the velocity of the Meyjoks, but they slid along with incredible speed just above the seabed. The Lingits and the Qails on Tantaul's back had darkened completely so that they would not be seen, and the darkness of the deep sea surrounded Saira again. She wondered why the Farkan did not use a sonar to orientate himself. She first feared he would collide with things at this high speed and held especially tight, fearing a crash at any moment. But nothing happened. The Farkan raced along with dreamlike assuredness, and without any collisions. The steady noise of his propulsion and his subtle movements soothed Saira noticeably. Once she had nearly fallen asleep and would have slid from Tantaul's back if Cherou had not given her a tender shove with his wing fin. The Farkan moved forward inexhaustibly at a steady speed until Cherou asked for a break, because he could barely hold on anymore. Saira felt the same, so Tantaul stopped and sank down for a short break.

"Are you not tired at all?" Cherou asked the Farkan, astonished.

"No, we Farkans are enduring swimmers," Tantaul explained in a sonorous voice.

Saira and Cherou relaxed their stiff bodies and limbs as best they could, while the Qails placed themselves at the corners of an imaginary rectangle around the two Lingits and kept their surroundings under close scrutiny. Tantaul stood completely motionless a little further away.

"How does he orientate himself without sonar?" Saira whispered.

"I don't know," Cherou replied quietly. "Why don't you ask him?"

"I don't dare," Saira admitted. "He's too scary."

"He won't eat you right now," Cherou said mockingly.

Saira gave him a sceptical look. "I'm not so sure."

"Excuse me, but we should move on," Mirgan said.

"All right," Cherou agreed.

A short time later, his passengers on his back, Tantaul was sliding through the deep sea again and travelled a long way, until the evening, when the Lingits rested with the Qails in a spacious cave, while Tantaul went hunting to strengthen himself for the next part of the journey. The Qails showed no sign of fatigue, while the Lingits where happy to rest at last.

"Are you not exhausted at all?" Saira asked, astonished.

"Our bodies function in a different way to yours," Silgai explained. "We don't need to rest as long as we can get enough energy."

"Oh, then you don't need to sleep?" Saira asked, surprised.

"No, we don't need any sleep," Silgai answered.

"That's quite useful," Saira said.

"It has some disadvantages too," Ravar admitted. "Our bodies wear out more quickly. So you live longer than we do."

"As you can see, everything has its consequences," Cherou said to Saira.

"You are certainly right there," Saira answered thoughtfully. Then the strain of the day demanded its tribute, and Saira fell asleep a short while later in Cherou's arms, while the Qails stood sentinel.

*

During the same night, the area where the Lingits and the Qails were spending the night was struck by a strong seaquake. It started so suddenly that even the Qails could not react quickly enough to warn the sleeping Lingits. The cave was already shaking with the heavy impacts when the Lingits woke up.

"Get out of here!" Ravar shouted as loudly as possible. At that moment, a large piece of the cave's ceiling came down. Cherou and Saira rushed away, but Saira fled in the wrong direction and was buried under falling rocks. The quake stopped a short time later as abruptly as it had begun. Although the cave was filled with whirling sand, the Qails rapidly obtained a first overview with their numerous senses.

"Oh no! Saira is buried!" Thorl shouted terrified and catapulted himself in the direction of the debris, followed by the other Qails.

Cherou could see nothing at first and was shaken by a cough attack caused by of the whirling sand. Then he managed to get a first view of the situation with the help of his sonar. The sand clouded the sonar picture, but Cherou could clearly see Saira's head protruding

190

from a pile of rocks. Frightened, he swam to her as quickly as he could. She was indeed buried almost completely by the rocks. Only her head and her left arm were free.

"She's alive, but unconscious," Mirgan explained with relief.

Cherou sat down beside Saira's head and lifted it carefully. "Saira, can you hear me?" he said loudly, but Saira did not react. "Saira!" he shouted again more forcefully and patted her cheeks slightly. She slowly opened her eyes, coughed briefly, and looked at him.

"Luckily you're alive!" Cherou said, relieved.

"What happened?" Saira asked confusedly and wanted to rise up. When she could not move, she realized with horror that she was buried. "Oh no!" she shouted, terrified and panicked.

"Don't worry, we will try to free you," Cherou said. "Are you in pain?"

"No, but I can barely breathe!" Saira gasped. She was very frightened.

The gap she was jammed into was so narrow that her breathing was quite constricted. "Please, stay calm, we will get you out of here as quickly as possible," Cherou promised and tried to lift the stones, but failed.

"We can't do it by ourselves. The rocks are too heavy. Tantaul must help us, but the entrance is buried too," Silgai explained.

At that moment, loud sounds of impact could be heard, bashing from outside against the rocks that buried the entrance. The crashing and bashing echoed inside the cave as though it was the inside of a bell and the unbelievable power caused the rocks to burst. A short while later, Tantaul had managed to create an opening through which he now entered the cave. Cherou was partly impressed, partly horrified by the tremendous strength of the Farkan.

"Are you injured?" Tantaul asked.

"No, we're fine, but Saira is buried," Cherou replied. "We need your help to move the heavy rocks off of her. But you must be careful so that Saira doesn't get squashed!"

Tantaul paused briefly, then he grabbed the first rock and lifted it carefully.

"Yes, that's fine! Carry on!" Thorl said. He helped to move away the smaller stones. The other Qails and Cherou also participated, but it was not easy to always take away the right rocks. The hill moved several times and threatened to squash Saira.

"Be careful!" Saira shouted, panic-stricken.

The rescue continued very slowly and Saira panicked even more. The cave was suddenly shaken by another lighter quake. Some pieces of the ceiling came down again. Saira screamed in horror, but the hill of debris that had buried her did not move.

"Get me out of here, please!" she shouted desperately, and on the verge of tears.

Tantaul, the Qails and Cherou worked as quickly as they could, but even so, it seemed to take an eternity until all the rocks were moved aside. Tantaul finally lifted the last rock that kept Saira stuck. Cherou carefully pulled her out of the rest of debris and laid her carefully on the smooth sand. It was a miracle that she was not heavily injured, there were only some scratches and contusions. The mental wounds were worse by far. She had started to cry while Cherou was carrying her out of the cave. He sat down outside and held her tight. The strain and the fear she had suffered now unloaded in a heavy crying fit.

"Oh, Cherou, I can't stand it any more! I want to be home again!" she sobbed. She cried for a long time that night, while Cherou tried to comfort her until she finally fell asleep through sheer exhaustion.

He could understand Saira well, and her sorrow nearly broke his heart. Her life had been in danger so many times in this world, and still she had taken it all so bravely, but gradually she was coming to her limit. It seemed a miracle to him how well she was taking it all. It was very clear to him that she would not survive much longer. The time had come to finally deprive the Duumars of power, so that Saira could finally return home. The farewell would certainly be hard, because he loved this young girl like she was his own child. But she was just not made for this world. This was not her place, and he had to accept that fact. It was now perfectly clear to him that she would perish here. And so, although he had finally found somebody he could love and care for again, he also knew that a farewell from her was going to come soon. He must let her go, for her sake. So that she could continue living and be happy again. He realized that their relationship here had no future, and that filled him with so much sadness! He looked down on her pretty face that he had come to like so much over all this time. Then he held her tenderly and silently started to cry.

*

Cherou woke up first the next morning and held Saira in his arms for a while longer until she opened her eyes, too. "Good morning, dream-swimmer," he greeted her smilingly. "How are you?"

Saira got up a bit stiffly. "Thanks, I'm well," she answered tersely.

Cherou looked at her, astonished. He hesitated for a moment, then he continued. "Saira, I know, what happened yesterday was bad ..."

He could not say anything more because Saira laid two fingers on his lips. "It's all right. I've regained control of myself," she said with a rough voice. "I had much time to think it over yesterday, and I have come to a decision. I will fulfil my duty, whatever happens. If I fail, I will perish with this world anyhow, but if I'm successful and there's a chance to return to my world of origin, I will take that chance. If there's no chance to see my home again, I will leave this world all together!"

Cherou looked at her, horrified. "You mean, you will ..."

"I mean it as I said it!" Saira interrupted him harshly. Her rigid, resolute look and her cutting voice frightened him. He had never seen her this way before. "But yesterday you were so frightened to die ..."

"I still fear a cruel and painful death. But if I can decide on my own how I'll leave, it doesn't scare me anymore," Saira said toughly

"I ... understand," Cherou answered hesitatingly.

"Well, then let's start now!" Saira said stringently, swam over to Tantaul and left Cherou behind, frightened and bewildered.

*

Again, they sped along on the back of the Farkan. Cherou was obviously churned up inside and kept looking over to Saira, but she avoided eye contact with him. She had made up her mind and had told him perfectly clearly. He could do nothing but accept her decision, as painful and shocking as it might be. That much was clear to him. But the fact that it had come to this horrified him very much. She was so very tired of this world, she wanted to get away from here, at any price! This bitter knowledge was a heavy burden to him, but still they had to save this world from destruction. They had a duty, a target, and that was of overriding importance now. He had better concentrate on the near future. It would determine what was to come after. Admittedly, this did nothing to expel the bitter feelings inside of him, but it eased his pain and diverted him from these confusing thoughts that were whirling around in his head. The time of rest passed silently. The Qails noticed the strained atmosphere, but kept a respectful distance, so that they would not confuse Cherou and Saira even more. Tantaul sank down to the seabed again when it finally grew dark, and the Qails searched for a cave to spend the night. At first, Saira would not agree to spend the night in a cave at all, after her frightening experience, but after some friendly encouragement she accepted the idea. Although she had been more abrasive towards Cherou all day long, she now sought his closeness again and clung to him with a grateful smile. Sometime in the night, Cherou woke up and realized that Saira was not lying beside him any more. He shot up, looked around and called her name. The Qails told him that Saira had found a place to sleep outside the cave beside Tantaul. Surprised, Cherou swam to the exit of the cave and saw Saira peacefully sleeping some distance away, close to Tantaul. She confused him more and more. Well, out there she was at least as safe as in the cave, for nobody would dare to come near a Farkan without permission. So he settled down again but could not sleep for a long time. He missed having Saira by his side. He realized now how much he had become accustomed to her closeness, and how far away from him she was at the moment. But he could well understand her actions. The terrifying experience of the last night was anchored much too deep inside of her now. At least, she wasn't afraid of the Farkan anymore. Cherou hoped he and Saira would soon come back together again. He did not want them to be so distant from each other. So he resolved to be especially pleasant to her for the time being, and to give her the support she seemed to miss so much. Then their former closeness would hopefully be restored. He finally fell asleep with this thought.

*

The next day, Saira woke up refreshed. She stretched and shook away the remnants of her tiredness. "Good morning, Tantaul," she greeted the Farkan.

"Good morning, little Lingit," Tantaul answered, surprisingly friendly. "I hope you've slept well."

"Oh yes, thank you!" Saira replied. "I thank you for allowing me to spend the night next to you."

"You're welcome," Tantaul said. "Swim to your partner now and strengthen yourself. The Qails have collected some food for you."

"Oh, that's wonderful, I'm really hungry!" Saira said and swam right over to Cherou.

He was already enjoying the seaweed when he saw Saira approaching. He waved to her and asked her to sit down beside him. "Good morning, Saira."

She sat down by his side. "Good morning, Cherou."

"Did you sleep well?" He asked kindly.

195

"Yes, thank you," Saira replied and lowered her gaze, embarrassed. "Please forgive me that I fled out of the cave. I just couldn't stay inside." "That's all right. You don't need to apologize," Cherou said understandingly. "I probably would have done the same if I were you."

"Thanks for your understanding," Saira said. "I'm also sorry for having been so dismissive yesterday."

"Now stop apologizing," Cherou said in his friendly way. "I wondered anyway how you could manage to be so brave about everything that's happened so far. It's more than understandable that you are now becoming aware of so many things all at once, under such difficult circumstances. You don't need to be ashamed of it." He gently stroked her head. "Now eat and regain your strength, before I eat it all up myself," he said grinning.

"I guess that would suit you just fine!" Saira replied with a smile and picked up a bunch of seaweed.

Soon after, they embarked on the last part of their journey. This time, Tantaul moved forward more slowly and quite carefully. The danger of being detected by a patrolling Galanx grew greater, the nearer they came to the city of the Duumars. The darkness of the deep sea worried Saira very much. Cherou and the Qails had completely darkened now, and Saira must not use her sonar, so she was enveloped in total darkness. The familiar noise of Tantaul's propulsion, the streaming water and the hard armour of the Farkan beneath her body were all she could perceive. So she held tightly onto the armour plates, because they were all she had to give her a feeling of safety. Memories of her time in the city of the Duumars returned. She saw herself working in the mine and experienced the cruel punishment meted out the slaves. What had happened to Jir? Had she become accustomed to the hard work in the mine? Was she no longer alive? Was old Flemm still alive? The many questions and memories threatened to engulf her. So Saira shook off the thoughts as well as she could and tried to concentrate on her duty, but she did not succeed completely. One or other experience rose up within her memory again and again. Past and present mixed up into a confusing kaleidoscope of thoughts and emotions, and her head soon started to buzz. Then Tantaul suddenly slowed up and finally came to a halt, which helped Saira to find back to the here and now again. "What's the matter? Why are we stopping?" she whispered.

"We've reached the target. Some way behind the rocks in front of us is the city of the Duumars."

Indeed, Saira could see light shining in-between the rocks in front of them: it must be the city's illumination.

"We will wait here until the dark phase starts," Ravar said. "I've contacted the other groups. They have arrived already and are in position. They haven't noticed any particular reaction. The city is calm. The number of guardians outside the city has been increased, but they are patrolling in the usual areas. The Duumars seem to be feeling safe and aren't expecting any attacks from the outside."

"Then we should ensure they'll continue to believe this, and should go about our plan most carefully," Cherou remarked.

"That's why we'll enter the city only after the dark phase has started, when many inhabitants are asleep and the illumination is dimmed," Silgai said. "You Lingits should have a rest too, until we start."

So Cherou and Saira went to lie down on the smooth sand in a niche between the rocks. When Saira clung to Cherou, he felt her excitement. "Oh, you're trembling! Are you frightened?" Cherou asked softly.

Saira looked at him as though she was seeking help, then she nodded. "This city scares me. So many terrible things are happening there. I never intended to return to this place ever again, but now I have no choice."

"I understand you very well. I'm feeling the same, but this time we are not as defenceless as before our escape," Cherou replied. "You can also use your magic powers now."

"That's true, but I'm no match for the Duumars," Saira argued.

"That's why I've taken the Qails along, they will help us in case of emergency," Cherou explained. "Don't worry. They will protect us. You'll be amazed when you see what they can do!"

197

"I hope you're right!" Saira said doubtingly. She could not imagine at all how these delicate, filigree creatures could be a match for the Duumars. But she trusted Cherou. His closeness felt good again. It was her fault that they were here now. She could have simply refused her help, but that would have been against her nature. And this venture offered her the only chance of returning to her world of origin. So she would simply have to get through this now. Then she would finally be able to leave this terrible world. This thought gave her new courage. She breathed deeply and tried to calm down, but succeeded only in part. After some time she felt sleepy, though, and snoozed in Cherou's arms until he gently woke her up.

"Wake up, Saira! We are starting now," he said euphorically.

Saira was immediately awake. But something was different. She became aware of a mighty noise and far thunder. "What's that noise?" she asked, worried.

"A storm is raging above the sea," Cherou explained. "It causes high waves and strong currents. They create this sound." When he saw Saira's upset expression, he said soothingly: "Don't worry, it's only uncomfortable and dangerous at the water's surface. We have nothing to fear down here."

"It's time to start!" Ravar urged.

"We're coming," Cherou answered and started to swim, followed by Saira. Carefully using every cover, the small group slowly moved closer to the city of the Duumars. Sometimes they saw Galanx patrolling around the city, but they were too far away to cause trouble. Then came the most risky part. They had to get to the exit of the old escape tunnel, but it lay in an open area without any hiding places. They hid at the edge of the area and made sure that the surroundings were safe in all directions. No Galanx or any other guardians were to be seen. They left the shelter of the rocks and hurried to reach the tunnel's exit. The first problem came up straight away: the Duumars had closed the exit with a grid.

Cherou briefly shook the grid, but it did not move. "Damn, how do we get inside now?" he growled.

"We could blow up the grid," Mirgan proposed.

"That would cause too much noise. Then they will detect us immediately!" Cherou argued.

"Maybe I can melt it," Saira said.

"Try it, if it's not too conspicuous," Cherou said.

Saira was just about to concentrate on the spell when Thorl shouted: "Watch out, a Galanx is moving closer!"

The rest of the group jerked around. "Oh no, not again!" Saira scolded. "These Galanx are making me furious! They somehow have the knack of always appearing at the wrong moment!"

"What shall we do?" Cherou asked, panic-stricken. "If we try to swim back to the rocks, he will surely see us!"

"He will also detect us here," Silgai countered.

"Crouch down together at the exit, quickly. I will draw a magic boundary around us, then he can't see us!" Saira shouted.

The rest of the group was sceptical, but followed Saira's order. Not a moment too soon she weaved the magic boundary, hiding them from the guardian. Saira hoped that the Galanx would not use his sonar. If he did, her spell would be ineffective and the Galanx would detect them. He had come close enough to see them by now, but the guardian moved smoothly along above them. His giant shadow fell on the small group, crouching motionless within the magic boundary. Saira saw how the spell twisted the shadow. If the Galanx had been more attentive, he might have noticed, but he swam on in a rather bored manner and was out of sight a short time later. Cherou and Saira drew a deep breath. Relieved, Saira removed the magic boundary after they had made sure that the surroundings were now safe. Her master probably would have been able to keep up the magic boundary and still weave the heat spell to open the grid. But her magic powers were not yet sufficient. So she concentrated only on the heat spell. At the beginning, she only made the water boil around the grid, causing treacherous gas bubbles to float up. Frightened, she looked around, but the process had apparently not been detected. She tried to calm herself and use the spell the right way. After some more trials she finally managed to melt some of the grid fixtures and Cherou bent the grid outwards, so an opening was created that was big enough to allow them through one by one.

"Swim through quickly! I don't know how long I can keep it open!" he groaned. Saira slipped inside first, followed by the Qails. Then they pushed against the grid from the inside to help Cherou. He finally managed to enter the tunnel too. Now they were safe for the moment.

"Let me swim ahead. If they have built in any magic traps here, I will detect them," Saira said. Cherou agreed and he and the Qails followed Saira. But the Duumars had been content with just blowing up the tunnel. With no further problem, the small group reached the place where the ceiling had come down.

"Oh, it will take a long time for us to dig a passage," Saira said.

"Then we'd better start immediately!" Cherou requested.

They started to move the debris aside. They had worked for quite a while when Ravar suddenly asked for silence.

"What's the matter?" Cherou said, rattled.

"Can't you hear it? Someone is moving debris from the other side, too," Ravar said. "Is the tunnel broader on the other side?"

"No, it has the same dimensions as here," Cherou said.

"Then they can't be Draughs. They wouldn't fit into the tunnel," Ravar said.

"A Duumar could squeeze through, but they would never do this kind of work themselves," Cherou agreed.

Ravar concentrated again, while the rest of the group waited in silence. "It could be Lingits, judging by their voices," Ravar said after he had listened for a short while. "They must be nearly through. Cling to the walls and darken yourselves!"

The group followed his order. The Qails placed themselves protectively in front of the Lingits and waited. They listened motion-lessly to the noise from the other side of the mountain of debris. A short time later, a small opening appeared in the upper part of the mound. Diffuse light shone through. More stones were removed.

"Hey, we're through!" a voice shouted from the other side. The head of a Lingit briefly filled the opening while he glanced through. Then the opening was widened some more.

"Be careful, don't let any more stones slide down!" one of the Lingits on the other side shouted.

Cherou was startled. He knew this voice!

Some more debris broke off the ceiling. "Watch out! I told you to be careful!" the same voice scolded again.

Now Cherou was absolutely certain. This was the voice of Old Flemm! A short time later his profile filled the enlarged opening, while he examined the surroundings. Cherou gave the Qails a sign, then raised and illuminated his body. Flemm jerked around, took a big stone and lifted it menacingly. "Who's there?" he shouted, surprised.

"Calm down old friend! It's me, Cherou!"

Flemm peered at him suspiciously. "Slowly come closer so that I can see you better!"

Cherou did as he was asked. When he hovered in front of Flemm, the old Lingit's eyes grew big.

"Cherou! Indeed, it's you!" he shouted happily and dropped the stone. "Come to me, boy!"

Cherou swam closer. Flemm bowed through the gap and joyfully hugged his old protégé . "You have really come back!" Then he released Cherou. "Have you brought Saira along?"

Saira rose up at the same moment and illuminated her body. "I'm here!" she shouted happily and waved to Flemm. Now the Qails illuminated themselves too and Flemm's eyes grew big again.

"You have even brought the Qails!" Flemm shouted in surprise. Then he turned around. "Hey, you young fins! Help me to widen the opening, so that Cherou and his companions can move through!"

In no time at all, they had made an opening wide enough for Cherou, Saira and the Qails to pass through comfortably. Flemm then hugged Cherou once more. Saira also got a big hug from him.

"It's been quite a long while since I held such a beautiful girl in my arms," Flemm said, winking, while Saira dropped her gaze, embarrassed. "I always knew you would return!"

"How did you know we would use the old escape tunnel to get into the city?" Cherou asked.

"I know you quite well, and I just imagined it, so I made some preparations with these young fins here." Then Flemm introduced his five helpers. Saira knew only one of them, Gorv, who had worked next to her in the mine. Cherou introduced the four Qails. They all greeted each other in a friendly manner.

"What's your plan?" Flemm asked inquisitively. So Saira told him about their intention to abduct the shard of the Fire-Crystal. "Then you will have to swim to the centre of the city," Flemm said and pondered this for a short while. "Even though it's the dark phase now, you can't just swim right across the city. That would be much too dangerous. The guardians would detect you immediately." He pondered some more. Then his expression brightened. "Of course, that's it! You should use the water shafts that supply the city with breathing water. Most of them will be wide enough for you to pass through easily. No one will detect you in there, and they'll lead you to the city centre!"

"That could work," Silgai said. "Are you sure they're big enough for Cherou and Saira?"

"Absolutely!" Flemm said. "But the entrance is closed off with a grid."

"The tunnel was closed off like that too," Saira said. "That's no problem for me."

"Really?" Flemm asked, surprised. "I didn't know the Duumars had closed off the exit, too."

"Well, they had," Cherou confirmed.

"We'll see whether you can open the grid," Flemm said.

"Do you know where the entrance to the water shafts is?" Ravar asked.

"I do, and it's not far from here," Flemm confirmed. Then he turned to his helpers. "It's better if I lead Cherou and Saira to this place alone, otherwise we might attract attention. Please return to your sleeping caves, and be careful that nobody detects you!"

"Thank you very much for your help!" Cherou said to the helpers before they swam away. Then the small group left the tunnel under Flemm's guidance and stealthily made its way to the entrance of the water shafts. The grid there was a lot bigger and much more stable than the one at the end of the escape tunnel. Strong suction made it even more difficult for Saira to loosen the grid, but this time she managed to break a sufficient number of fixings more quickly than before. Then Flemm twisted the grid open. Saira was surprised how strong the old Lingit was. The Qails entered the shaft first, followed by Saira and Cherou. The two Lingits had to hold on to the grid, otherwise they would have been washed directly into the giant intake-rotor by the water stream. The flat featureless walls provided no handhold for the Lingits. Only the Qails some-how managed to hold on to the smooth walls.

"Be careful and good luck!" Flemm said to them before he moved away from the grid.

"How do we get past this?" Saira asked and looked in fear at the intake-rotor.

"This thing doesn't move very fast. We'll just have to swim through it between the blades at the right moment," Thorl explained.

"That's easier said than done. If we're not careful we'll be killed or sliced by the rotor!" Cherou replied.

"Don't worry, we'll get you through this thing uninjured," Mirgan assured them. Ravar and Silgai then catapulted themselves between the rotor-blades to the other side and held onto to the wall there.

"You see, it's very simple!" Ravar shouted.

"Now stretch out one arm," Mirgan told the two Lingits. Saira gave Cherou a frightened look, but they did what they were asked to do.

The Qails drew out some of their tentacles and wrapped them around both Lingits' arms.

"Now let go of the grid," Mirgan ordered.

Cherou and Saira again exchanged glances, then they complied and were immediately swept along with the water stream. Saira screamed, but then the tentacles around her arm stretched and held her safely. She and Cherou reeled helplessly in the strong water stream.

"Wrap your wing fins around your body!" Mirgan told them. The Lingits complied again.

"Who wants to go first?" Mirgan asked.

Saira gave Cherou an imploring look, and he agreed to go through the rotor first.

"Well, keep upright and don't move. The water will pull you through the opening," said Thorl, who was holding on to Cherou. "Are you ready?" Cherou nodded and Thorl unclasped him at just the right moment. Cherou shot between the blades and passed through the rotor uninjured. Ravar caught him on the other side and pulled him against the wall.

"Well done!" he praised Cherou. "Now it's your turn, Saira!"

"Ready?" Mirgan asked, sounding friendly, but Saira shook her head.

"I'm scared!" she shouted desperately.

"Trust us, nothing can harm you," Mirgan assured her. "Cherou has passed though without problems."

Saira turned her head and looked at the giant rotor, extremely frightened.

"Come on, Saira. It's really easy. Nothing will harm you!" Cherou now assured her from the other side.

Mirgan waited patiently until Saira finally agreed. "Now don't move!" he ordered, then released the grip of his tentacles. Saira was catapulted screaming into the rotor. She got so frightened that she instinctively stretched out her fins. She started to spin and got stuck in the rotor frame. One of the giant blades moved towards her. Silgai reacted very quickly, shot out some of his tentacles, wrapped them around Saira's upper body and yanked her out of the frame just in time. Then he pulled her against the wall next to him.

"Are you all right?" Cherou asked, scared.

"Everything went well!" Silgai assured him. "She's uninjured."

Saira hugged Cherou although Silgai kept holding her. "Please accept my apology! I didn't want to act silly, but I was so terrified."

"It's all right, young fin!" Cherou said. "The main thing is you're all right."

"You are not angry with me?" Saira asked, embarrassed.

"There's no need to be angry," Ravar now said. "But now we're dependent upon your guidance. You must show us in which direction we have to swim."

"I will!" Saira confirmed. She had regained control of herself. "I can feel the Crystal Shard right now."

"Well, let's move on then," Silgai said.

By now, Mirgan and Thorl had passed through the rotor too and were following the rest of the group. A short time later, they came to a junction where several big tubes branched off. Saira quickly found the right shaft and the small group drifted along within. The water stream had become much more moderate, so the Lingits could now move along without the help of the Qails. They advanced deeper into the city without further problems. Saira felt the Crystal Shard more and more clearly. Then they had to pass through a narrow tube, which caused massive problems to the Lingits. Saira was more slender and managed to crawl through with some difficulties, but Cherou nearly got stuck. His wing fins were scraping along the wall when suddenly they heard the stomping of a Draugh beneath them. Cherou stopped moving to avoid making more noise, while the Draugh kept coming closer. If he detected them now, they were caught in a trap because they could barely move in the narrow tube. The guardian came closer. Every single one of his heavy steps could be heard clearly now. Finally, he was exactly underneath them. Saira got so tense she stopped breathing and the Qails stretched their bells, but the Draugh just stomped on. His heavy footsteps quickly moved away, and a short time later they had vanished all together. Saira drew a deep breath and Cherou relaxed too. He hastily tried to get through the narrow tube but it took much effort for him to pull himself forward on the plain surface, so he could advance only very slowly.

"Is there no other way than this terrible narrow shaft?" he grumbled angrily.

"I'm sorry, but this really is the only way," Saira confirmed.

"A short way ahead is another junction. After that, there will be more space," Ravar promised, who had swum ahead. The narrow tube presented no problem for him. He could move in even narrower passages without any problem.

"I should hope so!" Cherou grumbled crossly. It took him a great deal of effort to get there, but then he finally pushed himself out of the narrow tube and was glad to be able to move normally again.

"The Crystal Shard is very near now!" Saira said excitedly. She led the group through the next tube, which finally ended with a grid obstructing the exit again. A big dome, brightly illuminated, extended behind the grid. At the centre hovered the shard of the Fire-Crystal. They had arrived!

Crystal thieves

It was early afternoon on Wuun. The dogged pursuit of the magic marks left behind by the portal had finally proved successful! The magicians found an actual clue pointing to the place that Saira had been abducted to. The investigations of the Sunstone led to a world many light-years away, a world that was completely covered with water. The magicians were shocked at first. How would Saira be able to survive there? Apparently, there was plenty of life on this world, but all life was found in the giant ocean covering the whole planet. It was not a mistake: there was no doubt that the clues led to this world. But why had they abducted a land-dweller to a waterworld? That just didn't make sense. Even if Saira was still alive, how should they find and rescue the girl? Tormenting questions like these arose in the presence of this new knowledge about Saira's current whereabouts. At first, a rescue seemed impossible under the circumstances. But the magicians would not give up so quickly. Wuun also had wide oceans with plenty of life in them. Maybe they could find a group of beings there that were willing to search for Saira on the waterworld and perhaps save her. But first they had to work out how to get there. To build a magic portal capable of transporting several beings uninjured across such a long distance was a project which brought even the Sunstone to its limits. It would take some time to weave such a mighty spell. Also, a source of tremendous magic powers existed on the waterworld, which massively complicated the access to this world. What little information the Sunstone had collected about this strange world had been examined very carefully. It was doubtful whether larger-scale access would ever be possible, not to mention how to actually gain admission to this world. An attempt might even mean more danger for Wuun, because they could not determine what kind of power they were dealing with for the moment. If this power could create such a complex portal, it would surely be able to create other spells, which might cause enormous damage to Wuun. It was important to advance quite carefully, to avoid provoking aggression or even an attack. Otherwise they risked that Wuun would be subjected to a tremendous attack, which might well destroy all life on this world.

*

The Crystal Shard detected the intruders quite early on, while they were still moving through the network of the breathing water supplies. As their auras were bright and clear, they evidently did not mean it any harm, which is why it at first assumed an observant attitude. The Lingit girl definitely possessed magic powers, but she was nowhere near as strong as the Duumars. So she did not pose a threat. Her aura shone even brighter and warmer than all the others. The little group entered the crystal chamber a short time later, and the Lingit girl carefully contacted the Crystal Shard.

Saira opened her spirit to enable the Crystal Shard free access to her thoughts. At first, its spirit advanced with such intensity that it caused physical pain to Saira, but then the access weakened to a tolerable rate and Saira now felt the powerful aura of the Crystal Shard. It advanced unhindered into Saira's thoughts, perceiving her intentions and feelings and finally experiencing the aim of their mission.

"Your thoughts are pure and clear without any bad intention," the Crystal Shard told Saira in a soft voice. "So you have nothing to fear. Your courage is great, and your intentions are laudable. My most ardent wish, to be back again with the Mother-Crystal, may finally come true because of you. But I can't turn against my masters. If you are attacked by the Duumars, I can't help you much. So your project is very risky. Consider this before you continue your mission!"

"We're all conscious of the risk," Saira replied. "But if we don't fulfil our mission, your world will perish. You surely have noticed that I'm not a descendant of this world. It's my most ardent wish to return to my world of origin. So we can be of mutual help to each other, fulfilling our wishes and at the same time saving this world from destruction."

"You're speaking wise words, and I can see in your thoughts that you've nothing else to lose than your life," the Crystal Shard replied. "I'm ready to follow you, but first I must weave a spell, so that the Duumars won't notice immediately that I'm gone. That will give you a chance to leave this place."

Soon, the Crystal Shard had created a complex illusion of itself, which Saira could not distinguish from the original. Its magic power was indeed very strong. Then the Crystal Shard left its position at the centre of the dome and hovered across to Saira. She wanted to take it into her hand, but hesitated when she saw the magic fire that flared around the Crystal Shard.

"Don't have fear, my magic fire won't harm you," the Crystal Shard told her.

Saira hesitatingly grasped the Crystal Shard, which was barely bigger than her hand. It felt warm and smooth.

"I will reduce my signature as much as possible, so that the Duumars don't recognize me immediately. But I can't hide my existence completely. Keep out of the Duumars' way. That's our only chance of avoiding detection," the Crystal Shard warned. Then it darkened itself, and extinguished the fire that flared around it. Only a warm glow remained from inside the clear crystal.

The rest of the group had silently stood and watched. Saira now turned to them and told them briefly about her communication with the Crystal Shard, as she was the only one who could hear its voice.

"We should leave this place as quickly as possible, since the Duumars haven't yet noticed the loss of the Crystal Shard," Ravar urged. "That way, we have the best chance of avoiding contact with them since most of them are asleep right now."

And so the small group left the hall the same way they had come. Cherou was not enthusiastic about having to pass through the narrow tube again, in which he had nearly gotten stuck before. But eventually they passed through the narrow part without any problems. Saira had orientated herself on the way there with the help of the magic signature of the Crystal Shard. But she had completely forgotten to memorize the way back through the complex maze of tubes and pipelines. The Qails, however, had memorized the way precisely and were luckily able to lead them through the labyrinth. Saira suddenly heard a warning in her mind from the Crystal Shard, saying that a Duumar was moving closer to them. She immediately told the others, who stood motionless.

"Damn, they should all be asleep now!" Cherou whispered angrily and Saira told him to keep quiet. They could already hear the typical sound of the Duumar's swimming motions. Soon he was exactly in front of them. Then suddenly the swimming sounds stopped. It was completely silent for a while. Apparently, the Duumar was not moving on. Saira and Cherou stopped breathing from sheer fright, and the Qails stretched their bells. Then Saira heard another warning from the Crystal Shard, but it was already too late. A heavy explosion tore through the shaft in front of them. Just in the nick of time, the Crystal Shard was able to create a shield to protect the group against the flying debris and the pressure-wave. The head of the Duumar appeared in the gap. His big eyes stared at them furiously. The Qails immediately started a counter-attack and shot two powerful bolts of lightning at the Duumar. He was hurled backwards, giving the Qails the opportunity to leave the narrow tube. The Duumar quickly built a protective shield around himself, so that further attacks by the Qails had no effect. In a countermove, the Duumar hurled some powerful lightning at the Qails, which they absorbed quite easily. The Qails changed their tactics and turned highly focused beams of light at the Duumar. Those passed through his protective shield and burned his skin. He cried out in pain, pushed himself off and tried to rush at the Qails. But the Qails were faster and moved aside, so his attack missed them. The Qails turned their light-beams on the Duumar again, while he slowly rose up. He lost control of his protective shield because of the painful burns. Saira saw her chance and hurled an energy-disk at him, which penetrated the protective shield and hit the Duumar on his head. A moment later he sank down motionlessly. The Qails rushed at the defenceless body and filled it with poison, so the Duumar breathed his last breath soon after.

"Why did you kill him?" Saira shouted, terrified, when the Qails moved off the body.

"We can't risk that he goes and warns the other Duumars," Thorl explained briefly.

"We should get away from here," Cherou said. "The noise must have been noticed."

"Then follow us!" Ravar shouted and just wanted to swim along the corridor, when Cherou stopped him.

"Wouldn't it be better to swim through the water shafts?" Cherou asked.

"No way," Ravar replied. "We're lost if they attack us there again."

"Come on, this way!" Ravar urged and pointed down the corridor with one tentacle, when they heard the stomping of a Draugh from a side corridor. The small group left the place of the fight as quickly as possible and rushed down the corridor. They did not get very far. A Draugh who had hidden there suddenly stepped out of another corridor and blocked their way. He lifted his big shears menacingly, but the Qails had already fired several flashes of lightning at him. They hit his head and his forelegs, and the Draugh fell down. But the guardian would not be defeated so easily. He pushed off with his rear legs and tried to rush at the group. Saira hurled a magic pressure wave at him, which threw him off his legs and smashed him against the wall. The Qails gave him the rest, so the Draugh also sank down dead after a short time. Saira was terrified at the brutality of the Qails, but had to admit that their action was justified under the circumstances. They hurried on through the corridors while they tried to avoid any further contact with the guards. But this time, too, the clamour of the fight had not gone unnoticed. Directly in front of them an opening appeared in the wall and a tired Duumar came through. It was already too late when he realized the danger. The Qails rushed at him and finished him off in a few moments. The breathless escape continued. They had to keep changing direction to turn away from Draughs or Duumars. Then, suddenly, they found themselves captured inside a corridor with Draughs moving in from both sides, blocking their way. The Qails took the rear part of the corridor under fire and blew out big pieces of the ceiling with their lightning. The corridor crashed down a short time later and this side was now impassable for the Draughs. Saira was again surprised and terrified in equal parts about the capabilities of the Qails. But there was no time to think about this now, as the Draughs in front attacked them. Saira weaved another strong pressure wave that pulled the Draughs off their legs. The attackers behind them stumbled over their falling comrades and crashed down too. The Qails then fired their powerful lightning into the struggling heap of bodies. Several Draughs were torn to pieces, the ones behind them smashed to the ground. Saira hurled a bundle of energy-spheres through the gap, which were able to search out their targets unaided. Wildly rolling, they raged amongst the remaining Draughs and cut them down. The Qails used their lightning to create a passage between the fallen Draughs, through which the small group was able to escape again. They had barely left the guardians behind them when a Duumar blocked their way, grinning maliciously. Cherou could not believe his eyes when he recognized him. It was Thurgun, the leader of the Sergon mine! Cherou was just about to shout a warning to Saira when the Qails started their attack. Thurgun was able to block the attack with a strong protective shield. The Qails tried to burn the Duumar with their focused light-beam, but this time the Duumar used a reflector together with his shield and the attack was not successful. The Qails had to absorb bundles of lightning instead, fired by the Duumar. Saira weaved a

212

strong pressure wave, which only pushed the Duumar back a little way. She soon had to jump aside to avoid a direct attack by the Duumar. In a countermove, she caused a steam-explosion directly beneath him with a strong heat-spell. He cried out in terror and pushed himself off when the Qails joined together to create a tremendous bolt of lightning, hurling it at the Duumar. It did not pass through his shield, although it smashed him against the ceiling. His shield flickered briefly when Saira shot a big energy-disk at him. But the Duumar reacted very quickly and catapulted the disk back with a fast pressure wave, directly towards the Qails. They raced aside and so escaped the attack by a hair's breadth. In a last desperate attempt, the Qails then activated all their joint power once more and hurled more strong lightning at the Duumar. But he easily repulsed this attack, too. Close to the end of their powers, the Qails finally fired small poisonous needles at the Duumar, which also expired in his protective shield. The Duumar however now weaved a spell to remove the Qails' energy. Saira detected it and shot a lightning into the ceiling directly above the Duumar, where it exploded and smashed the Duumar to the ground and left him lying there, dazed.

"Move away quickly!" Saira shouted to the others. "You can't handle him, but I can!" Then she threw the Crystal Shard to Cherou. "Flee with the Qails. Wait for me outside the city. If I don't appear within a short time, you must finish the mission without me!"

Cherou wanted to contradict her, but the Duumar hurled a whole bundle of lightning bolts in their direction. Saira weaved a strong shield and repulsed the attack this way. "Now move, get going! I'll be all right here!" she shouted to the others. Then she had to concentrate on repulsing the next attack. The Qails shot a last weak volley at the Duumar, which was as ineffective as all the attacks before. Then they fled with Cherou into a side-corridor, where they refilled their lost energy by absorbing light and heat from their surroundings.

"We can't leave Saira in the lurch now!" Cherou shouted desperately and wanted to return, but was stopped by the Qails.

"Please, be rational," Mirgan tried to soothe him. "This Duumar is just too strong. Only Saira can cope with him. Our energy is nearly spent. There's no other choice at the moment. First we must absorb new energy. We can't help Saira while we do that!"

"How long will that take?" Cherou asked desperately, while again he could hear the clamour of fighting.

"Only a short time!" Silgai assured him.

"It'll definitely be too late by then! I recognized the Duumar you fought with. It's Thurgun, the leader of the mine we used to work in," Cherou explained in great panic. "He's very shrewd and cruel, and he hates us, because we've escaped from his mine ..." A heavy explosion interrupted him, burying the corridor in which Saira fought against Thurgun.

*

Saira defended herself with all her might, and Thurgun had to admit that he had underestimated his enemy. This little magician possessed remarkable powers. Otherwise he would have long defeated her. Although she offered fierce resistance and made it quite hard for him, she would not be able to resist much longer. Thurgun even enjoyed playing a little with his new enemy. He had encountered no enemy of equal rank for quite a long time, so he extended the fight against Saira to defeat her at just the right moment.

Saira's strength slowly waned, but she utilized all her skills and knowledge. Now all the long lessons with Master Torem finally paid off. Again and again she parried the Duumar's attacks and pushed him back. She had to detain him at least for a while, so Cherou and the Qails could escape. The Duumar strangely seemed to make no great efforts to defeat her, but Saira took advantage of every weakness to put her enemy under massive pressure. But

214

exhaustion finally claimed its tribute, and the Duumar went for the final strike when she was unobservant for a moment, and Saira's world perished in a tremendous explosion.

Good friends

Cherou and the Qails rushed to the site of the heavy explosion. A piece of the ceiling had indeed been blown up, and its debris now blocked the corridor.

"Oh no! Saira!" Cherou shouted, terrified, and wanted to move the debris aside, but was held back by the Qails. Then the Crystal Shard suddenly spoke to them.

"Don't worry, Saira is alive. She is unconscious for the moment and Thurgun is carrying her to his quarters."

"Then we must rescue her!" Cherou shouted in panic.

"That's not possible right now. The direct way to Thurgun's quarters leads through this buried corridor. Also, the Qails are still not able to engage in a new confrontation." The Crystal Shard paused before it continued speaking. "The fight has been observed. Several Duumars are moving closer. You are finished if they detect you here!"

But Cherou did not move and looked desperately at the debris. Only when the Crystal Shard promised to lead them on another route to Thurgun's quarters he finally moved. The Crystal Shard led them through a maze of corridors in the outer zones of the city, where it was a little calmer and they did not have to fear running into Draughs or Duumars the whole time. A shrill noise suddenly sounded throughout the entire city.

"What does that mean?" Cherou asked excitedly.

"One of the Duumars has sounded the alarm," Silgai explained.

"That means that all the inhabitants will hunt us now!" Cherou said, frightened.

"Then the time has come for some diversionary action," Ravar said and sent a telepathic impulse to the Qails outside the city. Several detonations sounded shortly after at the edge of the city, which certainly did not go unnoticed. The Duumars and their guardians redirected their attention and rushed to the affected areas, so Cherou and the Qails could advance more easily. Cherou had lost orientation long ago and just followed the directions given by the Crystal Shard.

"How far is it now?" Cherou finally asked impatiently.

"Just a few more turn-offs and we're there!" the Crystal Shard stated.

The small group was passing through another corridor when suddenly the alarm sounded again. Massive doors moved across in front of them and behind them at the same moment, blocking the way. They were caught in a trap.

*

Saira woke up in a big room. She was lying on the floor but could not move. She quickly found the reason: a magic fetter-field fixed her to the spot. Saira tried to break the spell, but it was too complicated and strong.

"Don't bother to try and defend yourself," she heard a malicious voice behind her. "You can't compete with this spell, little magician," the speaker said mockingly as he appeared above her. It was the Duumar against whom she had fought before. "The more you fight, the faster the spell drains your living energy! So you better don't move if you want to live for a while. Your friends might find you alive when they try to rescue you. But they don't have much time left," the Duumar scoffed and took delight in watching his defenceless victim. "Now I finally get to know you in person. You're stronger than I expected, and you caused me quite a lot of trouble even before the fight. Well, it was still a joy to compete against an enemy of equal rank. It's been a long time since I had the pleasure. However, you surely understand that I can't just let you get away. But first, having you here will ensure that your friends return the Crystal Shard, which you have stolen from us so brazenly. It will be a pleasure for me to watch you die afterwards." The Duumar grinned sadistically.

"How can you be so cruel to all the beings out there?" Saira shouted horrified. "Don't you realize that you're destroying this world?"

"Ridiculous!" the Duumar growled. "We're not destroying this world. We're just changing its appearance. We finally have the power to shape this world to suit our own vision, and nobody will get in our way, not even you and your silly friends."

"Oh yes, you're already on the way to causing the destruction of your own home. You're taking away the food. You're poisoning and heating up the water, so even the big streams are changing their direction. You and your wasteful use of energy are causing heavy seaquakes and volcanic eruptions with increasing frequency. A large-scale catastrophe is about to happen. I have seen all this out there. Stop before it's too late! You only have this one home!" Saira shouted desperately.

"We're strong enough to handle these developments," the Duumar replied stubbornly. "We're not headed for a catastrophe but for a new world, created by us and our vision!" He leaned menacingly over Saira. "You shut up! Your whimpering won't help you anymore. It's your own responsibility that you are lying here now. You just couldn't be grateful that you were the only slave who ever managed to escape. You've already caused enough trouble, especially to me. No! You had to return with this ridiculous idea of depriving us of power. That's what you get for your exaggerated opinion of yourself! But don't worry! Just as soon as your fine friends have returned the Crystal Shard, you won't need to think about your future any more. Unlike us, you won't have one!" Then the Duumar laughed loudly and spitefully.

*

"Oh no, we're trapped!" Cherou shouted, terrified.

"Come on, we'll blow up the gate!" Ravar said and stretched his bell.

"That's impossible," the Crystal Shard said. "These gates are too strong for you. Your energy isn't sufficient to break them."

"So what shall we do?" Silgai asked helplessly.

"I'll try to deactivate the closing mechanism," the Crystal Shard proposed. Then it reached out with its magic powers to the gate's controller, touched the shutter and finally interfered with the control. Nothing happened for a while and Cherou grew more and more impatient. The excitement of the Qails expressed itself in the flickering of their luminous organs. Then the gate in front of them slowly opened up and unblocked the way.

"Well done!" Cherou shouted eagerly and started to swim out, only to reach another closed gate a short time later.

*

Saira felt increasingly weak. The effect of the spell that drained her living energy was making itself felt. She very much hoped that Cherou and the Qails had managed to escape after all. If they could at least finish the mission, then her death would not be completely in vain. The Duumar wasn't likely to show mercy. He was already looking forward to Saira's final agonies, and would be glad to be rid of her at last. There was no help to be expected, so nothing was left for Saira than to put up with her fate. She had anyway intended to put an end to her life if she failed during this mission. Admittedly, she had not planned to die like this, but even this death would be painless. It just would take a lot longer until she could step over to the other side. A loud howling sound pulled her out of her thoughts.

"Oh, now they've closed the safety-gates too," the Duumar remarked, amused. "That means I can watch you die for even longer!" He grinned sadistically again.

Saira looked away in disgust. She just hoped Cherou and the Qails were outside of the city by now and on their way to the Mother-Crystal. This dreadful Duumar seemed to think he would be able to extort the return of the Crystal Shard by her captivity. She hoped that he would soon lose his great power instead, though this was no longer of importance to her. An enormous tiredness engulfed her.

*

The Crystal Shard managed to open the gate even more quickly this time. Admittedly, it risked that Thurgun would detect its presence, but the Crystal Shard could feel Saira's life fading away. Saira would soon be taking her last breath if they could not rescue her quickly. So the small group stepped from gate to gate and eventually reached Thurgun's quarters. The Crystal Shard ordered Cherou to stay away so Thurgun would not be alerted to their presence too early, while the Qails placed themselves in front of his door. They unified their power and created a strong bolt of lightning, which they fired against Thurgun's door.

*

Saira had by now lost consciousness and was not aware that the door suddenly exploded. The heavy pressure wave smashed Thurgun against the wall and he lay there, dazed. Ravar and Thorl sped in immediately, rushed at the Duumar and filled him with poison, while they removed his living energy at the same time. Thurgun died very quickly. The spell that held Saira captive vanished. Ravar gave the all-clear signal, and Cherou quickly swam in to look for Saira. Thorl was already examining the unconscious girl.

"What's the matter with her? How is she?" Cherou asked with great urgency.

"She is showing only very weak signs of life. Her energy has nearly faded," Thorl answered.

"Oh no!" Cherou shouted and moved to lift Saira up, but Thorl stopped him.

"Please move aside, maybe I can save her," Thorl said, his voice friendly but firm.

Cherou hesitated briefly but then complied and moved a back.

Thorl hovered above Saira while he drew out most of his tentacles to full length to create the biggest possible surface. Soon, they were stretching across the entire room. The Qail's body darkened until it was completely black, in order to absorb most of the light. In addition, he drew large amounts of thermal energy from the water with his tentacles. Soon, small layers of ice built up around some of them. The Qail transformed the energy into another form of energy, which the Lingit-body could use, and injected it via several tentacles directly into Saira's blood vessels.

Cherou watched the goings-on with great uncertainty while Ravar moved closer. "Don't worry. Thorl knows what he is doing. If anybody can save Saira, he can!" the Qail assured him.

Indeed, Saira started to breathe again after a short while, and first twitches moved through her body while Thorl supplied her with more energy. Saira's condition stabilized quickly and soon she even opened her eyes. She got scared when she saw the deep-black Qail with his spread-out tentacles hovering above her.

"Don't be frightened!" Cherou shouted overjoyed and bent down to Saira, so she could see him. A happy glow returned to her eyes when she saw him. "Thorl has just saved your life, young fin! Keep lying still until he has finished his treatment."

Saira relaxed again, laid her head back and closed her eyes for a moment while she enjoyed the warm stream of energy that pulsed through her body.

"Thorl, how long will this take?" Ravar asked, alarmed. "Mirgan and Silgai report a Duumar approaching quickly!"

"I need some more time, otherwise Saira won't be able to follow us," Thorl answered.

A brief clamouring could be heard outside a little later, then the silence returned. Cherou looked at Ravar questioningly.

"One less Duumar," Ravar explained tersely.

Even Cherou was frightened at times by the indifference with which the Qails accepted the death of other beings. But, as energy-transformers, they had a completely different view of the world than all the rest of the inhabitants of Turoon.

Thorl finally finished his treatment. Saira felt strong again and got up.

"She's well again and won't suffer any ill effects," Thorl stated while he drew in his tentacles and illuminated his body.

Overjoyed, Cherou hugged Saira and held her tight.

"Hey, you're squashing me!" Saira yelled jokingly, and Cherou eased up.

"Please forgive me, but I'm just so happy you're alive and well!" he said gladly.

"It's all right!" Saira laughed. "I'm glad too that you've saved me. I had certainly thought that the time had come to say good-bye to this world. You've taken so many troubles and dangers upon yourself for me," she said, embarrassed.

"You didn't really think we would leave you to this monster?" Cherou scolded and pointed at Thurgun's body with a disgusted expression. "Oh no! We have escaped together and we will finish this mission together, too!"

"Then we should get away from here before even more Duumars turn up!" Ravar advised.

"Please wait," they suddenly heard the voice of the Crystal Shard. "Maybe I can open the safety-gates with the help of Thurgun's control console." The shard hovered next to the device and touched the controls. It soon found the safety-gate control and deactivated the alarm. Then they heard the opening of the gates in the corridors. "All clear!" the Crystal Shard proclaimed and hovered back to Saira, who took it in her hand. Then it led the small group to the edge of the city.

*

They encountered only weak resistance in the corridors. A few Draughs tried to block their way but were easily overwhelmed by the Qails. Then they finally reached the end of the corridor-system that passed through the city, and slid out into the open ocean. The sound of isolated fighting could be heard, but it was restricted to single skirmishes outside the city. Using every cover available, the group sneaked along the buildings to the escape tunnel through which they had entered the city. Three young Duumars suddenly blocked their way. Before they could say anything, Saira weaved a strong sleeping spell, which let them sink to the ground unconsciously within a few moments. The small group swam on cautiously. Again they heard the sound of fighting near the escape tunnel, this time coming from the tunnel entrance. When they looked around the corner, they recognized Sembaja who was guarding the entrance with a group of Qails. They were defending themselves against several Duumars and Draughs. The group took a short diversion, which led them directly behind the attackers, who suddenly found themselves under attack from both sides. Soon, Saira had disabled the Duumars, while the Qails overwhelmed the Draughs. Then the group rushed to Sembaja, who welcomed them happily.

"There you are, finally! Did you have any difficulties?" he asked anxiously.

"Did we indeed!" Ravar said.

"I see the Crystal Shard is with you," Sembaja said happily. Another Duumar appeared at that point and attacked them again. Sembaja fired some lightning at him, which the Duumar blocked with his protective shield. Then Saira hurled several bundles of energy-beams at him, which she had equipped with a strong protective spell. Right before the Duumar could break the spell, the energy-beams passed through the protective shield and hit him. His unconscious, twitching body sank to the ground a short time later. "Thank you!" Sembaja said. Then he suddenly saw a huge group of Duumars hurrying towards them. They apparently had finally noticed that the Qails had invaded the city, and were launching a large-scale attack aimed at the escape tunnel. "You have to leave the city quickly. It'll soon be getting quite uncomfortable around here," he advised Saira.

"You can't overcome that many Duumars," Saira said.

"Don't worry, we'll get reinforcements soon," Sembaja promised. "Now get away from here! We'll detain the Duumars as long as possible!" While Saira still hesitated, Sembaja said soothingly:

"We'll manage. You absolutely must take the Crystal Shard back to the Mother-Crystal otherwise all this was in vain." Saira finally nodded and was just about to swim away, when Sembaja gave her an important piece of advice: "If you get attacked by Galanx, defend yourself with a magic shield. It makes the sonar signals ineffective!"

Saira thanked him for the advice, then she passed through the escape tunnel with Cherou and the four Qails. They had just cleared it, when they heard the sounds of fighting from the other side. The Duumars had started their offensive and were rushing at the Qails, who defended themselves desperately to obtain as much of an advantage for Saira as they could. Then the first Galanx appeared directly in front of the group and prepared to attack with a furious growl. But before the Qails could defend themselves, a Farkan raced up and rushed at the Galanx who snatched at the attacker. But the Farkan swerved skilfully and rammed his sting into the side of the Galanx, dealing the guardian a terrible electric shock just as he wanted to let off his sonar. The entire acoustic energy discharged inside the head of the giant, which burst like a bubble. The twitching corpse of the guardian sank to the ground, while the Farkan just rushed away. Saira and Cherou had watched this, terrified, and were once again upset about the cruel fighting. Then they saw, some distance behind them, a huge group of Hingais who quickly passed through the tunnel to assist the Qails in their fight. Cherou recognized Seveg, the oldest one, who had granted them asylum at the beginning of their escape. The clan furiously rushed at the dreadful Duumars and put them under severe attack with their poisonous stings. Many Draughs soon lay on the ground, unable to move, paralyzed by the Hingais' poison. Cherou and Saira followed the fight with bewilderment until the Qails urged them to leave. The small group, led by the Crystal Shard, was soon under attack by several Galanx. Saira protected Cherou and herself with a strong shield, as Sembaja had advised her, while the Qails and Farkans embarked on a counter-attack. The fight lasted for a long time, for the giant guardians were not easy to defeat. More and more Galanx appeared and joined the fight, while the Qails and Hingais in the city also met an increasing number of enemies. It almost seemed as if the Duumars and their guards would after all be victorious, when suddenly a giant swarm of Gamburas arrived. Some of them rushed at the Galanx, while the rest of the swarm invaded the city and rushed at the Duumars. And so the tide turned and the Duumars were pushed back with their guards. In the end, the Duumars withdrew completely and relinquished the fighting to their guardians. At that very moment, Saira felt the magic barrier around the city collapse. It looked as though the Duumars were defeated for the time being, and it was just a question of time until their guardians would be defeated too. But the attackers quickly stood corrected. The Duumars suddenly reappeared, but this time they were sitting in strongly armoured steel machines with driven by propellers! Unattackable within their protective casing, they now rushed against the aggressors, who were defenceless and at the mercy of their attacks. Saira and Cherou had to watch helplessly as more and more Qails, Hingais and Gamburas were killed. In his despair, Sembaja called on the last remaining opponents for help. A loud rattling was heard a short time later. Directly in front of Saira and Cherou the outline of a giant box-type head peeled out of the darkness of the deep sea. The giant swam directly towards them. The mighty bow wave, which he pushed along in front of him, simply washed the two Lingits aside, while the Wra activated his fighting sonar. Although Saira and Cherou were enclosed by a magic shield, the loud, increasingly faster rattling sound caused them to go nearly deaf. Each pulse would hurt the entire body, even though they were only hit by the outflow. More Wras peeled out of the darkness and started to attack. The rattling of their fighting sonar was like constant thunder, but then the first giant fired his pressure pulse in the direction of the Duumars. The energy of the pressure wave was so tremendous that even the waters around the head of the

Wra briefly flashed up. The pulse raced through the water, while the frightened Duumars tried to escape backwards. But the propellers of their machines, running at full throttle, cranked through in a cavitation bubble so they could not move away. The first pressure wave had already reached its target, and the first of the armoured boats of the Duumars was simply torn to pieces by the gigantic energy pulse. The other Wras also let off their fighting sonar a short time later, and more armoured boats burst because of the enormous pressure waves. The Duumars finally fled the remaining armoured boats before they exploded under the bombardment of the Wras. Soon, the resistance of the Duumars and their guards had broken down completely. The Duumars fled and hid inside the city, while the Draughs and Galanx moved away. This time, the Duumars seemed to be properly defeated, and so Cherou and Saira hurried to finally reach the Mother-Crystal.

The Fire-Crystal

Saira, Cherou and a swarm of Qails reached the hidden entrance to a cave a short while later. They were just about to enter the cave, when the Crystal Shard sent them a warning that a Duumar was inside. So they advanced quite carefully. The Qails took Saira and Cherou into their midst to protect them. They moved forward slowly, but could not detect the Duumar. They finally reached the centre of the cave after passing through a long rock-lined corridor. The sight took their breath away. A giant, round hall extended in front of them, the ceiling forming a mighty dome. A giant, red shimmering crystal lay in the middle of the dome of rock. Magic fire flared around it. Its spherical surface was divided into countless facets. Their beams were reflected from the nearby walls and the ceiling. This created a dreamlike, mystical atmosphere, which captivated all those present. A small, pulsating gap could be detected at the upper edge of the crystal, looking like a wound. This was where Saira had to join the Crystal Shard back with the Mother-Crystal. All of them were so fascinated by the sight that no one detected the movement in the shadows. Only when a strong bolt of lightning smashed into the ground in front of them and the Duumar rushed out at them, was the group woken out of its dreamlike state. The two Lingits were hurled aside, while the Qails jerked backwards and stretched their bells. Then a veritable inferno of lightning and flashes erupted, as the Qails went for the Duumar. But his mirrored protective shield seemed impenetrable. The Duumar harassed the Qails and began to draw away their energy, when Saira finally woke up from her daze. She recognized immediately the intention of the Duumar and created a steam explosion directly underneath him. The Duumar was hurled upwards. His protective shield flickered for a moment, so some of the Qails' lightning passed through and caused strong pain to the Duumar. He roared and catapulted himself aside, which gave him valuable time to recover. He attacked Saira with a poisonous spell, which Saira was able to block. Then the floor beneath Saira exploded. She quickly jumped aside and fired a whole swarm of energy-bundles at the Duumar, which he absorbed quite easily. He had to defend himself again against the Qails rushing at him. This gave Saira time to prepare a new attack. She shot a force field at the Duumar to overload his protective shield. But the Duumar transformed the spell and hurled it back at Saira, while he again started to draw away the energy of the Qails. Saira was hit by the heavy lightning. She was able to ease the effect with a shield, but it did not protect her from being smashed against the wall with great force. Dazed, she slipped down to the floor. Frightened, Cherou quickly swam over to Saira. The Duumar continued fighting with the Qails and did not take any notice of him. Cherou carefully lifted Saira's upper body.

"Saira, how are you?" he shouted, worried.

She opened her eyes a little and seemed to look at him from far away. The fight appeared to have drained her again. This time he would not tolerate that she ended up completely exhausted again. "Just relax, I'll handle this!" he said soothingly and laid her carefully on the floor.

Several Qails were lying lifelessly in the cave, and the resistance of the other fighters was lessening.

"Don't you imagine that you are a match for me!" the Duumar scoffed. "You maybe have disbanded us, but I'll never allow you to deprive us of our power! I haven't built up our whole empire to let it be destroyed by you parasites!"

Cherou trembled. So this was the Duumar who had once before taken over and enslaved his tribe! This was the leader of the Duumars, the one who had instigated the uprising that had started the reign of terror so long ago. He had been the trigger for all the grief, the pain and the sorrow bestowed on the inhabitants of Turoon! Boundless fury rose up in Cherou and made him shiver. He grasped a big rock and moved off in the direction of the Duumar.

Saira woke up from her dazed state and saw Cherou swimming away. It was already too late when she realized what he intended to do. She could only watch as Cherou raced up to the Duumar and smashed the rock directly on his head. The Duumar detected him at the last moment and hurled a flash at Cherou, while the rock crashed down on his head and he fell to the ground, unconscious. The lightning had hit Cherou simultaneously with full power, and he, too, sank to the ground, motionless.

"No!" Saira screamed in terror and rushed over to Cherou, while the remaining Qails raced to the Duumar. Filled with poison, the Duumar soon breathed his last breath, while the exhausted Qails sank down beside him.

"Is ... he ... dead?" Cherou asked when Saira cradled his head. He was breathing with great effort. Saira just nodded, her eyes full of tears. "Well ... young fin. So ... our mission ... is accomplished."

"Yes it is," Saira said, choking with tears.

"Heal ... the ... crystal!" Cherou breathed with his last power, then he smiled once more wistfully and closed his eyes forever.

Saira held him tight and started to cry bitterly. She did not notice the noise coming closer from the outside.

"Saira, you must rejoin the Crystal Shard with the Mother-Crystal! Sembaja shouted. "We are too weak and the Duumars are moving forward from the outside and are coming closer and closer!"

But Saira was so caught up in her sorrow that she did not react. Her pain about the loss of her beloved friend and mentor was just too great.

"Please Saira!" Sembaja shouted almost pleadingly. "Only you can fulfil the mission now! Heal the crystal!"

Saira still did not react, but looked at him, her eyes veiled with tears. Then a heavy explosion shook the corridor to the cave.

"Please Saira, the Duumars will be here quite soon. You must heal the crystal!" Sembaja shouted again desperately.

As another explosion shook the cave, Saira finally let go of Cherou's body and grasped the Crystal Shard. With eyes full of tears she hauled herself to the upper edge of the giant Mother-Crystal, directly next to the wound. Right at that moment the first

Duumars had reached the cave. Horrified, they looked up at Saira, who lifted her arm with the Crystal Shard, looked once more in despair at Cherou, and finally rammed the shard with a loud cry into the Mother-Crystal's wound.

Liberation

The crystal flashed and its magic fire blazed briefly all the way up to the ceiling. A mighty thunder reverberated through the cave as the crystal shone bright white and filled the dome with brilliant light. Saira was hurled away and found herself next to Cherou's body again. She carefully lifted him up, and again tears of indescribable sorrow filled her eyes. She gently hugged his body and cried silently. It was of no importance to her what happened around her. She perceived her surroundings as through a veil because of her sorrow, while the pain of her loss nearly deprived her of her senses.

The mighty Fire-Crystal had reduced its light to a tolerable level. Instantly, the Duumars lost their magic powers. They hastily left the cave and disappeared, while the Qails absorbed new energy. Then the thunder faded and a pleasant silence lay upon the scene. Only Saira's quiet sobbing could be heard, as the Fire-Crystal spoke to her:

"Thank you so much for my healing. The elemental order is restored again, and a new age has now begun for this world. Thanks to your courage, your bravery, and your strength this world will soon be as it was when I created it. Your sacrifice was not in vain!"

Then the Fire-Crystal turned a bright beam of light on Saira and Cherou. Saira lifted her head with her eyes full of tears and only now was able to perceive her surroundings clearly again. Then Cherou's body was suddenly and carefully lifted. With a last longing gaze Saira let him go and watched as Cherou's body slowly moved to the crystal, while he became more and more transparent. He finally merged with the crystal in a bright flash of light, while a lilting sound passed through the hall. A short while later, a radiant being appeared in front of Saira and gradually took on Cherou's shape. Saira gazed in surprise at the transparent figure. The radiant being stretched out one hand and gently caressed Saira's cheek. Its touch was pleasantly warm and expelled the sorrow from Saira's spirit. Then the radiant being smiled kindly and said to her: "Don't mourn me anymore. I'm now a part of the crystal. We'll heal the wounds of this world together and return it to what it was before. But I need your help with this. Tell the Lingits their time of slavery is over, and give them back their freedom. Then please lead all the abducted slaves here to the crystal, so that we can send them back to their worlds of origin, whence they were once dragged away. Then you too can return home. Will you do this last favour for us?"

"With great pleasure!" Saira said, deeply moved, and wiped the tears out of her eyes.

"We'll be very grateful," Cherou's spirit replied in a friendly voice and gave her a warm-hearted smile. Then he turned to the Qails that had gathered in the cave. "Thank you very much for your help. You have made a great many sacrifices to accomplish this goal. Now you can leave your exile and be free again. You're always welcome here! Just let us know if we can ever do anything for you."

"Thank you!" Sembaja answered. "We're very happy the reign of terror of the Duumars is finally over. Now we and our descendants can finally live freely and in peace. This is above all because of Saira's help. We'll always be grateful to her!" Then he turned to the exit and left the cave with his clan.

Saira embarked on her last task. The news of the Lingits' liberation spread quickly. Freed slaves were leaving this place of horror and swimming off in all directions again, to establish new settlements or to repopulate their old homes. That same day, Saira assembled all the abducted slaves in the cave. She had never expected that there would be so many of them. Soon it got very crowded in the domed cave of the Fire-Crystal. But finally the lines of victims thinned, as the crystal sent them, one after the other, back to their worlds of origin. Saira was very happy when she found Jir amongst the survivors. At long last she could keep her promise to free her. When finally the last of the abducted victims had safely reached its world of origin, it was Saira's turn to leave Turoon. Cherou's spirit appeared once more in front of her and they said a heart-felt good-bye to each other. Although Saira had yearned for her return so much, the farewell was very difficult for her now. But before the Fire-Crystal let her go, it asked her to swim to the exit of the cave again. What she saw there exceeded her greatest expectations. A giant mass of Lingits, Hingais, Qails, Gamburas and Wras had gathered and started to cheer loudly as Saira appeared. Then one of the giant Wras swam closer and hovered above Saira.

"All our thanks go to you! You have given us a new future with your courage and your hard work. We'll never forget this!" his mighty voice boomed, and loud cheering started again, until the Wra asked for silence with a shrill sonar signal. "May your path always be a happy one. We wish you all the best for your journey home. Farewell Saira, and thank you very much for everything!" Then all of them bowed down silently in front of her.

Saira was moved to tears by so much kindness and gratitude. "Thank you so much for all your help. We couldn't have done this without you! Farewell, and look after your world well!" she shouted as loudly as she could.

"We'll keep you forever in our memories!" the Wra said once more, followed by thunderous cheering. Then Saira waved good-bye to the inhabitants of Turoon, while she fought back her tears. The Fire-Crystal opened the magic portal in the dome for the last time and again thanked Saira. She waved one last time, gathered all her courage, and swam through the portal. Without her knowledge, the crystal had given her a present to take with her, which would thoroughly change the course of her future life.

Home again

Torem was just devising a plan for Saira's rescue in the early evening, when the magic portal suddenly appeared again at the same place where it had previously abducted Saira. A moment later, the Guardians of the Light were already materializing and weaving a strong spell to retain the portal where it had appeared. Then Saira fell out of the opening, together with a surge of water. She had her original shape again. Torem rushed to her and quickly carried the naked girl away from the portal. The Fire-Crystal had by now made contact with the Sunstone and was transferring the information of what had happened on Turoon. The Sunstone immediately relayed the information to the Guardians of the Light, who then dissolved their spell around the portal, which vanished a short time later.

Torem had wrapped Saira in his cape and examined her quickly, when Emnavuk, the first of the four guardians, came closer. "She seems to be uninjured and healthy," Torem reported to the guardian, who then examined Saira himself with his magic gaze.

"That's right. But she won't be able to move her legs for a short while. This condition won't last long, and she has not sustained any other harm," Emnavuk assured him. "But Saira mustn't use her magic powers for the moment."

Torem looked questioningly at the guardian. Right then, Saira woke up and looked around her in confusion until she realized that she was back home on Wuun. Instantly, she felt very happy and smiled brightly when she recognized Torem. "Master, is that really you? Am I really back home again?" she asked in disbelief.

"Yes, Saira!" he said. "You are finally back with us!" Happily, he hugged the Velbe girl

"We're so very happy you've returned safely!" Emnavuk said.

"Oh, you can't believe how happy I am to be here again!" Saira said joyfully and attempted to get up, but found she had no control over her legs.

"You won't be able to move your legs for a short time. That's a consequence of being on a waterworld for such a long time. But you'll be able to walk again in just a few days," Emnavuk reassured her.

Saira looked at him in surprise. "So you know where I've been all this time?"

"Oh yes, it required a great deal of effort to figure it out, but finally we discovered where you were," Torem explained.

"Don't be surprised. You've come back the same day you were abducted. The Fire-Crystal has contacted us and explained everything. It created a time-paradox when it brought you back, so that you have not been separated from us for too long," Emnavuk told her. "But now it's time for you to relax. I'll take you back to your parents. They don't know anything about your abduction." He lifted Saira with his magic powers and took her in his strong arms. A moment later Saira found herself with Emnavuk and Torem in front of her parents' cottage. "Keh, Hri, I bring you your daughter!" Emnavuk shouted in a friendly voice. A short time later, Saira's mother Hri opened the door, astonished. "Guardian Emnavuk, Master Torem, what happened?" She looked frightened when she saw Saira lying in Emnavuk's arms.

"Don't worry, Saira is all right!" Emnavuk said reassuringly. She just can't walk for the moment, but that'll last only for a short time."

By now, Saira's father Keh had come out too and taken his daughter from Emnavuk's arms.

"Please come in!" Hri requested, and Emnavuk and Torem entered the spacious cottage. Emnavuk had to bow down deeply, for he was nearly double the size of the Velbs. He took a seat by the door, while Keh carried Saira to her part of the cottage and laid her on her bed, while Hri asked the two guests to wait a moment. Then she followed Keh.

"How's my little girl?" Keh asked worriedly.

"Thanks, I'm fine, just a bit exhausted," Saira said.

"What happened?" Hri asked.

"Oh Mama, that's a long story," Saira answered tiredly.

"It's all right. You can tell us later," Hri said understandingly. "I'll fetch you some clothes."

"No Mama, I would prefer a blanket. Every movement is difficult for me at the moment," Saira answered.

"Stay, I'll get you a blanket!" Keh said and stood up, while Hri helped her daughter out of the cape. Keh returned a short time later with a blanket, and Saira stretched out underneath.

"Can we do anything else for you, dear?" Hri asked lovingly and caressed Saira's head.

"No, thanks! I just want to sleep," Saira replied, exhausted.

"Well then, relax now," said Keh and caressed Saira's cheek. "We'll look in on you again later."

Saira gave her parents a grateful smile. Soon, her deep, regular breaths showed that she had fallen asleep. Keh and Hri quietly left the room and returned to their guests. Hri gave Torem back his cape and thanked them for bringing Saira back.

"Do you know what happened?" she asked.

"Shortly after Saira arrived, she was abducted to another world by a magic portal," Torem began to narrate. "We tried the whole day to find her, and finally succeeded. But by then, Saira had already returned safely with the second appearance of the portal."

"How could that happen?" Keh asked, frightened.

So Emnavuk started to tell sequentially what had happened in the foreign world, as reported by the Sunstone. Keh and Hri were shocked when they learned what had happened to their daughter, and how long she had been on the waterworld. In the end, Emnavuk asked the two Velbs to advise Saira not to use any of her magic powers until she had recovered. It appeared that her magic powers had been massively increased by the Fire-Crystal, and Saira would not be able to control these powers at the moment.

"So how strong are her magic powers now?" Torem asked.

"They surpass even your powers by far," was Emnavuk's surprising reply. "That's why you can't complete her training. No magician on Wuun can control Saira's powers at the moment. Only the Sunstone remains a match for her. So it will have to take over her remaining training."

Torem looked at the guardian with big eyes. He could barely believe Saira had suddenly become so strong. But Emnavuk's expression left no doubt how serious he was. If Saira really was this strong and not yet able to control her powers, she would be a danger to everybody. And it really would be for the best if the Sunstone completed her training. But he kept these thoughts to himself, so that they would not disturb Keh and Hri even further. It was already difficult enough for them to comprehend the abduction of their daughter. Torem finally nodded understandingly and rose up with Emnavuk. "Now we'll just have to wait until Saira has recovered a little. I will explain everything to her later," Torem promised. Then the master-magician and the guardian said good-bye and left behind a confused Keh and Hri.

*

The next morning Saira woke up when the sun was already high in the sky. It took her a moment to realize that she was back in the safety of her own home. She appreciated and enjoyed this so much! And so she lay there for a while, dreamily watching the sunlight illuminating her room through the window. She still could not move her legs, but she had started to feel them again, which gave her hope to be able to walk again soon. Right at that moment, Keh peered through the curtain at the entrance of her room.

"Good morning, late riser!" he greeted his daughter jokingly and entered the room. "How's my little girl?" Sometimes he still used this pet name, although Saira was practically a grown up.

Saira did not mind, but mostly smiled to herself when he called her this. She yawned and stretched joyfully and rubbed the sleep out of her eyes. "Thanks, I'm fine. And I'm getting some feeling back in my legs."

"I'm happy to hear that!" Keh replied. Hri also entered the room.

"Oh, you're awake already! Good morning, dear!" she greeted her daughter.

"Good morning, Mama!" Saira said and propped herself up.

"Did you sleep well?" Hri asked.

"As well as never before, at least not in a long time!" Saira answered enthusiastically, while Hri gently stroked her head.

"By the way, we've kept some of your favourite meal!" Keh remarked with a grin. "You should have seen Mama, she defended it like a Tjoa!" Then he imitated the deep growl of the well-armoured animals. He promptly had to take a hard stare from Hri, while Saira started to giggle.

"Oh Paps, you're still outrageous, but that's why I love you so!" she said and laughed happily.

"I love you too, dear!" Keh replied and held his daughter close. Then he got serious. "There's something important I have to tell you. Guardian Emnavuk and Master Torem ask you very seriously not to use your magic powers. Apparently, the Fire-Crystal enhanced your powers massively while you returned. So it could be dangerous if you use them now. That's why the Sunstone and the Guardians of the Light want to complete your training."

Saira looked at him, astonished. "I will of course weave no magic if they don't want me to. But why can't I study with Master Torem anymore?"

"It seems that he can't control your power now. At least that's what Guardian Emnavuk told us," Hri explained.

"Oh what a pity! I felt quite comfortable with Master Torem. Does it really have to be this way?" Saira asked, a little desperate.

"Master Torem has agreed. He will soon visit us again and explain everything to you," Keh answered. "Now don't be sad, you can visit Master Torem and his apprentices anytime," Keh said when he saw Saira's disappointed face.

"Sure, but the guardians are a bit scary," Saira finally admitted.

"I can understand that you don't feel at ease with them, but you don't need to be frightened. As you know, Emnavuk has raised me. The guardians sometimes seem a bit reserved, and many of the things they do are hard to understand, but you certainly don't need to fear them," Keh assured her.

"I know, but I'd rather stay with Master Torem!" Saira said uncertainly.

"Now you'd better wait what Master Torem has to tell you. Maybe there's another solution," Hri said soothingly. Keh and Hri helped their daughter into her new clothes and served her a good meal. Saira helped herself quite well and enjoyed the tasty meal.

"Didn't you get anything to eat on Turoon?" Keh asked jokingly.

"I did, but the food there didn't taste as good as this by far!" Saira answered eagerly, and all three of them started to laugh.

Master Torem visited later and explained the situation in detail to Saira. Unfortunately, the matter ended with the decision that she would have to complete the rest of her training with the Guardians of the Light, which did not exactly fill Saira with enthusiasm.

*

As Emnavuk had promised, it took just a few days until Saira could walk again. The fact that she now had to complete her training with the Guardians of the Light did not make her happy. The mighty guardians had always seemed frightening, although Emnavuk once had been her own father's foster-parent. Even Keh could not succeed in dissipating her doubts, so on this day, Saira waited with a dull feeling for her first lesson with the guardians. Emnavuk finally materialized in front of her cottage and called for Saira. She stepped out of the door with Keh a short time later. Her father encouraged her again in his friendly way, then Saira dematerialized with Emnavuk to appear again immediately in the Temple of Lights beside the Sunstone. The shimmering white walls of the temple caused an enchanted atmosphere, intensified by the bright sunlight that flowed in through the crystal dome. Directly beneath it, the bright white shining Sunstone was enthroned on its rock pedestal, flooding the surrounding area with a magical light. It was the first time that Saira had seen the Sunstone so close-up, and its sight drew her immediately into its ban. She was greeted in a friendly manner by the other three guardians and returned the salute, feeling a bit shy. Then she suddenly heard a voice.

"Don't have fear, nobody will harm you," the Sunstone spoke with a friendly voice. "Please come closer!" Saira haltingly took two steps towards the Sunstone. It wrapped her in bright light for a short while. "Indeed, your power is tremendous!" it then said appreciatively. "The Fire-Crystal from Turoon has given you a great present, but you're not yet able to control your powers." Then a small bowl filled with water materialized next to her. "Please, make the water boil with a heat spell," the Sunstone requested.

Saira was a bit confused at first, because she did not understand what the Sunstone's intention was, but finally she followed the order and concentrated on the water. Almost immediately, the bowl was torn to pieces by a heavy explosion. Saira would have been seriously injured if the Sunstone hadn't instantly placed a protective shield around the explosion. She jumped aside with a frightened outcry, and then looked at the smoking debris of the bowl, terrified.

"Now you understand what I mean," the Sunstone said in its friendly voice. You must first learn to control your great powers, otherwise you could cause a catastrophe by mistake! You are so strong that no magician on Wuun can control your power. Only the guardians and I are able to guide your magic. That's why we ask you not to use your magic powers outside of the temple for the moment, until you can control it properly. Will you promise us that?"

Saira looked around in confusion at first, but then she made the requested promise to the Sunstone.

"Well then, let's continue with your training," the Sunstone said, satisfied.

*

Emnavuk took Saira back to her parents in the evening. She was completely exhausted and very quiet for the rest of the evening, which was not at all her style. Keh and Hri were somewhat unsettled and concerned, in case their daughter had overexerted herself. Saira retired soon and reclined on her bed for a while, lost in thought, until her father sat down beside her and lovingly took her in his arms. "What's the matter with you? What's so disturbing to my little girl?"

Saira hugged him and started to cry hard the next moment. Keh let her have her tears and just caressed her gently until she had calmed down a little. "Oh Paps, I'm so scared of myself!" she sobbed.

Keh carefully moved her back a bit, so that he could see her face. "There's no need for that," he said soothingly. "You may have great magic powers, but you would never harm anybody. That we all know!"

Saira swallowed hard and wiped the tears from her face. "That's right, but I have grown so strong I could burn down the entire village with a single thought by mistake," she said with a terrified look. "I don't know whether I will ever be able to control my power properly. I'm a danger to all of you at the moment," she explained and started to cry hard again.

"Oh no, you mustn't believe that!" said Keh and caressed her gently. "Don't worry, you will soon learn to control your power. The guardians and the Sunstone will take care of you until then. You aren't a danger to anybody, and you never will be. That much I know for sure!"

"You really think so?" Saira asked after she had calmed down a bit.

"Oh yes! I'm yet quite sure of that. You mustn't have so many doubts about yourself. Mama, I and all the others know that you will be able to handle it," Keh said encouragingly.

Saira looked at him, embarrassed. "Thank you," she then whispered with tears in her eyes, but the sorrow did not leave her face. "There's something else, which I haven't told you yet," she said, looking down. Keh looked at her inquisitively, until Saira found the right words. Her mother had also joined them and put her arms around Saira, too. "You know, on Turoon, there were many ferocious fights at the end," Saira finally continued. "I caused the death of some inhabitants with my powers ..." She broke down crying again. Her parents looked at each other, frightened, but then waited patiently until Saira had regained control over herself.

"Did you kill them?" Hri asked carefully.

Saira shook her head. "No, but I disabled them, after which they were killed by the Qails!" She started to cry again. "So I'm to blame for their death!"

"No Saira, you aren't! You only defended yourself. You can't help that others killed them. You aren't to blame," Keh said soothingly, but Saira did not want to believe him.

"Look, you had no choice. You had to defend yourself. Besides, you had to rely on the help of the Qails. Perhaps they had their reasons to act so brutally, but you carry no guilt for the death of your enemies. They didn't die because of you, but because of others. Please believe us, you're not responsible for their death! Most certainly not! The Sunstone would have never been willing to look after you if you were someone who would be likely to kill. To the contrary! He would have most certainly rejected you," Keh explained calmly.

"Now stop reproaching yourself," Hri said gently. "You're really not guilty. Believe me, we've experienced it ourselves. Sometimes awful things happen during a fight, and it often hurts very much that it had to come to this. But you've kept your heart pure during all the things that happened, and you've done nothing bad. You are much too loving and helpful for that. No, you don't need to feel guilty about anything. To the contrary, Turoon was saved because of you! Such things sometimes demand great sacrifice, and many lose their lives. It also happened on our world not too long ago. None of this is your responsibility, but the responsibility rests with those who plunge the world into misery and harm. Be assured, you only helped to restore the old order, and you saved many lives, but you never took even a single one!"

"Is that really true?" Saira asked uncertainly.

"Yes, quite so!" Keh confirmed the word of his partner.

"Now don't reproach yourself any more! You're not responsible for those things."

Saira gave her parents a thankful look with her eyes full of tears, and held on tightly to both of them.

"And now stop those tears!" Hri grumbled with pretence disgust and gently wiped her daughter's eyes.

A visitor from Turoon

The lessons with the Guardians of the Light were feeling much easier for Saira the next day. She gradually got to know the guardians better too, who took great care to make her training as pleasant as possible. With much patience and understanding they taught her to control her tremendous power and returned a sense of steadiness and strength to the unsettled girl. Saira learned quickly and soon was much steadier in the execution of her magic skills. But also the high regard, the understanding and the love granted by her parents and all the inhabitants of her village helped Saira to adjust to the new situation quickly.

One evening, after the lessons, Emnavuk appeared once more beside Saira and asked her to come to the Temple of Lights with her parents. He did not tell her why, but just said smilingly that a surprise would be waiting there for Saira. Soon after, the three Velbs and Emnavuk materialized directly next to the Sunstone in the Temple of Lights. Saira could not believe her eyes: Cherou's spirit hovered above the Sunstone!

"Hello young fin! We haven't met for a long time," Cherou said smilingly and slid over to Saira.

Saira was completely baffled and at first could not say a word, she was so overcome by her surprise. The Guardians of the Light had retreated discreetly and were watching the scene from some distance, obviously amused.

"H ... how did you get here?" Saira asked, surprised.

"The Fire-Crystal contacted your Sunstone on my behalf to enable me to see you again. I can only stay for a short while, because it costs a lot of energy to keep the contact over such a far distance," Cherou explained. "As I can see, you have done well since being back in your world of origin."

"Thanks, I'm fine," Saira replied, still a bit confused.

"That's nice to hear," Cherou said. Then his look wandered past Saira. "Are these your parents, young fin?"

"Oh, yes, please forgive me! This is my father Keh and my mother Hri," Saira hurried to introduce her parents. Then she turned to them. "Mama, Paps, that's Cherou, my mentor and friend from Turoon."

Keh and Hri took a step forward and bowed down slightly. "Be greeted Cherou!" Keh then said in a friendly manner.

"I greet you!" Cherou answered politely and intimated a bow too. "You can be proud of your daughter! Without her efforts our world wouldn't exist any more," said Cherou.

"We thank you too, for you have taken care of our daughter and protected her!" Hri answered. "Thanks to you she has safely returned to us."

"It was a pleasure!" Cherou assured them and turned to Saira again. "So that's your real shape," he said smilingly. "I liked you better as a Lingit-girl!"

Saira gave him a hard stare. "You are still outrageous!" she then scolded in pretence annoyance, and her parents exchanged an amused look. This comment seemed somehow familiar to them!

"And you still look sweet when you're angry!" Cherou countered, grinning. Now even Keh and Hri could not suppress a short laugh. Saira put her hands on her hips, seemingly disgusted, then dismissed it laughingly, as she noticed how her father was suddenly inspecting ceiling and walls with great interest. "You haven't changed at all!" she said to Cherou, amused.

"But you have, at least with regard to your magic powers!" Cherou replied. "Can you handle them properly, or is it difficult to control them?"

"It was tiring for me at the beginning. But by now I can control it quite well, thanks to the help of my instructors," Saira said and pointed briefly at the four Guardians of the Light, who nodded at Cherou.

"I'm happy to hear that. I was worried our present had turned out to be a burden to you," Cherou said.

"It's all right!" Saira said. "I can handle it quite well by now." Then she paused briefly. "What about your world?"

"We managed at the last moment to avert a catastrophe. Step by step, we are returning Turoon to its old splendour. The wounds of the past are healing gradually, and Turoon will once again become the paradise it used to be.

"Oh, that's wonderful!" Saira said happily. "What about the Lingits and the Duumars?"

"My tribe now lives a free and untroubled life again, like it did before. The Duumars have scattered across the wide ocean and now live a very secluded life. Many of them still fear the rage of their victims, although no attacks against them have occurred so far. They've learned their lesson. The Fire-Crystal will continue to guard them and ensure that such a reign of terror never again happens at Turoon." Then Cherou seemed to listen. "It's time to go now. The contact is getting weaker." He hovered close to Saira and they hugged affectionately. "Take good care of yourself, young fin!" Cherou said and waved one last time, while his image faded until it had gone. Saira waved in tears until he had disappeared. Then her parents surrounded and comforted her. Emnavuk took them back to their cottage a little later.

As Saira went to bed a short time later, she could not get the encounter with Cherou out of her mind for a long time. She remembered the hard times she had experienced at Turoon. But finally she wiped away the memories with an energetic move of her hand. It was over! She had managed to escape from there! She was at home again, living her normal life, that was the only thing that was important now. She finally fell asleep, soothed by these thoughts.

Life

By now, Saira's abduction was well in the past. Although she was a very strong magician now and could control her tremendous powers very well, she still wished to live the same simple life as before her abduction. The support of her parents and all the inhabitants gave her much strength. Her experiences on Turoon had naturally affected her very much and some of them had left deep scars. But the love and respect she experienced from those around her allowed most of her mental wounds to heal quickly.

Saira had known Tju, one of Torem's apprentices, for a long time. After her abduction the boy, who was nearly her age, visited her quite often and looked after her with touching care. She felt comfortable with him, because he was a patient and understanding listener and supported her wherever he could. Saira never felt beleaguered by his loving and diffident manner. To the contrary! She felt safe with him, in a way that was very helpful to her while she was coming to terms with her experiences. Her parents also got on well with the boy, and so he soon became part of the family.

This evening he came to visit again. Hri sent him directly to the rear part of the cottage, where he pushed his head, a bit shyly as usual, through the curtain at the entrance to Saira's room. Saira asked him to take a seat beside her. She had just settled comfortably on her bed and greeted the boy happily. A little embarrassed, Tju handed her some little nuts that Saira loved to eat.

"Thanks! But you shouldn't spoil me so," she grumbled jokingly and soon ate the first nut.

"Yes, I know," Tju replied, still embarrassed. "But I like to give you treats ..."

"You're really a lovely guy," Saira said, touched.

"How are your lessons coming along?" Tju asked after a short pause.

"I'm doing quite well at the moment. How about you?" Saira asked.

"Oooh, quite well," Tju whispered.

"That doesn't sound very convincing," Saira said, amused.

Tju hemmed and hawed a little before he came out with the truth. "We brewed some healing potions today. One of mine would have exploded if Torem hadn't prevented it at the last moment."

Saira started to giggle while Tju lowered his head, embarrassed. "Don't worry! When I was learning the fire-spell I nearly burnt Torem's beloved cape during my first attempt," Saira admitted.

"Really?" Tju asked, chuckling.

"Oh yes!" Saira confirmed.

"Mefi nearly blew up Torem's best telescope!" Tju continued his tale, and Saira had to laugh even more loudly.

Both of them continued to tell all kind of anecdotes about their misadventures during Torem's lessons.

"Oh dear, I suppose it's really not easy for poor Torem to handle us!" Saira finally said laughingly.

"Indeed. He sometimes really has a dangerous life," Tju admitted and chuckled.

Right then, Keh stuck his head through the curtain. "Oh, hello Tju!" he said happily.

"Hello Keh!" Tju greeted him.

"Do you have some time during the next few days?" Keh asked with a grin.

"Oh ... yes," Tju answered uncertainly. "What can I do for you?"

"Well, maybe you could persuade Saira to go swimming." Then he made a grimace and held his nose, as though Saira exuded an unpleasant smell.

Saira shot straight up, jammed her hands on her hips in disgust, then picked up one of her shoes. "Paps, you're outrageous!" she scolded and lifted her shoe menacingly, while Keh hurried to get out of the way. This time, Tju could not deny himself an amused grin.

"Don't you laugh at me!" Saira scolded in mock annoyance and boxed Tju on the shoulder. She had not been swimming since her abduction, and it had nothing to do with a lack of cleanliness!

"Ouch!" Tju shouted in exaggerated pain. "What was that for?" he asked and displayed an innocent expression.

"That you know quite well!" Saira grumbled, apparently cross. "Cheeky fellow!"

"When I think about it, we really should go swimming one day soon," Tju said, grinning.

"I see," Saira said and looked at him sceptically, but then could not stop an amused smile. "All right, maybe during the next few days," she finally agreed half-heartedly.

Tju looked out of the window, where the sun had sunk worryingly close to the horizon. "Oh, it's getting late. I should go now!"

"Wait, I'll come with you," Saira said and got up. The boy said good-bye to Keh and Hri, then he and Saira stepped out of her front door together. "Oh come on Saira, let's go swimming tomorrow!" Tju begged her once more when they were outside, looking all innocent.

Saira gave him a sceptical look again, but then agreed with a smile, and Tju turned to go home. She looked after him, smiling, until he turned around again, made a grimace and held his nose, grinning. Saira put her hands on her hips again, but then waved at him, laughing, and Tju winked at her happily. She gave him a bright smile and returned into the cottage. Her parents could not fail to notice Saira's dreamy smile and exchanged an amused glance. "I suppose our family will soon grow," Keh said with a grin, and Hri boxed him in his side and ordered him to be quiet with a fierce gesture, because she feared that Saira would hear them.

Their daughter meanwhile had settled comfortably on her bed again. She had no idea that her world and her feelings would soon be severely tested, but that is another story ...

Acknowledgement

Special thanks to my lovely wife Monica, because this book would have never been conceived without her. She always encouraged me to continue with this project and supported me even in my darkest hours. Her helpful advice and the patient corrections of my writing errors were a great help to me!

I am also indebted to my parents. They always backed me up and have given me every possible support.

I also want to thank my loyal colleague and friend, Sabine. She helped me to better understand a great many things and was always there to listen and to offer her help and understanding whenever required. That's why this book is dedicated to her!

Turoon and its inhabitants

Turoon is a waterworld. There is no mainland on this planet. It is completely covered with water. There are mountainous regions, canyons and high plateaus, but they are all beneath the sea. These environments combine to create a complex network of wide streams, which run through the entire ocean. With the help of frequent and often very ferocious storms that develop because of the enormous evaporation of water at the ocean's surface, they cause a massive mixing of the water-layers. This enabled a rich variety of life to develop in the ocean.

The axis of planet Turoon remains nearly vertical. This means that there are practically no seasonal temperature and weather fluctuations. This stable climate also encourages the ocean world's rich flora and fauna.

The following chapter describes some of the higher developed creatures of Turoon.

Cherou, a Lingit

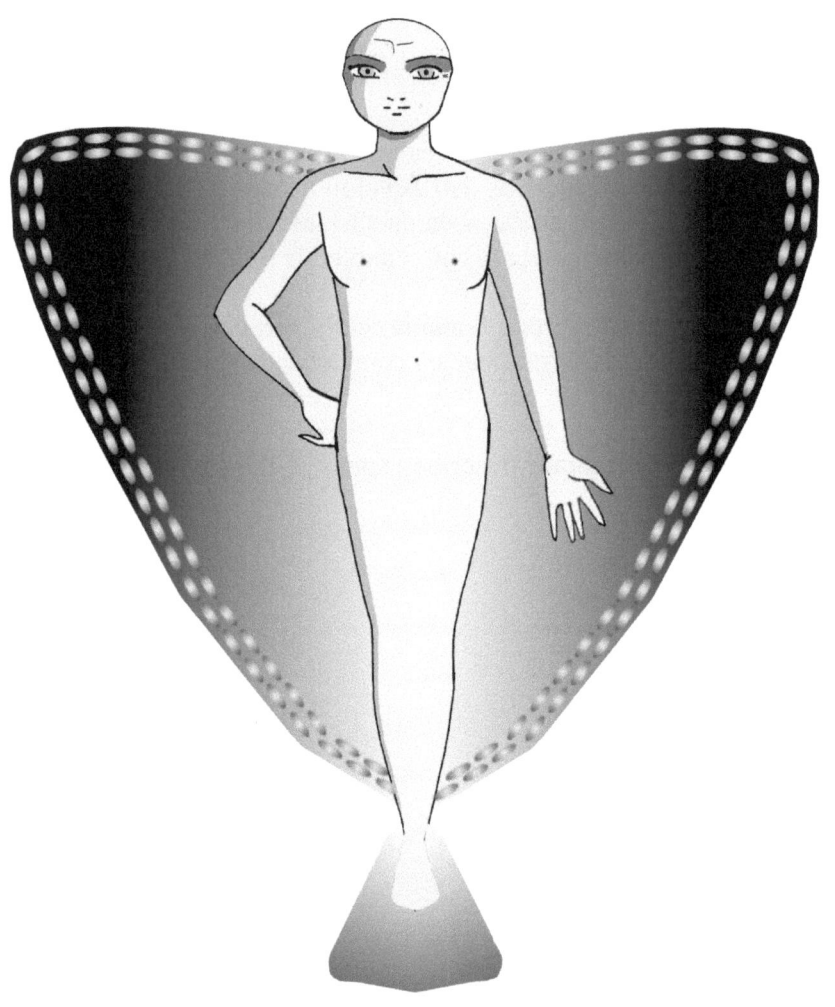

As the big wing fins with the numerous luminous organs already show: this is a dweller of the deep sea. Lingits have no gill-slits. Their organs for the exchange of substances reside inside their body, which is why they have the same breathing-motion as men. They are elegant and enduring swimmers. Their eyes work well even in very weak light conditions. However, in the complete darkness of the deep sea, these creatures orientate themselves with the help of a bipartite sonar system. For large-scale orientation, they use loud whistling sounds, which they produce with their vocal cords. They receive a rather indistinct "image" of their surroundings through these echoes. They have a special organ at the base of their throat for the detection of details. Its click-sounds can be adjusted very precisely. These echoes only show a rather small section of their surroundings, but the "image" they receive is more detailed. Although Lingits have very sensitive hearing, they receive sonar echoes with their entire body. Especially the big wing fins are used for the reception of echo sounds. They also carry sensitive streaming-sensors, which also serve for orientation purposes. Lingits live on vegetation only. They are sexually dimorphic and live together in huge groups for mutual protection. Lingits have many enemies who eat them. Descriptions of these are amongst those provided below.

Saira, as a Lingit

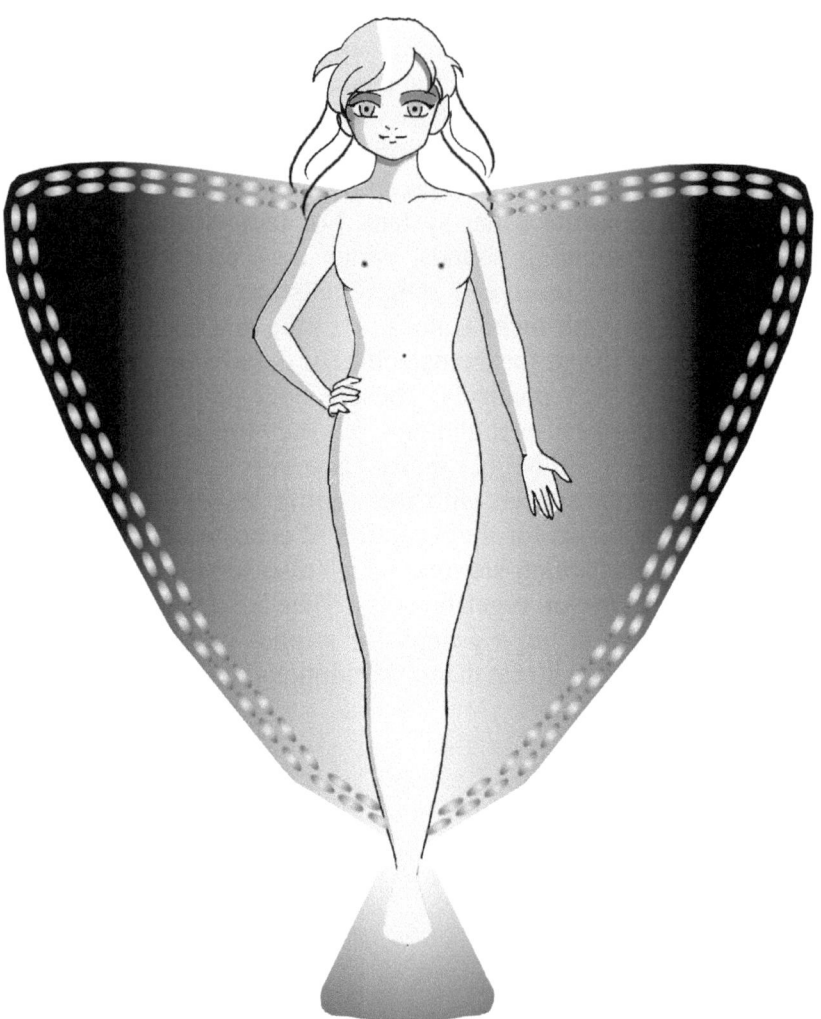

Saira is the protagonist of this story. Once she lived as a human-type land-dweller on the planet Wuun. She was abducted by a magic portal to Turoon and transformed into a Lingit.

Dorgons

Dorgons hunt in the twilight zone of the ocean, where the lightless deep sea begins. Their giant eyes perceive even the smallest amount of light. That's why they are easy to blind, which is how some of their prey escapes them. They themselves carry no luminous organs and are therefore difficult to see, even though they are nearly five times the size of a Lingit. They swim very slowly, which enables them to move absolutely noiselessly. They surprise their prey and catch them by throwing open their giant mouths, which act like suction-traps. They have no sonar system. Their highly sensitive eyes and their streaming-sensors are quite sufficient for their orientation.

Draughs

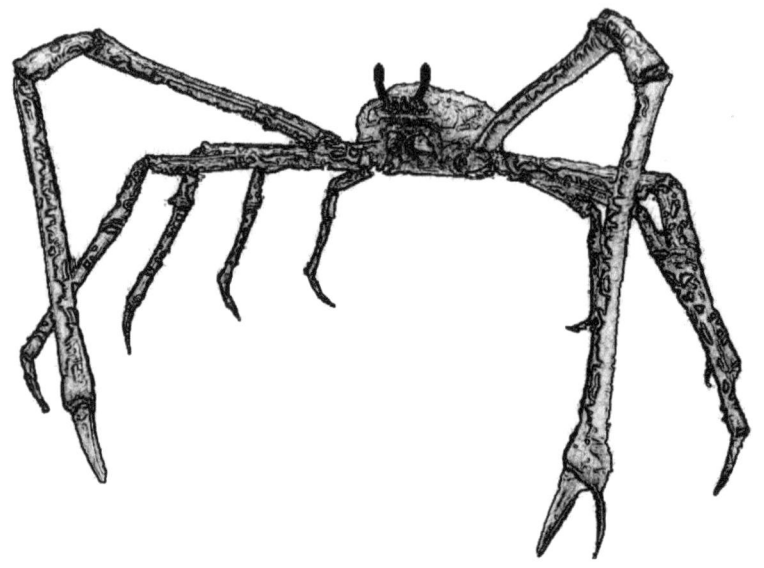

Their triangular body and its extremities are massively armoured. They possess four pairs of walking legs. A fifth pair of extremities in the front carries huge, powerful shears. The Draughs also have very strong mouthparts. The eyes are positioned on stalks and can be folded into the head-armour for protection. Their body is nearly three times the size of a Lingit, but they seem much bigger because of their long extremities.

Draughs live only on the ground. They cannot swim, but they can walk very quickly and for a long time. They have the same bipartite sonar system as Lingits, but they can create much louder sounds, which causes physical pain to other creatures. So they use their sonar not only for orientation, but also as a weapon.

They are quite aggressive and moody, which is why they live as loners. Draughs are omnivorous.

Durkas

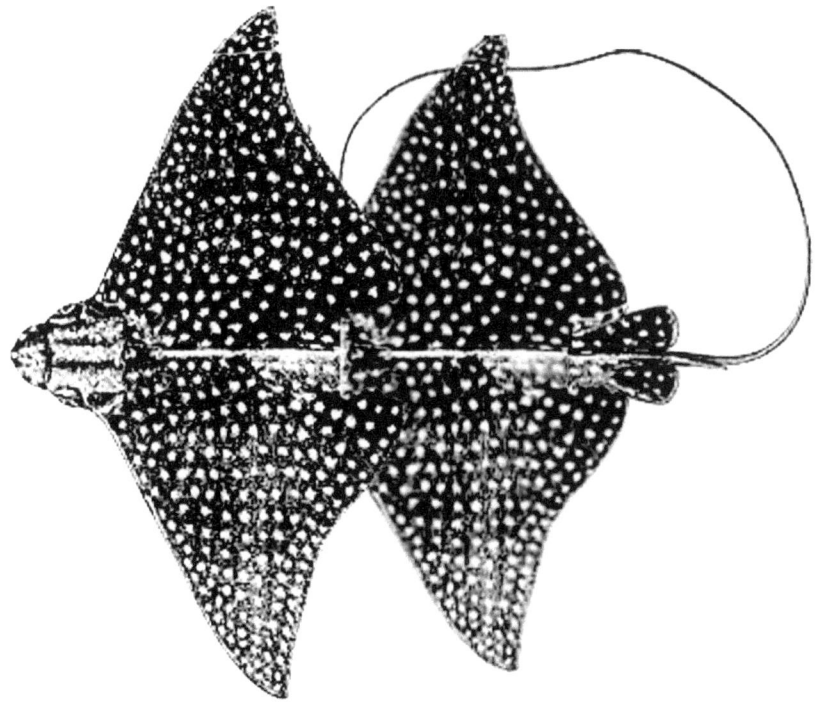

Durkas look like double skates, whose pair of rear wings is somewhat smaller than those in front. They live in the higher light-flooded water-layers, where they filter small organisms either in the open water or from the sand of the seabed. They swim slowly and leisurely and therefore cannot escape fast hunters, but they possess a very long whip-like tail, which they use as an effective weapon for their defence. Durkas are nearly three times the size of a Lingit and often appear in large groups.

Duumars

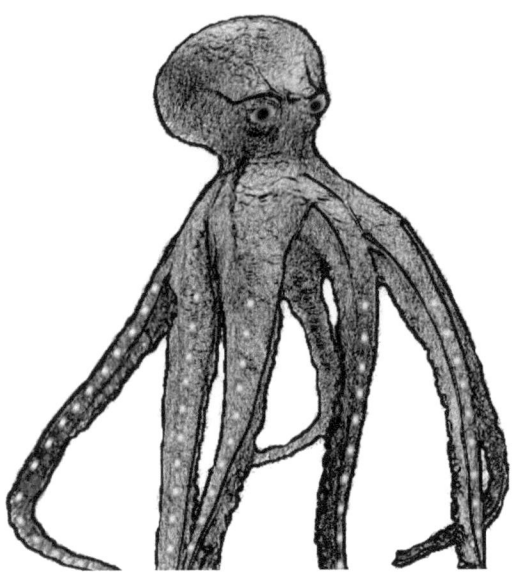

Duumars look very much like octopuses. Their eyes are quite big and function very well even in weak light. The eyes are positioned close together, which gives them a good spatial view. The Duumars' eight arms carry numerous luminous organs. They do not use sonar to orientate themselves in complete darkness. For this purpose, they have highly sensitive streaming-sensors, which are distributed over their entire body and can perceive even the slightest movement in the surrounding waters. They are able to determine a rough image of their immediate surroundings from the discernable anomalies and changes of the streams, and so are able to detect the movements of other beings close to them too. As their body is made up of soft parts, they are able to squeeze into most narrow gaps and cracks. Duumars are nearly five times the size of a Lingit, and often live in groups spread out over a wide area. They are meat eaters.

Dyx

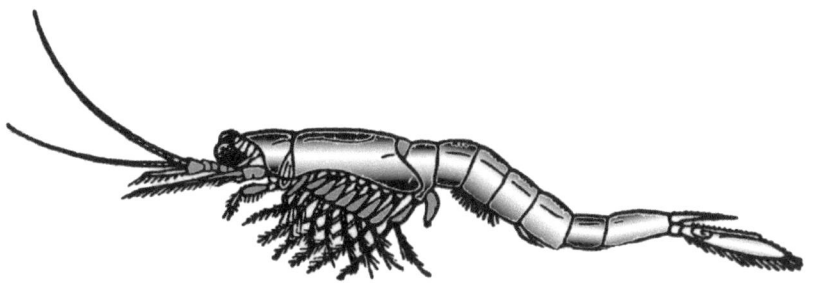

Dyx are tiny crab-like creatures, only as the size of a Lingit's finger. They appear in giant swarms and serve as main food supply for many big ocean-dwellers. They can glow in many different colours, depending on their mood or condition. Thus, they create the most beautiful and intensive sea-light imaginable. They feed on plankton.

Farkans

Although Farkans are six times the size of a Lingit and their body is heavily armoured, they are able to swim. In order to do this, they move their extremities close to the body and enlarge the three rear segments of their side-armour to form wings, as can be seen in the image below.

They possess a jet-propulsion system with exhaust-openings positioned at the front and the rear on both sides of the body. The exhaust-openings can be turned in any direction, giving these creatures enormous agility. They are able to hover in the water, because the jet stream can be adjusted very precisely. It is produced by several parallel working hollow muscles inside the body. While some of the muscles expel the water contained within them, others suck in fresh water, thus creating an almost continuous stream of water, which is distributed to the four exhaust-openings as required. The water suction takes place through the gaps in some segments of armour. Farkans move very much faster than Lingits, but they can never reach the speed of the Meyjoks - who possesses the same jet-propulsion - because of their massive body and their protruding armour. Farkans have no sonar system. Instead, a special organ is located at the base of the tail that discharges weak electric pulses into the surrounding water for orientation purposes, but can also discharge extremely strong electric shocks via the tip of the tail. Farkans perceive their surroundings and everything that moves around them even at quite some distance, by observing the inter-ference of the electric field-lines. For this purpose, their whole body is equipped with highly sensitive electric sensors, which perceive the smallest changes in the electric field that permanently surrounds these creatures. That's why Farkans have only eight small spot-like eyes, which show only a narrow, restricted image of their surroundings. Their main orientation occurs via their electric sensors. They are omnivorous and also hunt creatures bigger than themselves. In addition to their mighty shears, they also have a red glowing tail sting, which can not only discharge strong electric shocks, but can also inject a strong poison. The tail can be moved in any direction and is very strong, so they can also deal devastating blows with it. Farkans live and hunt in small groups. They are surprisingly social.

Galanx

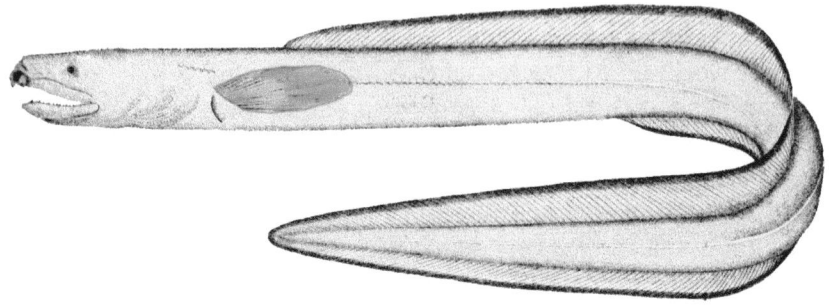

Galanx are twenty times the size of a Lingit. Their laterally flattened body enables them to pass through very narrow gaps and openings, despite of their size. Their powerful jaws show that they are meat eaters. Although they can't swim fast, they are very agile because of their flexible body, and can hide in small caves, where they lie in wait for their victims. Their sonar is so strong they can stun even larger beings for a long time.

Gamburas

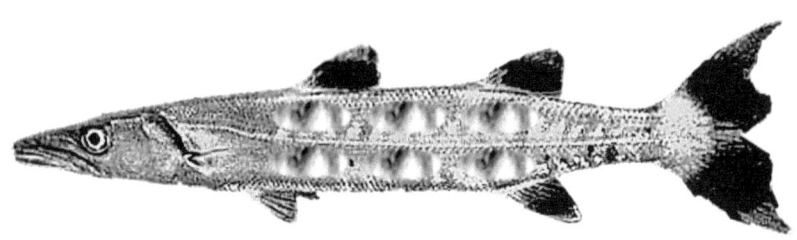

Gamburas are feared hunters, which roam the ocean in giant swarms. They are Lingit-sized. Their slender, laterally strongly flattened bodies with the big tail fin show that they are very fast and agile hunters. They do not need sonar because they mostly hunt in the light-flooded upper layers of the water. Almost nothing escapes their sharp eyes. They possess highly sensitive electric sensors, distributed across their entire head area, which can easily detect even those creatures that are immobile and well hidden. Gamburas are always on the move and will even hunt creatures many times bigger than them. Even the giant Wras can barely withstand a swarm of hungry Gamburas and seek safety in flight. Gamburas behave very socially with members of their own species.

Ganvas

Ganvas look like swimming-crabs, and are indeed able to swim short distances with the help of a pair of flattened rear extremities. They are barely bigger than a Lingit's hand. Their strongly armoured body with its spiky outgrowths is an effective protection against their numerous enemies who feed on them. Luminous organs on the body and the strong shears identify them as inhabitants of the deep sea. Ganvas are aggressive loners. They orientate themselves with the help of short sensory hairs that are distributed over their entire body, and can perceive the slightest movement in the surrounding waters. Their eyes are very sensitive. They can detect even the weakest pulses of light, enabling them to evade approaching enemies in good time, as well as aiding them during the hunt for small organisms. Ganvas are meat eaters, but will also eat carrion, so they play an important part in the removal of cadavers.

Hingais

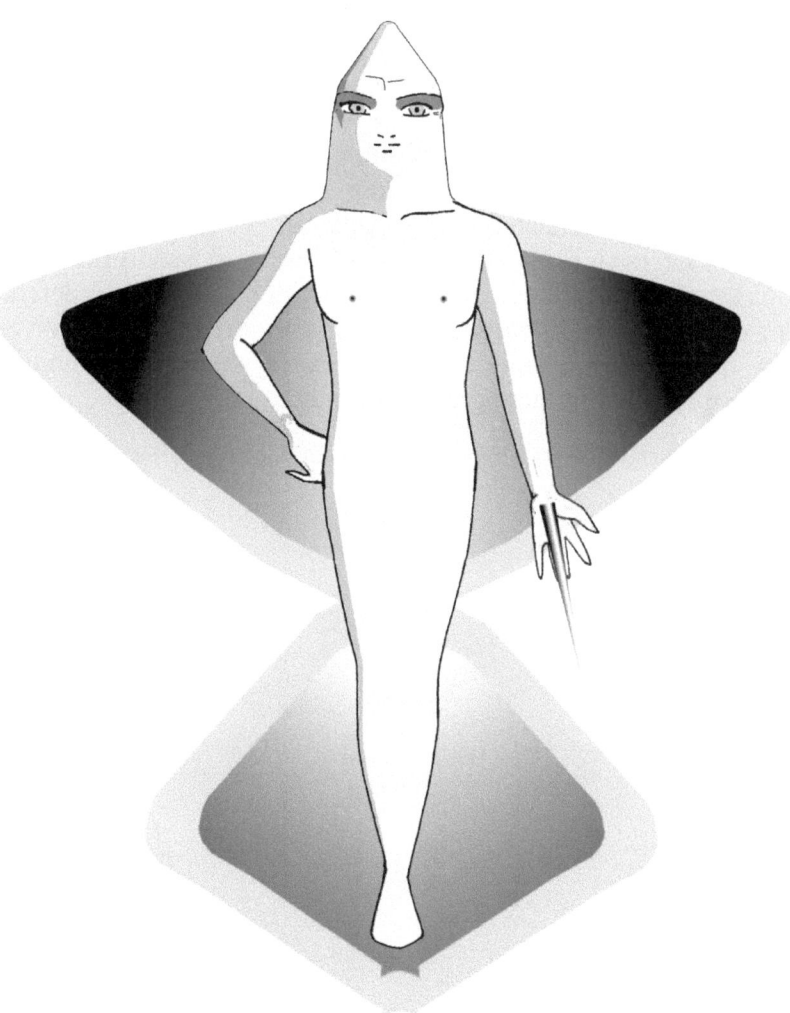

The body of the Hingais is similar in shape to that of the Lingits, but they are only about half the size of a Lingit. Instead of one huge pair of wing fins, they carry a bigger pair in front and a smaller pair at the rear. Around the outer edge of each pair of fins runs a luminous organ. Although they are small, Hingais are fast and agile swimmers, which is very helpful during hunting as they are meat eaters. From each forearm they can draw out long pointed spikes, which are connected to poison glands. The poison is so strong that it can kill even beings the size of a Duumar in a short time. The Hingais use these spikes not only for hunting, but also to defend themselves. As they live in the deep sea, they orientate themselves in the dark with the same bipartite sonar system as the Lingits. They live together in huge groups for mutual protection.

Meyjoks

Meyjoks are the fastest creatures on Turoon. In addition to the normal propulsion provided by the big tail fin, they possess the same jet-propulsion as the Farkans. Huge amounts of water are sucked in through the broad mouth and ejected with high speed through nozzles at either side of the tail-base. These tube-like nozzles can be moved freely, enabling the Meyjoks to retain full manoeuvrability even at high speed. The water jet is produced by several parallel working hollow muscles in the body. While some of the muscles eject the water, others suck in fresh water. So a nearly continuous stream of water is produced. As a proper metabolism cannot be guaranteed at high speeds because water would run too fast across the gills, these are located in sealable pockets, which open only as required and suck in a small amount of water. This ensures that the flow speed of water along the gills is greatly decreased, which guarantees a suitable metabolic exchange at all times.

Meyjoks are meat-eating nomads. If they have fed on an area and food is getting rare, they move on to other feeding grounds. With the help of their jet-propulsion, they can cover huge distances in a short period of time. They live in the upper light-flooded layers of water, and have very good eyes - barely a movement escapes them. They possess highly sensitive electric sensors distributed over the entire head area, which easily detect immobile, well-hidden beings. All those skills make them extremely successful hunters. Meyjoks are nearly four times the size of a Lingit.

Peltais

Peltais are blind meat eaters, who hunt only with the help of their sonar and their highly sensitive hearing. They bury themselves in the seabed and wait until they hear a potential prey above them. When they have located it, they rush upwards with very high acceleration and pierce their victims unerringly with their long, pointed upper jaw. If they should miss their prey, they'll try to locate it with the help of their sonar system. Some of their potential victims confuse the Peltais by emitting loud sonar sounds themselves. These are then reflected back and forth throughout the surrounding area and cause enough interference to make accurate locating difficult. In this way, they are able to escape from the Peltais. Peltais are nearly four times the size of a Lingit.

Qails

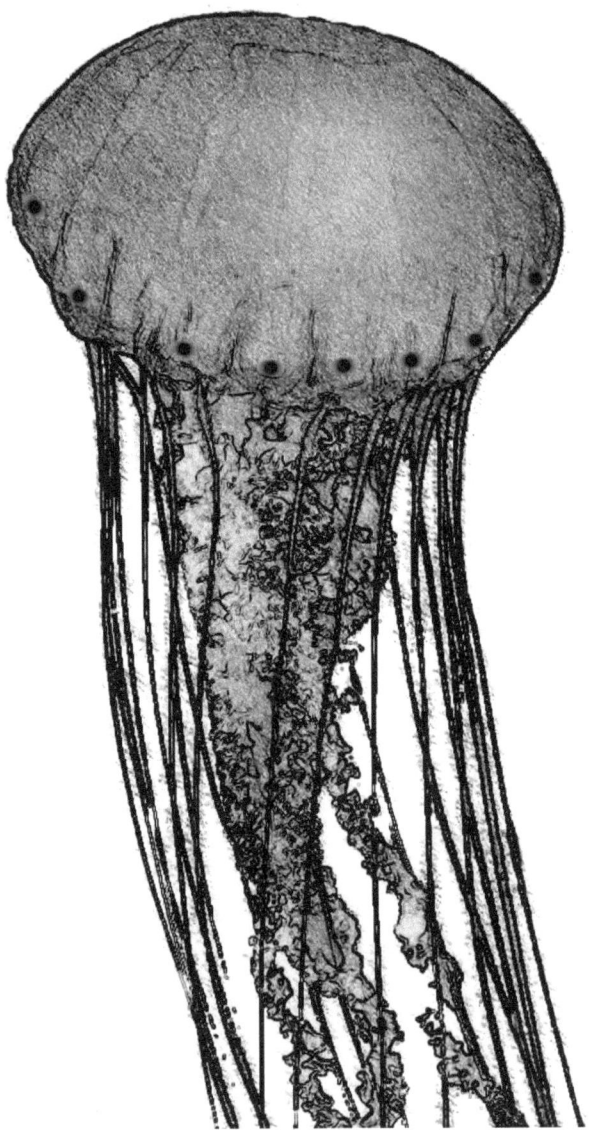

Qails are the most unusual creatures on Turoon. They are energy-transformers, which means they can absorb nearly any type of energy and transform it into another type. That's why they are not implicitly reliant on organic food, although they somewhat prefer it. Their numerous tentacles have different functions. Some of them are covered with highly poisonous nettle-cells for hunting and defence purposes. Their poison is so strong that it kills even Duumars very quickly. Qails orientate themselves not only with their numerous eyes located at the edge of their bell, but can also detect streaming and magnetic-field anomalies in the surrounding waters. They can create nearly every type of energy, which is why their poisonous tentacles are not the only weapons they can make use of if required. However, Qails are perfectly peaceful and very social beings. They live in huge swarms and prefer spacious caves, which protect them against their biggest enemies, the Galanx. Qails are about the same size as Lingits.

Tister

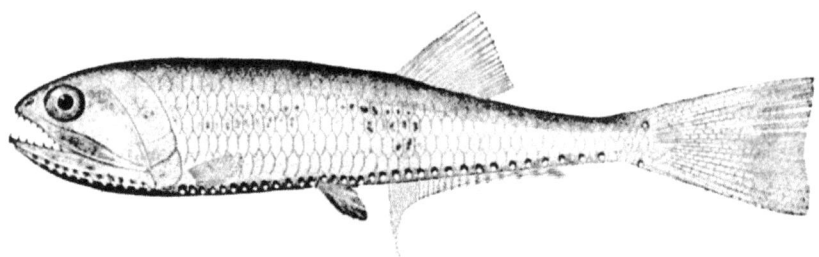

Tister are small meat eaters who are barely bigger than a Lingit's hand. They appear in big swarms. When hunting, the members of the swarm hide in the sand, with only a single guardian swimming above them to watch the surroundings. If he detects a potential prey, he swims closer and bites a small piece out of it. If the prey is edible, he gives a short sight-signal with the luminous organs on his abdominal region, at which the entire swarm comes racing out of the sand and eats the prey alive. A single swarm is able to reduce even a creature the size of a Galanx to its skeleton in a very short time.

Wras

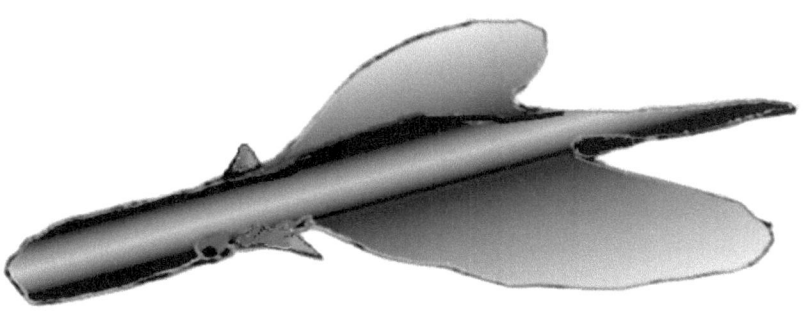

Wras are the biggest creatures on Turoon. They grow up to eighty times the size of a Lingit. They mainly feed on Dyx, who exist in giant swarms. Wras are peaceful loners who always travel and never settle anywhere. Because of their giant size, their only threat would be a swarm of Gamburas. But they have an effective defensive weapon against them. As well as the bipartite sonar, which they use mainly for orientation, they also possess a so-called fighting sonar, which first charges through a sequence of accelerating clicks. Then the accumulated acoustic energy is released with a single explosive pulse, which creates either a directed or a spherical pressure wave. This pressure wave is so strong that it can blow up hard rocks. However, the Wras use this tremendous weapon only in case of emergency, if their own life, or that of another Wra, is in danger.

Explanation of the term „cavitation"

Cavitation happens in liquids streaming around objects at high speed. During acceleration, the pressure sinks below the steam-pressure of the liquid, which causes the development of steam bubbles. The ensuing increase of pressure through the deceleration lets the steam bubbles condense again. The sudden change of volume induced by this process causes strong pressure pulses. They emit very loud noises. In times past, this happened quite often due to badly constructed ship propellers. Big steam bubbles developed during fast rotation, so the propeller turned inefficiently. In time, the extreme pressure pulses and the strong noise being emitted often caused massive damage to the propellers.

Michael Kerawalla was born in India in 1963 and moved to Germany as a child. He is a biologist and software developer. After losing his job, he followed his vocation as a writer and published his first fantasy novel entitled "Stein der Finsternis" in October 2006. His second fantasy novel entitled "Turoon" followed in 2011. Michael Kerawalla lives with his wife near Stuttgart in Germany.